"AH, CASSIE,
YOU DO PLEASE ME."

Like strong drink, his voice mesmerized her, stilling her every impulse to turn from him. Cassandra did not protest when his hands slid under her and raised her up to lean against his broad chest. She must stop him, she thought, but no longer cared to. It was as if he had cast a spell to remove her reluctance and fear, and replaced it with strange rough desires for which she had no name.

Reaching out blindly, she found the strong column of a masculine neck and her arms encircled it. One of her hands scored into the thick black hair at the nape and her fingers flexed, drawing his head down hard to hers.

Stealthily, his hands began a gentle roaming of her slim body. When his fingers grazed the long curve of her spine she arched involuntarily against him. His palms molded the sides of her waist, then rose slowly to her ribs, where his thumbs hooked under the glorious full softness of her breasts.

"Do not fear me," Merlyn murmured, cupping her face in a strong hand. "Let me hold you, touch you, as I wish. Do you not yet know there is only pleasure to be had from me?"

Dear Reader,

We, the editors of Tapestry Romances, are committed to bringing you two outstanding original romantic historical novels each and every month.

From Kentucky in the 1850s to the court of Louis XIII, from the deck of a pirate ship within sight of Gibraltar to a mining camp high in the Sierra Nevadas, our heroines experience life and love, romance and adventure.

Our aim is to give you the kind of historical romances that you want to read. We would enjoy hearing your thoughts about this book and all future Tapestry Romances. Please write to us at the address below.

The Editors
Tapestry Romances
POCKET BOOKS
1230 Avenue of the Americas
Box TAP
New York, N.Y. 10020

Emerald and Sapphire

Laura Parker

A TAPESTRY BOOK
PUBLISHED BY POCKET BOOKS NEW YORK

An *Original* publication of TAPESTRY BOOKS

A Tapestry Book published by
POCKET BOOKS, a Simon & Schuster division of
GULF & WESTERN CORPORATION
1230 Avenue of the Americas, New York, N.Y. 10020

ISBN: 0-671-46415-9

First Tapestry Books printing May, 1983

10 9 8 7 6 5 4 3 2 1

POCKET and colophon are registered trademarks
of Simon & Schuster.

TAPESTRY is a trademark of Simon & Schuster.

Printed in the U.S.A.

For Theresa,
Tony and Christopher

They say best men are molded out of
    faults,
And, for the most, become much more
    the better
For being a little bad.

William Shakespeare
Measure For Measure

Chapter One
London: Newgate Prison
October, 1754

"GOD IN HEAVEN, SET ME FREE!"

Lady Cassandra Briarcliffe collapsed in the rotting hay as the cell door of Newgate Prison slammed closed behind her.

"Less than a full day at Newgate and already ye be stirrin' trouble." The voice of Dowerty, the gaoler, came to her through the small grille set in the heavy door. "Now listen to me, ye fancy slut. Had ye give them whores in the common cell what they wanted, ye'd not have been roughed up. Ye'll be safe enough alone in here till mornin'. Then the magistrate can decide what's to be done with ye."

He watched, eyes narrowing in interest, as the girl crossed her arms self-consciously to shield the naked expanse of her throat and upper bosom from his gaze. Her complexion was as white as the silk undergarments she wore. A skinny bit of goods, Dowerty thought. But then, his tastes were easily accommodated to need.

And the luxuriant fall of dark chestnut waves down her back made him think of wrapping his broad body in it while he . . .

Dowerty reined his thoughts in reluctantly. That kind of thinking would keep him from finishing his rounds, and he had rounds to finish. But later . . .

Raising tear-brilliant eyes to the figure blocking the peephole, Cassandra said, "Please, sir, I beg you, a blanket against the dampness of the evening."

"Damme!" came the answering coarse chuckle of the turnkey. "Damme, but ye're a proper one! A voice what could turn a swell's head. Mebbe there is somethin' to the rumor ye're a gentlewoman. More like, ye're an actress." The gaoler turned the key in the grate. "Mind yer manners, me genteel slut, and ole Dowerty will be back afore midnight to do right by ye. I'll be findin' ye a scrap of blanket, too—if ye please me."

Without another word, he slammed shut the peephole in the door, closing out the meager hall light that had illuminated the cell.

Her head ached and she was out of breath, so Cassandra did not at once rise from her knees. The long thin silk shift that covered her would not keep out the damp chill that crept from every corner. The brown velvet traveling gown she had worn was gone now, lying in shreds on the floor of the huge common cell that served for men and women prisoners alike. She had not known what the women wanted until they began pulling at her. "A ticket of admission," that was what one woman cried at her. They wanted her to pay a penalty for having been thrown into the same cell with

2

them. Wild with fright, she had fought them, knowing in this stinking dampness she would surely catch pneumonia and die. In the end they had bested her, one holding her face in the foul hay scattered on the floor while the others tore the gown from her. Soon they were fighting over ownership among themselves and the gown was ripped beyond use.

Frightened laughter rose and caught in Cassandra's throat. She had possessed nothing when brought through debtor's door three hours earlier; now she had even less.

She squeezed her eyes shut, curling slender fingers against the drumming at her temples that had plagued her all day. A shiver of fear chased a chilly ripple up her slender spine. She was a prisoner in Newgate, a prison whose name was a byword in the farthest reaches of England, and she could remember neither her own name nor that of any soul she called friend.

"No, no!" she whispered silently, uncurling her fingers to hide her face in her hands. If only the pain in her head would cease she might think, might remember the events that had brought her here.

Outside the tiny barred window of her cell the bump of a cart and stumbling clomp of a horse's hooves broke the silence as the minutes passed. Slowly memory wafted about her, as real yet intangible as the London fog outside the walls. The breath of the moors seemed to seep into the stench that permeated the prison, teasing her memory with the soft, damp smells of peat and heather.

She raised her head, eyes searching the darkness as if the clues to her present misery were stealing into the room's black corners. If only she could recall a single name she would not feel so frightened.

Faint stirrings of recall skirted her thought. Horses. Yes, there had been horses, a coach and pair. Other memories stirred and she remembered a man, a beautifully handsome man, a fairy-tale prince with hair brighter than the sun and eyes as clear a gray as the sea off the Devonshire coast. Long ago he had entered her life, offering love where once there had been only disdain and indifference. His name was . . .

Cassandra moaned under her breath as the memory failed. It was like a candle flame's death: a gentle flicker, a sputter, and then darkness.

Beyond the doorway all was silent. The chattering and swearing and raucous laughter of the common room were locked away for the night. But the morning, what would it bring?

She shuddered, not needing light to tell her that she was pale and bruised as she rose to her feet and brushed the straw from herself. Where the weals on her arms made by the brawling women had bled, filthy decaying bits of straw stuck to her skin.

She had been too frightened and hurt to think properly when she had been ushered before the London magistrate on charges of vagrancy. Unconcerned for her discomfort and fright, he had ordered her placed in Newgate until the matter could be pursued.

Cassandra bowed her head and gritted her teeth, fighting the panic that rose like bubbles in her mind. If her memory had not betrayed her she might have fabricated a lie which would have set her free. If she could only recall the name of . . . of . . .

Again the tantalizing sensation of memory curled through her thoughts. She had been running when she struck her head and the confusion began. *Running away.*

The thought was so swift and certain Cassandra moaned under the weight of the knowledge. She had been in flight, not from but toward a man who meant safety and love.

Suddenly aware of her surroundings once more, she strained against the pain behind her eyes to find a chair or cot, but nothing would reveal itself to her eyes. This blackness was not like the invisible cloak of night. The smoky shadows seemed to writhe and breathe before her eyes, alive with a malevolence that sent fresh terrors skidding along her spine.

A shadow scurried past her, the claws of its tiny feet rustling the hay. Rats! Cassandra leaped for the door with a shriek.

The rodent, terrified by the disturbance, turned and rushed again across the open ground. As it passed the source of the scream, it brushed human flesh.

Her second scream came quickly, freeing the panic like bubbles from a bottle of champagne, and it was followed by another and then another.

At the far end of a corridor a man lay in the darkness, not for lack of candlewax or oil but for lack of interest. It was not an unusual attitude for a man who was to be hanged outside debtor's door with the dawn.

He was tall, six feet in his stockings, and with the lean, wiry physique of a fencing master. All that spoiled his elegant figure was the concentrated power

5

of a professional brawler in the broad shoulders. The face was too harsh for handsomeness, the nose long and blunt-ended. The left eye was covered by a patch, but many found the gaze of his single green eye too direct for comfort. Coal-black hair covered his head, thick and wild, a memento of his gypsy ancestors. It was a face which reflected reckless daring and spirited passion. Yet always about him was an air of self-possession and a hardened contempt for life's vagaries.

Sprawled on his bed of newly purchased linens, Merlyn Ross reached for the new brandy bottle that rested on the floor by his cot. The rattle of the iron fetters that encircled one wrist and leg and held him chained to the wall reminded him too well of what the dawn would bring. He muttered a curse in the rich, deep voice that had once earned him a living on the stage and, setting the bottle against his lips, swallowed deeply.

After a long moment, when the level of the rich amber liquid had dropped an inch in the bottle, he set it down. It felt good to be drunk, he thought, a bitter smile settling on his wide, firm mouth. Not that he was drunk yet. That was his intention before the night had spun out its final hour. He had paid a small fortune to spend his final night in comfort and ease. When they came for him at daybreak, he would be as drunk as any lord. He would need that false courage to play the boastful unrepentant sinner on the morrow. He meant his final hour to be the best bit of acting of his checkered, sometimes nefarious life.

A low rumbling chuckle issued from Merlyn's lips. The irony of his last night lay like molten lead within him. From the age of reasoning he had known he was destined to die by the bullet or the gibbet. A man born of a whore and subjected to the worst life had to offer could entertain no other thought. But it should not have been like this.

Merlyn touched the patch that covered his left eye. Few knew that behind it lay a perfectly good orb. It was a secret that was at once a bonus and a liability.

Twenty years earlier the secret had brought him to the attention of a nobleman who had taken him, a filthy little thief, from a village street and brought him to live in his London residence. Under the dilettante's protection, he had learned to ape the manners and speech of a gentleman, losing his rough country accent as easily as his grime. Only later did he learn that the nobleman's largess had a price tag.

Merlyn sat forward suddenly with an angry oath. It was still too sore a spot to probe and he'd as soon not think on it. It was not his last betrayal, but it taught him to never again trust a living soul.

He had taken the nobleman's lessons and put them to use, as both an actor and a thief. By these means, he had moved from the life of a cutpurse to that of the most accomplished jewel thief of London. His touch with a gentleman's purse strings had equaled the delicacy of an art. With it he had once slipped a diamond necklace from the throat of a most sensitive lady. He preferred stealing from wealthy ladies. They wore their wealth on display, no need to wonder the worth of the item. Sometimes it had been accomplished during the dance figures, at others during a genuine enough passionate embrace in the shadows beyond a ballroom.

Merlyn smiled in self-amusement. He was good, he did his work quickly, deftly, and always without the nastiness of violence. That luck he owed to his many disguises.

None thought to look behind the powdered peruke and black silk eyepatch of the Comte de Valure for the culprit. To be sure, the comte's finances arose from a source altogether mysterious and apparently inexhaustible. There was speculative talk of the comte's many holdings in New France, and veiled jealous references to dealings with the fearsome pashas of the infidel Turkish Empire, but none entertained a thought for the true fount from which sprang his monies.

Merlyn's smile widened as the brandy sang warmly through his veins. For the last six years he had passed through the elegant salons of London Town known as the bewigged aristocrat, the Comte de Valure. To his acquaintances of Covent Garden, he was the tall, black-haired actor known as Merlyn Ross. To the criminal element of the city he was known as the pockmarked petty thief named Old Jack. No one suspected that the three were one and the same.

Merlyn chuckled. That was the great jest. His condemnation to the gallows had nothing to do with his disguised lives. It had come from an altogether too common source of a man's fall.

Who would have thought he would find his death for the ill luck of having bedded a *petite amie* with a jealous protector?

Merlyn reached for the bottle again. He had been drinking that night, too. If not for his belief that they were safely tucked away from the eyes of Bella's mysterious lover, he would never have stayed so late with her. Neither would he have remained afterward drinking at the public tavern below the room they had shared. The Bow Street Runners had arrested him as he sat drinking. The murderer was clever. The witnesses swore that only he had entered Bella's room that night.

The distant screams were slow to penetrate Merlyn's consciousness. The sounds of Newgate were well known and seldom given heed. But, as they continued to reverberate down the long empty corridor, the quality of their despair drove Merlyn from his self-contemplation.

He sat up to an accompanying clink of his chains and strained an ear. There was nothing gin-soaked or coarse about these clear high notes of hysteria. It must be the young woman's first visit to Newgate.

For a moment something close to sympathy stirred in Merlyn's breast. Spurred by that unfamiliar emotion, Merlyn moved as if to stand, but the chain around his wrist caught in a kink and stopped him. Frowning, he looked down at the proof of his own helplessness. The raw strength that gave him a catlike grace coiled in rebellion against the reminder of dawn. Anger quickly replaced the weakness of sentimentality as he jerked the chain straight, uncaring for the sharp pain that shot up his arm.

Easing back into a comfortable sprawl, Merlyn let the anger pricking him fuel his resentment toward the unseen young woman. Was he to spill tears for every young scrap of life who found the moment too much to bear? He had only hours left of his own life. Why should he give up his comfortable stupor for any soul?

As his long-fingered fists curled tightly a stray flicker of light from the burning taper on the wall opposite his door caught upon the stones of the heavy gold ring he wore. The light slipped into the emerald, radiating like an icy fire from its depths, then shot through its mate, a huge sapphire that burned deep as blue flame.

"How are ye holdin', guv'nor?"

Merlyn raised his gaze slowly to the pair of eyes peering into the gloom of his cell. "A good evening to you, Master Fletch," he intoned in the aristocratic voice that had so pleased the ladies in his disguise of the comte. "You will forgive me if I do not rise. The privilege of the condemned, I believe."

The biting sarcasm was lost on Fletch, the evening turnkey. It was all of a same to him. The only difference between hangings was seeing how the "gaol bait" passed his last night. This particular prisoner was a mystery. He was Jack Commoner for the court records because he refused to give his real name. It was not important. The woman he had murdered was just a slut and her protector did not want the publicity a sensational trial would have brought. Quietly and quickly the man had been tried and found guilty. Rumor said he was a thief, but none would confirm it. The London underworld had its strange code that looked to its own. If Jack Commoner wished to remain an enigma, it was his right.

No matter, thought Fletch as he rubbed his runny

nose on his coatsleeve. Commoner would die just like all the other Jacks and Johns and Jamies who passed through the condemned cells.

The turnkey reached for the ring of keys that he wore at his waist. The weight of the metal felt good in his hand. The small pieces of iron were worthless in and of themselves, but because they fit the locks of the doors along this corridor, they gave him a power the world should never have been obliged to give a man of his birth and drinking habits.

"Just givin' a look-see, guv'nor," the turnkey explained as he pushed the cell door open and raised the candle he carried.

"Douse your damnable flame!" Merlyn roared, throwing up an arm to shield his eye, sensitive after weeks of confinement in the shadows.

Although the command sent a shiver of disquiet through the turnkey, he did not pinch the flame until he had looked his full. The prisoner was dressed in a full-sleeved shirt, unfastened nearly to the waist to reveal a mat of fine black chest hair. One well-muscled leg lay sprawled out before him while the other he had drawn up to rest on the mattress. He appeared to be in a half stupor, but it was hard to tell when a man wore an eyepatch, Fletch decided.

But of most interest to the turnkey was the bottle of French brandy that sat on the floor by the prisoner's foot. Greedily his eyes marked the level of liquid still remaining and saliva filled his mouth in anticipation of a swallow.

"Most ever' bit o' coffin meat to sit these condemned

cells goes out debtor's door his head so full o' spirits he never feels the halter's embrace. Leastways, with the lucky ones that's so."

Fletch took a step toward the prisoner, not because he wanted to get any nearer the man with the cropped wild black hair of a gypsy but because the lure of the brandy bottle was stronger than his superstition in that moment.

"Wouldn't serve, now, was ye to come out crowin' tomorrow. Folks might git the wrong idea, like me and the other turnkeys is given to takin' bribes and such."

He edged a little nearer, his eyes constantly moving between the lounging prisoner and the bottle. "Best let old Fletch share a spot with ye. Folks is expectin' a proper hangin', come the mornin'. Wouldn't want a riot on account ye spoiled things for the crowd. Ye have too much of the devil's spirits in, ye'll not strut up the steps o' the scaffold like ye promised."

Merlyn let the man come close enough to touch with an outstretched hand, but he did not move until the turnkey bent to grasp the bottle. Then his action was swifter than the poor gaoler had thought possible.

One moment the cool glass of the bottle was under Fletch's fingers, the next he was dangling in air, his feet six inches off the ground as the prisoner lifted him up by a handful of his shirtfront.

"'Tis not polite to help oneself without asking," Merlyn said in a deadly whisper, ignoring the violent struggles of the man who was beginning to choke. "A condemned man is to be left in peace on his last night. I will have peace, one way or—"

The woman's screams began again, suddenly, whipping Merlyn's attention toward the open door of his cell. "Who the devil is that?"

Fletch, finding himself released, sank bonelessly to his knees. Immediately he gained his feet and staggered toward the door, out of the reach of the prisoner's chains.

"Hold!" Merlyn called after the turnkey and bent to scoop up the brandy bottle. He waved it enticingly at the man. "Wasn't this what you wanted?" His smile grew cunning. "Who's the woman?"

Fletch pulled himself up straight, tugging his long red coat with the brass buttons into order, but his rummy stare never left the bottle. "That'd be the young lady they brought in this afternoon."

"Why is she here?" Merlyn took the cork out of the neck and poured a small amount between his lips before giving a satisfied sigh.

It was all the prompting Fletch needed. Speech poured out of him. "Wanderin' the road north o' London, she was. Got no purse or jewelry or nothing. Says she can't even remember her name. The magistrate locked her up in the debtor's cell till inquiries is made. 'Cept, guv'nor, ye knows well as me, she ain't lost. More like she's come for to enter the trade. Mother Tess is makin' her rounds after—" The turnkey swallowed, unsure that he should mention the hanging again. "Leastways, she's young enough for Mother Tess to take an interest in." Fletch cackled with laughter. "She didn't like above half givin' her gown to them bawds in the common room. She's got a bit o' spirit." He winked at the prisoner. "Dowerty says he's goin' to have a look for himself, just to make certain."

Merlyn's expression did not alter. The turnkey's snickering meant only one thing. Dowerty would rape the girl before turning her over to Mother Tess, one of the most notorious madams in the district.

"Is that why she's screeching, because Dowerty's in there with her?"

Fletch shook his head, the long greasy locks of his hair trailing over his coat collar. "Not a bit o' it, guv'nor. The lady's scared. Reckon she ain't familiar with the inside o' a prison cell. She's the kind I seen set up to a champagne breakfast in a tavern window across the way to watch some poor blighter kick at a rope's end. A real genteel whore."

Merlyn said nothing for a long while. So long, in fact, that the turnkey began to shuffle anxiously in the doorway. Finally, Merlyn raised himself up to his full height, and the look in his one good eye made the turnkey fall back another step.

"You asked me how I'm holding, Master Fletch. I'll tell you, not well. Aye, I've had a bath and a fresh change of linens, brandy and a full belly. But there's one appetite left me." He leaned nearer, his one good eye glittering like the icy emerald on his finger. "I want the girl."

Merlyn felt no compunction about his action. The girl probably earned her keep as a slut. If not, he was merely claiming the right to teach her the skill Mother Tess would demand of her. There were worse ways to learn the trade.

He stretched out the hand with the brandy bottle until the length of chain around that wrist checked him.

"Bring me the girl, Fletch, and you'll have your brandy, and gold besides. I want her untouched. If Dowerty's been at her, then our bargain's off. I'll not have another's leavings. Understood?"

Fletch nodded rapidly. He had earned a pretty penny bringing the prisoner brandy and tallow; the girl should earn him even more. All he had to do was sneak her out of her cell before Dowerty was any the wiser. If the chief gaoler found her missing, he could always say he didn't know the girl had been marked special. Besides, Jack Commoner offered gold for her.

Fletch reached for the brandy, to have it drawn back from his reach. "How's a body to know ye're to be trusted?" he complained. "This here is Fletch ye're dealin' with. I know what's o'clock, guv'nor, and I'll be takin' somethin' handsome for me trouble." His avaricious gaze dropped to the magnificent ring the prisoner wore.

Merlyn smiled, a steely cold smile to match the chilling fire of his green eye. "Would a thousand pounds open these fetters and set me free?" he demanded.

"A thou—" Fletch's tongue stammered to a halt as a delirious, delicious moment of pure greed shivered through him. The greed died quickly. He had seen the color of the prisoner's gold before. The man did not possess the means in hand, and he doubted a note to the outside world could procure the coinage before morning. His greedy eyes weighed the ring's gold. The ring alone was not worth the risk.

"Sorry, guv'nor. Ye know as well as the next 'tis a

dozen barred doors 'twixt here and freedom. Was I to be caught, they'd string me up beside ye, quick as light."

Fletch shook his head with a regretful sigh. 'Twas not fair, a thousand pounds offered when he could least afford to gamble on it. A sulky look further drooped his thin features. "Should've asked sooner, guv'nor, afore the case came before the courts. Ain't much a thousand pounds couldn't buy, not then."

He turned on his heel, dragging the cell door closed behind him until he remembered that Commoner had offered him gold for the new female prisoner. A smile flickered on the turnkey's face. It would not be a thousand pounds, but it would be enough to buy a few more bottles of brandy. "Ye still of a mind for the lady, I'll see to it," he called as he turned the key in the lock.

Merlyn flung himself back among the bedding. He knew what the turnkey thought. The irony of it was he did have the thousand pounds. They were sewn into the lining of the velvet coat he had worn when arrested. He had not thought of it before because, until this night, he had not truly believed that he would die. A tremor close to fear rippled through him. It was not death he abhorred but the thought that only jackals would profit by it.

Merlyn looked down at the ring on his hand. The emerald and sapphire jewel was his talisman, the key to his secret lives. The gold meant nothing, but he would swallow the ring before he left it to ride the bloody hand of the hangman.

He eased his heavy frame lower in the bed, realizing the girl's screams had subsided. It had been a long time since he had felt a woman beneath him, even longer since he had truly enjoyed it. What would she be like, this wandering lady of the highway? Perhaps, he thought, raising the bottle yet again, she could make him hate less his impending loss of the world. He had been too little loved in this life. It was the grudge he bore the world. It was all he would regret in dying. But he was not a man given to wasting precious hours in bitterness. He would take what was offered and ask nothing more.

Chapter Two

HER SCREAMS HAVING RUN THEIR COURSE, CASSANDRA stood rigid in the center of the room. The hysteria had released the pent-up fears of the last hours, but as the terror retreated so did her strength. Her mind, bruised and aching, resisted any effort to flex or operate.

A tremor shook her, but she felt disembodied as she stood in the blackness. Without conscious thought, she wrapped her arms about herself, swaying slightly from side to side as if comforting a crying child.

"Miss? Ye awake, miss?"

She had not heard the shuffling footsteps moving along the corridor, but the sound of a human voice at her door sent her spinning around. The grille hatch was open and she saw a pair of eyes staring into the darkness of her cell.

"Ye be the wench Dowerty brought in afore dark?"

Cassandra's heart began to pump, slow thick thuds that shook her as she remembered the gaoler's promise to return before the night was over.

Don't answer! her mind urged. *Don't move and he'll move on!*

She knew it was a futile hope even before the key scraped in the lock. In full panic, she threw herself against the far wall, pressing her slender body to the cold, slimy stones as if she could force herself into the mortar that held them together.

Fletch moved cautiously into the room. He had made certain that Dowerty was sitting to his evening meal before coming for the girl. Even so, he did not trust candlelight. It would cast suspicious shadows along a corridor that should be quiet this time of night. The smoking torch on the hall wall stretched dull yellow fingers of light into the cell and Fletch followed them with his eyes until he found the girl.

"Here, miss. Ye'll catch yer death, pressed up agin' them stones." He took a step forward, but a whimper from her made him halt. "Sh!" he cautioned softly. "Ye'll get the pair o' us in a mort o' trouble. 'Tis only Fletch with a bit o' good news. There's a gentleman waiting for ye."

"A gentleman?" Cassandra turned her face toward the light, and Fletch swallowed an oath in astonishment.

She was as pale as linen and some woman's nails had left thin red trails along her left cheek, but these did not detract from her youthful beauty. The delicate planes of her face, even though muted by shadows, proclaimed that she was no common slut. His eyes moved from her face to her slender throat, then to the tempting roundness of her bosom where the soft sheen of her skin slipped out of his sight into the low,

19

square-cut neckline of her shift. She did not wear her dark hair powdered and dressed high in ringlets like London ladies, but he doubted the prisoner would mind. The heavy fall tumbled nearly to her waist.

Fletch expelled his breath in a greedy chuckle. One look at the girl and Jack Commoner would pay through the nose. "There's aplenty o' gold to be had tonight, and don't I know it!" he murmured delightedly to himself.

"Come along, be a good girl, and I'll have ye to a warm, dry place afore Dowerty knows what's what."

Cassandra narrowed suspicious eyes on the man. "There's a gentleman to see me?"

"Aye! That's the ticket. Asked special for ye, he did."

Who had come for her? Was it rescue? Had she remembered a name, sent for someone, after all? Cassandra closed her eyes briefly as drowsiness washed over her. The minutes were blending together, confusing her. "How—how did he know I'm here?" she questioned softly.

Fletch threw a worried look to the open cell door. Dowerty was not the sort to linger over a meal, especially if he had marked a female for his attentions afterward. "Time's awastin', miss. Ye don't come, Dowerty will, that's a fact."

Cassandra started in fright when he stepped up to her, but she did not pull away when his hand slipped under her elbow to guide her from the cell. Anything was better than remaining where Dowerty might find her, she told herself.

"Well? Come on!" Fletch hissed when the girl moved reluctantly into the corridor. "And quiet, mind."

They moved through a serpentine maze of corridors that never seemed to end. One after the other, the darkened doorways of many cells passed through her vision. So many that she finally lowered her head to shut out thoughts of the misery that lay behind each.

"Here we are, miss," Fletch said finally, pausing to reach for the ring of keys at his waist. He fitted one into the lock of the nearest door and it opened.

Cassandra watched the yawning opening of another cell in disbelief. "You said a gentleman wanted to see me." Her heart hammered painful strokes as hysteria began working like fermenting yeast through her veins, rising to the surface of her mind once more. "I thought I was to go free!" she whispered faintly.

Irritated by her reluctance, Fletch reached out to take her by the arm, but she struck him in the face with the flat of her hand and swung wildly away.

"Cor!" Fletch cried. "Ye can't do that! Come here, ye sneaky little slut!"

The cry did not stop Cassandra. She tore down the hall, only to nearly collide with the burly figure of the chief gaoler who suddenly appeared in the end of the corridor. The light from the torch in his meaty fist briefly illuminated his gross features and what she saw made the bile rise to her throat. He was grinning at her, the black stubs of his rotten teeth revealed within thick lips. "Come here, girlie," he said, raising his arms to her.

Sickened by the possibility of being swallowed in his

filthy embrace, she turned to run in the opposite direction, but Fletch blocked her path. Fear hung like an icy splinter in her throat as she realized she was trapped. Then, suddenly, she saw the open cell door, inviting her to seek shelter in the darkness it offered. In desperation she launched herself across the threshold and into the blackness.

"Had I realized my offer would be so repugnant to you, I could have saved us both the trouble."

The deep masculine voice, as soft as velvet, sounded in the darkness as strong arms reached out to halt her headlong flight. A moment later she was enfolded against the firm hard warmth of another body. In speechless surprise, Cassandra looked up to the man towering above her.

Shadows dulled the details of his features, but she had the impression of a harshly handsome face striped by a leather patch which hid one eye. And power, a power so strong that her fear momentarily subsided. Yielding once more to instinct, she stayed within the stranger's embrace. She felt no fear, no inkling of danger, as she accepted the heat of his body against hers, his dark form like a mast about which sailors lashed themselves in a storm. There was only the feeling of power, of security, of safety, that she had felt once long ago in the arms of another stranger. Without conscious thought she spoke the words forming in her mind.

"Please, have mercy! Save me!"

Two loud belches rumbled up from his belly as Dowerty moved into the dim cell. He did not like interruptions at mealtime and his natural inclination to dyspepsia flared at the sight that greeted his eyes. There before him, her slender arms locked about the waist of a condemned prisoner, stood the flighty bit of muslin he had labeled his own this night.

"What's this?" Dowerty swung around and grabbed Fletch by the collar. Twice the size and weight of the turnkey, Dowerty shook Fletch with the tenacity of a bulldog with a bone. "Try to cozen me, will ye?" He thrust the man's head against the wall, and it made a sickening thud as it connected with the stone.

Fletch shrieked out his pain, blood gushing from his broken nose, as Dowerty cast him bodily into the corridor. "Out! Ye scum! Out!" Scrambling to his feet, the turnkey fled into the dark.

Dowerty hoisted his breeches with a hand and turned back into the cell, his torch lighting the way. He recognized instantly the prisoner's posture of challenge, and his eyes slid from the man's broad shoulders to the fetters circling his right wrist. His gaze lowered to the iron ring around the prisoner's right ankle, and he smiled for the first time. The prisoner was hampered by the weight and length of his chains.

All of this passed quickly through the gaoler's mind. His real interest was the girl. A frown scored his narrow brow as he realized that she now was nearly hidden by the barrier of the prisoner's tall frame.

"Stand free o' the prisoner, wench!" he ordered.

For a moment Cassandra held her breath, in expectation of a challenge from her defender, but the tall man said nothing, his shadow the only comfort offered.

Swallowing her bitter disappointment, she forced herself to step beyond the shadow, her fingers tightening into white-knuckled fists.

"Aye, that's better," Dowerty exclaimed in smacking satisfaction as the girl's half-dressed figure came into his view. He watched as the torch's flame slipped up and over the curves of her breasts, dancing in the valley between and seeking the places where his own fingers would soon delve. Lust swelled his dirty breeches, increasing his impatience.

"Come along quiet, girl. We've a bit o' business to pass between us." He reached out grinning for her, but Cassandra drew back out of his reach, a shiver of revulsion sweeping her.

Dowerty's gaze narrowed, the puffy flesh about his eyes nearly swallowing them. "So! 'Twill be that way." A malicious grin drew back his thick red lips from a jumble of blackened teeth. "I've showed better tarts than ye how to give a man his due."

"No!" Cassandra whirled on the silent chained man, despair making her bold. "Please, sir, can you do nothing?"

Merlyn turned his emerald gaze on the young girl who did not quite reach his shoulder, and the smile he offered her was bittersweet. "You ask for my help," he said gently. "What you truly expect is protection for your virtue. That I will not promise, but I can spare you this."

Dowerty's piggish eyes darted from one to another, understanding at last why the girl had been allowed out of her cell. A cunning look came into his muddy brown eyes. "The bitch's mine, and there's an end to it."

Merlyn knew what was expected and reached into the pocket of his breeches to withdraw a coin purse. His gaze never left the girl's panic-stricken face as he said to the gaoler, "'Tis all I have. Take it and leave."

Dowerty's eyes moved mockingly over the prisoner and a sly grin creased his features. "I could bash yer head in with this torch and take yer gold and the wench to boot."

Merlyn shrugged. "If you wish to cheat the hangman of his fee, 'tis no matter to me."

Cassandra looked up, amazed by the indifference in the stranger's tone, and came once more under the blaze of his single emerald eye. His was a hard face to look upon, pale from weeks of imprisonment. When she had rushed unknowingly into his arms and been cradled briefly against the warm solid flesh of his broad chest, their momentary contact had made her believe that safety lay with him. Nothing in the dark shadows of his face promised that now. Yet the feeling persisted, compelling her to speak. Uncurling her fingers, she held out a cold, trembling hand to the manacled man. "Please," she whispered.

Immediately, it was caught up in a warm strong hand half again the size of her own.

Dowerty licked his lips, still slick with grease from his meal. "Have it yer way, me cunning little baggage. Come the morn, I'll have ye singing a different tune." Chuckling, he displayed a thick-palmed hand. "The gold."

"When you've handed over the key to these." Merlyn rattled the chain attached to his right wrist.

Dowerty started to protest, but his covetous gaze

fastened on the purse of gold. He could see the shapes of a dozen coins against the cloth.

Merlyn smiled slightly, reading the man's thoughts. "I cannot make the lady comfortable chained like a beast."

Dowerty nodded numbly. Backing out of the cell, he dragged the door with him, mumbling, "Ye can't escape. Even without them chains, there's a door 'twixt ye and me."

Cassandra felt little relief as the victory in the battle of wills fell to her champion. She had only chosen between the lesser of two evils.

Sensing her discomfort, Merlyn released her hand and took her instead by the waist, pressing her close until she was scored from shoulder to thigh with the heat of his body. Bending down, he whispered in her ear, "Be easy, my lady." His firm lips brushed her cheek and then settled in calm deliberation against her own.

For an amazed instant Cassandra felt the tantalizing pressure of the stranger's brandy-warmed breath upon her lips. The touch of his lips, too subtle to call a kiss, was as light as the brush of a butterfly's wing. Yet it left a burning impression upon her mouth such as if he had touched a live ember to it. And then he gently set her away from himself. Shocked by the power of his touch, she shivered in the chill darkness.

"I'll have the key now," Merlyn called to the gaoler in a tone that had nothing to do with the sweet taste of the kiss he had just sampled. That showed in the tiny smile curving his mouth.

"Come and get it, me tart," Dowerty replied, inserting the key through the narrow space of the peephole.

Merlyn handed Cassandra the gold purse. "The key first, then the gold."

Like a sleepwalker, Cassandra did as she was bid, feeling no part in the actions which sealed her fate. When she turned from the door, listening to the gaoler's retreating footsteps, the small iron key lay in her palm like an omen of her future.

Merlyn reached for the candle and tinderbox that had been of no use to him an hour before. The spark caught the wick and light sputtered, fluttered, and then brightened into being.

Cassandra's first clear impression of her protector was of his darkness. A thick unruly mane of black hair covered the well-molded head. Not even a dusting of powder dampened the sheen of the raven-black hair curling against his pale olive complexion. *Gypsy. Pirate*. The leather patch angled across his brow made her think of dangerous company and adventure. Repulsed yet attracted by his exotic countenance, she looked away, to have her gaze snagged by the mat of fine dark hair revealed by his opened shirt. Eyes sliding lower, she found narrow hips and well-muscled thighs and then the fetters that held him chained to the wall behind.

She stared at the chains. He was a prisoner the same as she. She had thought the turnkey would bring her to a gentleman who had come to give her her freedom. Instead, he had brought her to this man. The implication of that action struck her fully for the first time. Abruptly her gaze rose to his face again.

Oh, Lord! she thought. *Why did I not think of that before?*

"You are pleased by your assessment?" Merlyn's tone was amused as he turned and found two great dark eyes on him. Until now he had seen very little of his purchase, but he already knew more of her than she might suspect. Her manner and speech bespoke a gentle breeding, but those had not convinced him that she was not an experienced streetwalker. It was her response to his embrace. No whore would have remained unmoved under his kiss. One softening of her lips, the smallest surrender to his invitation, and he would have caught her out. Not that it mattered. The urge was strong within him. He did not expect her to be a virgin, but it gave him satisfaction to know that he would not share his bed with a seasoned slut.

She was not a great beauty, he saw that at once, but neither did he find any cause for complaint. The long tangle of soft brown hair framing her young face was more unusual, and he marveled at it. She must be a country mouse. The dirty damp shift she wore left little to his active imagination as he quickly noted a tiny waist, softly flaring hips, and the enticing curves of firm young breasts. Yes, he liked what he saw. Washed and properly dressed, she would prove a diversion for a time.

The pattern of his thoughts brought a sudden scowl to Merlyn's features. Unlike the times before, he would not have the luxury of growing tired of the girl. One night. It was all he had. The brandy he had consumed made him impatient to spend it as best he could.

"The key, my lady."

Exhaustion had made her lids fall shut, but now Cassandra looked full into the stranger's face and met a stare that made her very aware of her half-dressed state. Flushing deeply, she clutched the front of her shift to fold it high on her bosom, but the clinging silk, pulled tight, outlined more fully the curve of hip and rounding of breast, sights she wanted to keep hidden.

Watching her, Merlyn's smile became a grin. "The key, if you please."

"No!" Her cry surprised Cassandra more than it did the man before her. As she backed away from him, she heard the rich disturbing sound of his laughter.

"So, you have a little courage. I had begun to wonder. Perhaps you would care for a sip of brandy?" He pointed to the bottle by the bed.

This time Cassandra merely shook her head as her hand closed tightly over the small key in her palm.

"You would feel more at ease if I introduced myself," Merlyn continued as if she had politely agreed. "Here in Newgate I am known as Jack Commoner, but I will tell you a secret." He winked at her. "Merlyn is my name. And you?"

"Cass—" Cassandra paused. She had known her name until the moment she began to speak it, then the knowledge winked out ahead of her tongue.

"Cass? Cassie? Is that it?" Merlyn encouraged. He saw her frown, her spiky dark lashes fluttering to her cheeks in a childish gesture of confusion, and wondered at her mercurial nature. It seemed she had no skill in the art of deception, that her expressions were a perfect reflection of her emotions, but he had lived too long to trust even his eyes. The sudden thought struck him that she might be dim-witted. Merlyn smiled. His interest was in that portion of her where wits were of least value.

"I have kept my part, Cassie. You must know what I expect in return. Believe me, it would pain me to hand your lovely innocence over to Dowerty. Yet I will do it and without hesitation if you do not give me the key. Now."

Cassandra looked up. He had made no move toward her, but she felt the full force of his will come to bear on her in his unwavering green gaze. He might have been invoking a spell, so strong was the lure. The strangely familiar sensation of helplessness before a superior force washed over her. The feeling was so clearly remembered that she knew a moment of panic. The urge to defy him made her lift her hand to throw the key away, beyond his reach.

"You won't like keeping Dowerty company," Merlyn warned when he understood what she meant to do.

With a cry halfway between a sob and a moan she flung the key at him and whirled away.

Merlyn caught up the bit of metal easily and inserted it into the locks holding the fetters about his wrist and ankle. If his conscience pricked him for having frightened the girl into submission he paid it no heed. He wanted her.

"No! No!" Cassandra cried when strong hands took hold of her and spun her around to face her captor. Using all that remained of her waning strength, she kicked out at him and twisted her body to be free.

"Don't," Merlyn said and brought her hard against his chest. Her slippered feet beat harmlessly against his legs as he captured her arms between their bodies in an enfolding embrace.

He met her gaze. "You have no choice, my dear. You are alone with me. There'll be none to come in answer to your cries. Do you understand? And I am not a man to be swayed by a few tears." When he saw that she was about to scream he quickly lowered his head to stop the cry.

The kiss fell unexpectedly upon Cassandra's mouth, the warm firm persuasion of his lips. The method of his attack momentarily surprised her and she accepted the hard pressure of his mouth. After a moment she felt the parting of his lips on hers, then the touch of his tongue like a flick of flame against her tightly closed mouth.

A tiny shock went through her and she tried to struggle against the intimate gesture, but her resistance made scarce any impression on the man holding her. He merely tightened his arms until she could hardly breathe. The skin of his chest under her fingertips seemed to scald her as she pressed against him until, finally, she recognized the heavy steady stroking of his heart beneath her right palm. He was a man, only that, she thought. Whatever she might suffer from him, womanly intuition warned her that it might be tempered by her response.

Her actions were those born of an unreasoned desire to lessen the torment to which she expected to be put, not from any knowledge of men. But later, when her knowledge was greater, she knew her actions would have been no different.

When his lips parted once more she followed his example and this time his seeking tongue met not the barrier of tight lips but the warm sweetness of her mouth.

Merlyn murmured his approval of her surrender as his tongue curled into her mouth, drawing from it a measure of her unique taste. Pleasure scored through him when, hesitantly, she met his tongue with the tip of her own. The action, so shy and uncertain, convinced him that she was new to the intimacy. It did not lessen the pleasure.

When he raised his head, breaking the long, deep kiss, he felt her shuddery hiss of indrawn breath and knew he was not the only one affected by their contact. Reluctantly, he put her away from himself, smiling tenderly at her. "There, Cassie. Tell me you find me not too much to your distaste."

Cassandra looked up into his face, wishing to gauge the effect of her actions. The glittering in his eye promised much, but it did not offer freedom. "Please, do not—" She swallowed and closed her eyes to prevent the pricking of tears. He had said they would not help.

"Innocent," Merlyn murmured softly, reaching out to touch her wounded cheek. He frowned. "Who clawed you?"

Cassandra shook her head, lifting her face from the cradle of his palm. "The women in the common cell. Horrid creatures!"

Merlyn understood. His eyes went briefly over her. Her shift was of the finest silk, embroidered with tiny rosebuds along the neck. It was a wonder they did not strip the girl bare, he thought with a cynical twist to his lips. Of course, she would not be here now if they had.

The common cells housed male as well as female prisoners, and gang rape was common. Common cells, common crimes, how aptly it applied.

"You are not a slut, are you, my dear?"

A spark of hope flared in Cassandra's throbbing brain. "You think . . . you believed!" She almost laughed as she put a hand on his arm in a pleading gesture. "Oh, sir, I swear to you, I am no tart. If that is the reason you had me brought to you I must—"

"Nothing will spare you," Merlyn inserted calmly into her frantic speech, and the effect was like a splash of water on a flame. As if bitten, she jerked her hand away. All the light that had animated her face, flushing her cheeks and widening her dark eyes, died.

Angry with himself for giving her even the momentary belief that she might somehow escape him, Merlyn decided the moment for conversation was past. She would learn for herself before the night was over that her fate at his hands would not be all unpleasantness. Without hesitation, he reached for her again. This time he lifted her up against him, an arm about her shoulders, the other under her knees, and carried her to the pile of rugs that made up his bed. The feel of her small weight reminded him again of the taste of her mouth and he sought her lips with his own.

Cassandra made no resistance when his arms went about her, lifting her up with ease. She felt as helpless as a shuttlecock, batted back and forth between her will and his. But when she felt his lips on hers, she gave up to tears that flooded her cheeks.

Merlyn bent and placed her on the bed, surprised by the taste of salt that had mingled with her kiss. He had been honest when he told her that tears would not affect his desire, but he was not unmoved. He could see her gaze clearly now and he was amazed to discover that her eyes were not brown as he had first supposed but the rich dark gold of clover honey. He pushed a silky strand of hair back from her brow, wishing that she would close the thickly fringed eyes staring up at him. They met his gaze with a hope he found touching and made him feel emotions he thought had died within him, things like compassion—and pity. But none of them altered his own need.

"Life is not fair, my lady. You would have had to learn that lesson one day." He smiled a little. "You cannot turn me from my desire to bed you. Your kisses would never discourage a man. But I will make you a bargain. I paid the turnkey to bring you to me. I am not so miserly that I will not offer you something, also. What would you have of me?"

"My freedom," Cassandra answered without hesitation.

Merlyn smiled ruefully. He had expected as much and was ready. "If I could arrange that, what would you offer me in return?" This she did not answer. He did not expect her to. "One night of your company, little one. That is what I want. Then I will buy you your freedom."

Cassandra gazed at him, unaware that the mysterious golden depths of her dark eyes made the man more determined than ever to bed her. She did not know that her direct gaze of innocence also held within it the subtle lure of an unwitting temptress.

"You can purchase my freedom?" she whispered.

The dark face above her did not alter a whit; he might have been made of granite but for the pulse at his throat.

She licked her lips self-consciously. Confused images animated the corners of her mind, just out of reach. But one clear thought finally emerged. She was lost and alone, without memory or protection. This would be her only hope to escape Newgate, and she knew it. "I agree."

Inexplicably, Merlyn found her answer annoying and he frowned. "Is it that simple for you? Why should you trust me? I could take you now and forget on the morrow."

"That's true," Cassandra answered, her eyes never wavering from the forbidding face so near hers. "But if I have the choice, I'll accept the embraces of a clean man over the . . . the other."

The reasoning was childishly simple, but Merlyn's mouth tightened against the curious softening he felt toward her. Innocence was a thing lost to him before he learned to cherish it. "I wish I could believe your naïveté. To have found an honest soul on my last night on earth would make up for a great deal."

The words startled him; he had not meant to say them aloud. It must be the brandy, he decided and quickly looked about for the bottle. "You must share my brandy, for it will make things much easier—and then we will learn together your mysteries. If you are frightened and fight me, you will only hurt yourself."

He saw her cringe and wondered for the first time what would become of her when dawn pinked the sky. "Why are you in London, Cassie?"

Cassandra's head moved fitfully on the pillow, new tears splashing free from beneath her lashes. "I don't remember."

When she fell silent, he reached for the brandy bottle and bucket of water he had used earlier to bathe himself. There was one thing more he was determined upon before climbing into bed. He would bathe her. Perhaps she had been clean before she arrived at Newgate—her undergarments certainly were expensive —but the filth and odor of the place had quickly attached itself to her. The whores who jumped her had probably rubbed her face in filthy hay. That would be like them.

Cassandra closed her eyes. What miseries would he inflict upon her? she wondered wretchedly.

Hands lifted her into a sitting position and the cold hard touch of glass against her lips made her eyes fly open just as brandy ran onto her tongue. She gasped in surprise, inhaling a drop of the fiery liquid, and choked. Then another drop of brandy found its path down her throat, smoothing over the searing pain of the first.

"Drink, little one," Merlyn commanded, grasping firmly the slender column of her neck and tilting the bottle to her lips once more. "I've precious little patience with maidenly tears this night." He urged the lip of the bottle against her soft mouth once more, holding it steady until he was certain she had accepted enough of the potent liquid to relax her.

"Now," he said in satisfaction, pressing her gently back down on the bed, "my lady should be ready for her bath."

Cassandra jerked under the pressure of his hands. "You cannot be serious?"

"But I am, my sweet," Merlyn replied silkily. "Your kisses are pleasant enough, but you smell of the sewer. I've a remedy for that." So saying, he reached down to pick up the cloth he had dipped in the bucket. He wrung it out before her astonished gaze. "I'm unskilled in the art of lady's maid, but it's my belief we shall deal well together."

Cassandra gasped in outrage as the cloth touched her cheek, but he held her firmly to the bed with a hand on her shoulder. "Don't, Cassie," he warned, and she closed her eyes. Why, oh, why could she not be left alone? She wanted only that. The brandy roiled in her, reminding her of the stale bread and bowl of gruel she had been too sick at heart to eat. When had she last eaten? Was it yesterday, the day before?

Behind closed eyes she began to drift. After a while, she forgot that the cool cloth bathing her cheeks and throat was wielded by a stranger who had bought her for his lusty pleasure. The brandy was a blessing, she decided. A swallow more, perhaps, and she would never remember this night.

Merlyn watched her face intently as he wiped the grime from it. Beneath the layer of dirt he discovered fine blue veins throbbing at her temples, the tender curves of her cheek, and a small dimple in the fullness of her chin. How old was she? he wondered. His eyes lowered to the swelling fullness of her breasts above the low neck of her chemise and he smiled. Old enough.

Dark lashes lay like tiny feathers against her skin and he reached out to touch one lightly. She blinked and looked to him, her sherry-gold eyes enormous in her face.

"Ah, Cassie, you do please me," he said softly and bent to place his lips lightly against hers. She trembled under the caress of his lips, and Merlyn murmured softly into her mouth, "If you would make me desire you less, do not quiver at the mere touch of my lips to yours."

His lips moved to her ear and breathed in tantalizing whispers, "Be cold, Cassie. Turn your lips to steel, drain the warmth from your skin." He moved to kiss her throat and then each temple, saying, "Do not allow the pulse to beat so strongly here . . . and here . . . and here."

Like strong drink, his voice mesmerized her, stilling her every impulse to turn from him. He said be cold, and yet her skin felt inflamed wherever he touched her, his thigh against her arm, his hip pressed alongside her waist. He said do not shiver, but she could not still the tremors or steady her pulse or even keep her lips stiff against the assault of his tongue. When it dipped into the moist valley behind her lower lip, the world seemed to explode in a shower of tiny silver stars. What was he doing to her? she wondered. Was it the brandy? Or was this magic that he worked upon her with only his voice and mouth?

Cassandra did not protest when his hands slid under her and raised her up to lean against his broad chest. She must stop him, she thought, but no longer cared to. It was as if he had cast a spell to remove her reluctance and fear, and replaced it with strange rough desires for which she had no name. Dimly she remembered he had called himself Merlyn, the most powerful of magicians.

Again there was the maddening brush of his lips upon hers. It triggered a memory of another kiss, a sweet chaste brushing of lips that had won her totally to a man whose name she could not recall. The memory blended with the present behind her closed lids, and the desire she had felt in that moment urged her to hold this time what once she had lost.

Reaching out blindly, she found the strong column of a masculine neck and her arms encircled it. One of her hands scored into the thick black hair at the nape and her fingers flexed, drawing his head down hard to hers.

With a fleeting moment of surprise at her burst of passion, Merlyn allowed her to direct the kiss. He held back from her, forcing her to hold him close. It was her lips which parted first, her seeking that brought the intimate return of his own.

Stealthily, his hands began a gentle roaming of her slim body. When his fingers grazed the long curve of her spine she arched involuntarily against him. His palms molded the sides of her waist, then rose slowly to her ribs, where his thumbs hooked under the glorious full softness of her breasts.

Caught yet again in surprise by the mystery of his touch, Cassandra gasped, her eyes flying wide in wonder upon the raven-haired stranger before her. It was the memory of the golden-haired man she sought, not the embrace of this man. But a thick sweet stirring of her blood began as his hands smoothed lightly over her face. The throbbing at her temples had found new, unexpected places to inhabit, in her breasts, her belly, and her thighs, and she was helpless against the stirrings.

"Do not fear me," Merlyn murmured, cupping her face in a strong hand. "Let me hold you, touch you, as I wish. Do you not yet know there is only pleasure to be had from me?"

Confused by her own body's reaction to his fondling, Cassandra murmured, " 'Tis wicked."

"If 'tis wicked, my lady, 'tis the most delicious wickedness ever devised." Merlyn eased her gently down onto the mattress. "Let me work. You need do nothing more."

She had best do nothing more! The thought echoed in Merlyn's mind as he drew a shuddery breath and reached for the lacing that closed her shift. She lay acquiescent and pliant under his hands. An accomplished mistress could have been no more provocative, he thought, savoring the tautening at the base of his belly.

Cassandra tried to remain calm under the path of his hands, but they seemed to feed the fever within her. When he removed her shift cold night air rushed across her flesh, making her gasp.

Merlyn echoed her gasp, but for a very different reason. He had revealed to his sight her full, exquisitely formed breasts.

Cassandra watched his face, waiting for him to speak, but he did not. Instead, he reached down and cupped a handful of water, then let it spill in a tiny waterfall from his palm onto one breast. Before his fascinated gaze, the soft areola darkened instantly, the nipple at its center forming a hard ruby pebble that dared his touch.

Merlyn bent his head to take first one, then the other of the taut peaks of her breasts between his lips.

Cassandra sighed as the heat of his body settled onto her, his warm heavy weight both a comfort and a torment. Hands moved up her sides, caressing the bare skin, then seeking and finding the precious weight of her breasts, touching her in ways she had never before experienced. It was wrong, wicked, she told herself, to garner any pleasure from this, but her body would not deny itself.

Merlyn's parted lips left a trail of wet flame across her throat and breasts before rising to still the throb of her lips. His fingers found the slender column of her throat, worked down the lushness of her bosom, and then began a gentle massage of her belly.

As his thumb dipped into the tiny well of her navel, he said urgently, "You are my last love, Cassie. You were made for this night—for me. You will remember it, always."

His fingers dipped lower, into the secret recesses of her being, and Cassandra cried out in astonishment, but his tender assault did not alter or lessen.

"Lie and enjoy, Cassie," he urged in a bare whisper against her ear. His teeth raked the lobe as he said, "Is this not pleasure? Is it not the most splendid wickedness you've ever known?"

Heated waves of sensation swelled and foamed in and about Cassandra's senses, the surgings of emotion too complex and confusing for her to give them name. There was only the feel of his lips and tongue and, ah yes, his hands. The tightening of her womb was a new experience, yet she knew he must hold the answer to the aching swiftly becoming unbearable. His fingers sought and found, only to give rise to a quickening desire for something more, something as yet unattained.

With a low sigh of surrender, she flung her arms about his neck to pull him down on her, as if by pressure alone she could ease the nearly painful aching that tautened her body like a bow. It no longer mattered that he was a stranger. So was she, even to herself. All that mattered was the magic, the glorious torment of which he was master.

When the instinctive clasping of her thighs loosened, Merlyn knew he had won. She was ready for him, more ready than she realized in her innocence. Quickly, he divested himself of his clothing and then he braced himself on his knees, one on either side of her waist.

Looking down, he found that fear had once again crept into the dark honey of her eyes. As he gazed at her, thoughts crowded his mind. It was his last night on earth, his last time ever to lie with a woman. Her mere acceptance of him was not enough. She would be the last thought of his life, yet he must expect to be forgotten by her.

The thought scored like a blade through the brandy heat of his intoxication. He did not want to be forgotten, to have his memory pushed aside. He wanted . . . needed . . .

And then knew what he desired: something of himself to be left behind in a world that had never wanted him. He desired to fill her belly with the seed of his loins, his life, which might flower and bear fruit after he was gone.

"Cassie, look at me."

Cassandra opened her eyes to the serious dark face above her. There was still the intense green flame of his gaze, but now a new, more tender expression rode his strong features. Her gaze fell before his to discover his nakedness. There, below his belly in a nest of black hair, she saw for the first time the naked perfection of a man.

Merlyn reached out and took her hand firmly in his. "Come. Do not be afraid to feel what your eyes have seen." Slowly but deliberately he uncurled her fingers and wrapped them about his warm hard flesh, sighing as her hand trembled and his flesh answered with a surge of desire.

"There," he said raggedly. "I am but flesh and blood, no more than what you hold in your hand. As my fingers give you pleasure, so my flesh will please you. Trust me, Cassie. Let me share your innocence." Without waiting for a reply, he lowered himself onto her, crushing her softness with the hard warmth of his body.

Again Cassandra felt the magic of his fingers; then he lifted his hips slightly and a new probing began. He lifted her, holding her buttocks, and slowly entered her. The pressure built quickly and then a quick deep thrust brought him into her.

He smothered her cry with his mouth, but a tear slipped out of her, trickling down her cheek. In natural response to the invasion of her body, Cassandra lifted her hips to throw him off. But he, too, moved, meeting her surging with strong deliberate thrusts of his body which drove him deeper and deeper till she believed she would split in two. Where was the pleasure he had promised and first given? she wondered in misery. Was it all a lie to keep her from fighting him?

Yet, even as the questions formed, the thrusting found a new rhythm, an irresistible pattern that her body adopted as its own.

Merlyn made himself move gently at first. He knew and understood the gift of her virginity, and exulted in the victory. She would not be able to forget him now. He had made her a woman.

When, at last, she found the ancient rhythm, he gave a chuckle of joy and made her his with the swift long shooting out of his seed.

"Now! Now! You belong to me!" he whispered fiercely. "Always!"

Cassandra lay awake listening to the rhythmic breathing of the man sleeping by her side. *What have I done? What have I done?* Over and over the single thought tolled in her mind.

The curtains of doubt parted and memory burst upon her, complete in every detail. She was Lady Cassandra Briarcliffe, wife of Nicholas Briarcliffe, and a fugitive from the care of her father-in-law, the Marquess of Briarcliffe.

Tears spilled upon the bedding beneath her head. She had been running away to London, in search of her husband, when a carriage accident and a blow to her head left her at the mercies of an unsympathetic magistrate. And now she had shared the lust of a Newgate criminal.

Cassandra closed her eyes, not wanting to see the cell in which she lay, but she dared not move away from the arm that encircled her waist and held her firmly against the naked length of the man beside her. Twice this night he had made love to her, whispering in her ears words of passionate longing such as one might offer a lover. And she had listened because they matched so closely her dreams of lying in her husband's arms and hearing the same words. But now she dreaded his next awakening because it was all a lie.

"Cassie?"

Cassandra shuddered at the sound of his voice, heavy with sleep but warmly persuasive. She felt him move, and then he was looking down at her, an infinitely tender smile on his mouth.

"You are here. I thought—I believed I'd dreamt you." Merlyn touched her cheek with a fingertip. "I wish I had time to make you love me, Cassie. I have only the night, too far spent already." Suddenly he jerked the emerald and sapphire ring from his hand. Reaching out, he took her left hand and placed the ring on her third finger. "It's all I have, Cassie, that's of any value to me."

He paused, searching for words which would make her understand. "I would wed you, if only there was time. I would wed you and love you and give you babes aplenty."

Cassandra stared up at him through tears and Merlyn saw it as her recognition that he was to hang in a few short hours. "Don't cry for me, Cassie. You've nothing to fear with the dawn." He reached out, his fingers combing back the hair from her face. "Ah, but it's a joy simply to touch you. You're silk and velvet, my love. I have money enough sewn in the lining of my coat to buy your freedom ten times. You must take it and leave here. Go home, leave London. No one but you and I will ever know of the hours we've shared."

Merlyn suddenly lay his cheek against her heart and whispered, "Generous, sweet Cassie, do not deny me this night. I've never begged a soul on this earth for anything since I was a boy of eight. But now I beg you, for the time left me, be my love."

Later she was to marvel at the power of his voice, this mortal Merlyn with the gift of magic at his command. His voice, so tenderly pleading, had drawn her across the barrier of her uncertainty. It was as though she heard in it the fierce tenderness that was his soul. He was a stranger, for all that she had shared his bed, yet he no longer seemed so. He was right. No one need ever know of the hours they spent here or of the words they spoke or of the joy they shared. In the morning she would obtain her freedom and he—he would reap the harvest of his life. This was a moment never to touch the reality of her life.

"Come," she said, reaching out hesitantly to touch his face. "Come and hold me tight!"

Chapter Three

THE MARQUESS OF BRIARCLIFFE SAT BEFORE THE BLAZING fireplace of his London residence. The long tongues of red flame did not penetrate the cold of his bones as he sucked steaming tea through the pleated lips of his toothless mouth. Once it had been a fine mouth, wide and thin-lipped to suit a handsome face. Veins worked only a spiderwebbing of color through the now-faded parchment of his bony nose and thin cheeks. The once copper-bright hair was bleached with age and covered by a red velvet turban. Those who remembered him as a high-spirited rake who had gamed and whored and drunk his youthful way through London Town would hardly have recognized him. They would look at the blue piping of his hands, large-knuckled with rheumatism, and exclaim in pity for the musician who had fiddled a tune worthy of the king's ear. They would say nothing remained.

And yet they would be wrong. One had only to look

into his gaze. The eyes that had once been a perfect foil for his fine aristocratic features now protruded from their sunken sockets, the last vivid evidence of the spirit of the man locked now in a shell of rigid bone and flaccid muscle. The clear irises, so pale a blue they appeared like lake water, were sharper than ever.

A narrow crinkling of his lips that might have been a smile moved the marquess's mouth. He might hate his disabilities, but they had their uses. They earned him a kind of power over his household he had never attained as an active man. When he sat so still his household thought he dozed, he listened to learn the guilty secrets of others that he might later turn against them. He had learned to foil, bedazzle, and direct the lives of every man, woman, and child within the boundaries of his property, everyone but Nicholas.

Enraged by the pain and frustration of his useless body, he had quickly come to a malignant dislike for those who still possessed youth and vigor, in particular his only child, Nicholas. They were too much alike. As the father's resentment of his son's inherited beauty and charm turned from envy into hate the son had merely flaunted his dissolute pastimes in his detested sire's face for spite.

"Confound the boy for a fool!" he muttered suddenly and flung his Chantilly teacup toward the fireplace, where it smashed against the brass screen and littered the marble hearth with porcelain splinters. He would settle the score with Nicholas. But first, he must find his runaway daughter-in-law, the discarded bride Nicholas had left on his doorstep two years earlier.

"My lord?" A faint rustle of petticoats accompanied the cry as his housekeeper appeared in the doorway.

The marquess did not look up but tucked his chin deeper into the folds of the tartan blanket spread about his shoulders. "There's a damnable chill about. Colder than a witch's tit and twice as bitter!" He thumped the arm of his chair with a gnarled fist. "Where's Dermont? Am I so ill served that I must go myself to do my business? Call for a sedan chair. I will take to the streets of this Sodom myself!"

"That won't be necessary, m'lord." Kendal Dermont stepped into the room, the edge of his cloak streaming with damp from the fog.

The marquess was not often affected by the sight of the tall, slender man who served as his secretary and companion. On any other occasion he would have castigated the plain-featured second cousin for his overt attempt to impress his employer by appearing in his street garb. However, the success of the mission upon which the man had been sent was too important. The older man could not quite control the tremor in his voice as he said, "Well? Where's Lady Cassandra? Haven't you found the girl?"

Kendal heard the sharp tone with an inward smile. So, the old bastard was worried. The hell-for-leather carriage ride from Derbyshire to London had made him wonder, but the marquess was not always motivated by the needs and greeds of most men. He might only have seen the chase as a form of exercise, a chance to catch out and humiliate the girl.

Kendal moved quickly across the room, thinking that

it was too bad Lady Cassandra had not importuned *him* to help in her escape. It would have made his position as the marquess's bloodhound less difficult. Still, he had news.

"I've news, m'lord." Kendal snatched his tricornered hat from his head to reveal a poorly groomed peruke. "The news I'm bringing—" He faltered in his country speech, hardly daring to reveal his news lest his pleasure at angering the old man betray him.

"God's bones! Speak up, you jackanapes!" The volume of the marquess's voice shook his frame as it thundered forth. "The girl's dead, that's it? Well? 'Tis so?"

Kendal took a nervous step back. "I daren't say, m'lord. Questions to the authorities fetched me the news that a coach overturned on the highway a few miles north of London yesterday morn. The Bow Street Runners say 'twas the work of highwaymen. They've stopped the regular stagecoach from Leeds before."

Kendal watched the old man digest this piece of information and was annoyed to find that his employer's hand had stopped shaking. He was in control again. Well, thought Kendal, he wasn't finished yet. "One passenger was killed. The runner says the passenger was gentry by dress, and with a large ruby birthmark upon the back of his right hand."

" 'Twas Simmons," the marquess said heavily. "Did you have the wits about you to demand to see the body?"

"Just so, m'lord," Kendal replied, lowering his eyes so that the man would not see his flash of anger at the high-handed tone. "They'd buried it. The man's lace and watch chain, even his shoes, were gone. His neck was broke when the coach went off the road. The coachman ran off, but they expect he'll turn up in a day or two. Too bad about Mr. Simmons, though."

The marquess snorted. He'd waste no thought on Simmons. The music master had been a simpering fool; it was one of the reasons he had hired him to squire Lady Cassandra about the halls of Briarcliffe. The chit's depression had deepened over months as she fretted over Nicholas's failure to return. If he hadn't thought there'd come a time when he needed her he would not have cared. But a decline in the girl's health might have left him with an invalid, so he had made inquiries and found Mr. Simmons to be a suitable male companion for his son's wife.

The marquess directed a sharp look at his secretary. "'Tis your fault, Dermont. I hold you entirely responsible. Had you made a few sheep's eyes at the silly cow, she'd not have gone off with that fop. God's death! It galls a man to think that a simple-witted peagoose could get the best of—of *you*. Where were you the night they escaped?"

Kendal bowed his head even lower. "My—m'lord, 'twas your orders I was following two nights ago. Went to see the vicar about the leaks in the chapel roof. You'd a been the first to hear of it, had I sniffed a plot." He raised his hands, palms up in apology. "I'd give anything to have stopped them. No one in the village would dare take so much as tuppence from Lady Briarcliffe without your word on it."

"That's so." The marquess's lip lifted in a contemptuous smirk as he eyed the nervous man before him. No one in his employ ever crossed him; the price was too great. Yet Lady Cassandra, that meek bit of fuzzy-headed womanhood, had dared to catch the Leeds coach!

Once more his eyes raked Dermont, their baneful stare like a splash of icy water. "We've had a traitor amongst us, Dermont. Do you understand me?"

"Aye, m'lord." Kendal licked his suddenly dry lips. "'Twasn't me," he added softly.

A cackle of laughter erupted from the marquess's bony chest. "You? Damme! 'Twould do my heart good to think you capable of it. You haven't fathered a single brat in the scullery yet. Ha! You think I'm too old to hear, too tired to see you sneak up the backstairs after dark. You've been pleasuring yerself with Bess and Sally, so I know you're a man—of sorts. If you'd any real fire in your breeches, you'd have scratched my daughter-in-law's itch instead of letting her make cow eyes at that skinny-shanked music master. Damme! That's an insult I'll not let her forget!"

Kendal voiced with astonishment, "Yer lordship can't think I'd . . . well, dishonor a member of his fam—"

"Rubbish!" The marquess drummed the chair arm again. "Had I been thirty years younger I'd have seen to it meself, and made the lady glad for it, besides. Were you a real flesh-and-blood man, you'd have had at her and damned this old cock to crow for his honor!"

The exertion of his heated speech left the marquess wheezing for breath and his head fell back against the chair back as his eyelids fluttered shut.

His meekness abandoned, Kendal ordered of the

servant who lingered in the doorway, "Bring His Lordship brandy."

The housekeeper stood a moment, one hand over her mouth, digesting the revelations of the evening. The marquess was a rare visitor to London, never once in the past two years. When he had arrived on the doorstep that morning, without notice, she and the household had been thrown into paroxysms. Now she knew why.

"Poor little lamb," she murmured as she fled the salon in search of brandy. Until this night she had not known directly of the marquess's daughter-in-law. It was rumored two years earlier that the marquess's son had wed, but the lady had never been seen. And certainly Nicholas himself acted as if there were no such bride, not if the accounts in the London scandal sheets were of any account.

The marquess allowed a sip of brandy to be administered, then waved Kendal away. "Enough, Dermont. I've no desire to be torpid with brandy before I've heard the last."

"But, m'lord, it's all been said."

The marquess gave the younger man a long look. "'Tis best not be all. If that's all, then you may pack your bags and quit my sight."

Kendal set the brandy glass on the mantel. For the moment his back was turned he thought hard about what his next words should be. Another day, perhaps two, and Lady Cassandra might be dead or certainly beyond the marquess's saving. Newgate Prison was a notorious place. A young girl, unused to the ways of scoundrels and whores, she would be a perfect victim for the human vermin who inhabited the place. If she were not beaten to death for her belongings, she might be driven mad by those men who took enjoyment in rape.

The thought of being present when the marquess learned the fate of his stupid little daughter-in-law nearly made Kendal hold his tongue. He was not a mover nor a schemer, but he knew how to squeeze the most out of any opportunity. The marquess was old and ailing; this might be the trick to send him to hell.

Kendal bit his lip anxiously. He needed forty-eight hours more—but he dared not risk it. If the nobleman learned that he had kept information from him Kendal knew he would be turned out, the poor cousin and beneath contempt. No, there would be other, better opportunities.

"There's something, m'lord. A young girl was found wandering the road later that same morning. A highway coach stopped and picked her up. When she couldn't pay her fare, the coachman took her to the magistrate. She's locked up in Newgate till inquiries can be made."

The news had an electric effect on the old man. Color shot through his face and a wide grin parted his lips to reveal lumpy gums. "It's Cassandra. It must be!"

"Dunno, m'lord." Kendal shook his head slowly. "There are questions need asking. If it is Lady Briarcliffe we'd best be cautious. Don't want word reaching the common ear."

"Balderdash! You will go yourself, at once, to Newgate and drag the sly bitch out. Go now!" the marquess cried as he reached for the small statuette on the table by his chair and flung it at his secretary. "Don't bother to return without her!"

When the door in the hallway slammed closed behind Kendal, the marquess slumped back in his chair. "To think I've housed a common strumpet these two years. Should have known it when Nicholas brought her to me." *The only virgin bride to be had in the land* was how his son had described the girl.

The marquess nearly choked on his phlegm. He should have known better. The fast piece had no doubt opened her thighs to Nicholas before they wed. Fifteen years old and a slut even then.

"It's no wonder. The whey-faced brat, who else would have her?"

And now, running off with a spindle-shanks like Simmons, how she must have burned to be ridden.

The marquess pounded his chair arm with a fist. "God's death, but she'll pay for this night! If Nicholas put her—"

He paused. His son had not shown himself at Briarcliffe since leaving his bride there the night after their exchange of marriage vows. It was simply that the slut was running true to form. Nicholas had picked a hoyden bride from the mire of West Country gentry as an insult and torment.

"Nicholas will rue the day he sought to cross his father," the marquess vowed with an easing of his ire.

And the slut would be the bait in the trap he set for his son. Two years was a long time to wait for the method of laying that trap. But he could wait. He had nothing else to do.

Chapter Four

Derbyshire, England
December, 1754

BLASTS OF FRIGID AIR BLEW THROUGH THE SNOWDRIFTS, splattering slush on the small leaded glass panes of the sprawling stone mansion called Briarcliffe. In the distance, the cottages that housed Briarcliffe's tenants were nearly swamped by the deep swells of snow.

Cassandra sighed at the sight of the winter morn upon which the sun refused to shine and began tracing patterns on a frosty pane. Two months had passed since the marquess had found her in Newgate and brought her back to Briarcliffe. The shock of that ordeal had faded and now she was left with a sick empty feeling of hopelessness. The frigid landscape of northern Derbyshire reminded her how far away lay London—and her husband Nicholas. She was no closer to him now than before. Cassandra bit her lip. She was still the marquess's prisoner.

Closing her eyes, Cassandra willed before her mind's eye the perfect beauty of Nicholas's face. The golden head with winged brows above eyes of new-leaf green, the image formed itself in loving detail. Even now, after two years' absence, she could remember the thin, firm lips that made his mouth, the long, slim nose with its elegant nostrils. Their days together had numbered only four, and yet she knew all she needed to know. He was the parfit gentil knight. *Le chevalier sans peur et sans reproche.* Yet even as she strained for that image it faded and disappeared.

"Nicholas!" she cried, opening her eyes.

At that moment a whirlwind of snow and ice splattered the windows before her and she saw her own image reflected in the glass. A petite girl with great eyes filled with bitter anguish stared back at her. And she was not alone. Behind her shimmered another figure, the dark, eyepatched stranger of Newgate. He was smiling, a tender lover's smile of desire.

Memory worked on memory, invoking images she thought she'd left behind in the grim shadows of Newgate. All of it came back to her, the sweet plunder of her body by a stranger, the shameless delight she had taken in his forbidden embraces, the embraces of Merlyn Ross. For a horrified instant she stared at the image in the frosty window; then it, too, faded.

Cassandra spun around, sweat beading up on her brow, to face the room. She was alone. "Please, please let it stop!" she moaned, shutting her eyes and willing away the nightmare. It was not the first time the shadow of that dark and haunting dream had invaded her thoughts, but never more clearly than today. In some mysterious magical way the man had willed himself into her thoughts, never to be forgotten. If Nicholas was Sir Galahad, then the sorcerer of her dream world was, indeed, a Merlyn.

Cassandra shook her head impatiently, warning off further thoughts of him. She had abandoned her pride to prevent a brutal rape and survived. The pleasure she had derived was her punishment, her guilt and shame. She had done a foolish, dangerous thing in running away, but she had done it for love of Nicholas, and she prayed that she could one day make him understand that. With his forgiveness, she could survive. "One can endure anything if one must!" she said aloud to herself.

"One need not 'endure' if one is clever—or obedient."

Cassandra lifted her head, eyes widening, to find the marquess was being carried into her sitting room in a litter-chair. She had seen him but once since Newgate, and that was just after Kendal Dermont obtained her release. Then she had been too exhausted to tell whether he wished her dead or if it gave him a kind of macabre satisfaction to see her misery at having failed to escape him. Later, when she was stronger, he refused to see her. Once they returned to Briarcliffe, she was forbidden even the freedom of the hallways.

"You're a stupid girl, Cassandra," the marquess continued as he directed the two men bearing him to place him down in the middle of the room. "I'd have expected better of you. Of course . . . Oh, do come in, Dermont. Lady Cassandra will not bite."

As the two servants withdrew, Cassandra's attention turned to the secretary. They were related by marriage, but they were not friends. Dermont, who possessed a rough version of the Briarcliffe profile in which each subtle difference worked against him, was too much under the marquess's thumb for her liking.

The marquess noted the untouched tray of food by the fireplace and his eyes came back with significant interest to his daughter-in-law. "You've no appetite, m'dear? Tsk! Tsk! Bad conscience, perhaps?"

"I've nothing to plague my mind," Cassandra assured him acidly, not wanting to give him the satisfaction of knowing that recently the sight of food was repugnant to her. Too late she remembered the sedan chair which meant that his rheumatism was in full flare. To ease his own discomfort he often chose to vent his spleen on some unlucky soul. With a sinking feeling she realized that this, perhaps, was the reason he had chosen to visit her after weeks of neglect.

The marquess stiffened, his gums working behind caved-in lips. "Dare use impudence to me, you, who've the propriety of a slut? Aye. You've the manners of a miss when it suits you, but tell me, did you win Music Master Simmons to your bed before or after you'd addled his simple wits to suit your scheme?"

Cassandra made no reply. She saw that she was, indeed, to be his whipping boy.

The marquess's piercing gaze swept over the petite young woman dressed in a tight-waisted rose gown. He sniffed in disapproval at the unfashionable dressing of her heavy brown hair which had been tightly drawn back from her high, smooth forehead. The thought that she was his only son's wife gave him a twinge of pain.

"Gad, but you're plain! To think even Nicholas would stoop to this just to spite me." He shook his head impatiently as he dipped into the jeweled snuffbox he had produced from his pocket. The pinch of doctored tobacco left a dusting of ashes on his nightgown front, but he did not seem to notice.

When he raised his head, his silver-lashed eyes regarded her unblinkingly. "The ancient laws are best, don't you think? Comes to mind one for adultery: the branding of the palm with a hot poker."

Shaken by the hatred that gleamed in his ice-water eyes, Cassandra found that her voice trembled as she said, "What I've suffered cannot be held against me."

"Tripe!" the marquess replied. Curling his gnarled hand into a fist, he pounded the arm of his chair. "I'll not be made a fool of beneath my own roof. So, you think you're clever, do you? Did you think the physician I called in wouldn't tell me the truth? Ah! You didn't think of that? Stupid, wantonly stupid. You thought I'd accept your mewling protestations that Simmons never laid a hand on you. By God! Get me a stick, Dermont, a great thrashing stick to take to the girl!"

Surprisingly, the marquess's distemper had a calming effect on Cassandra. Two years had taught her many bitter lessons, and a shrewd appreciation for her father-in-law's moods. In many ways he was like her own father, she thought with a surge of anger. Like him, the marquess's most violent tempers never lasted long. It was his calm moods she feared the most, when he was thinking, watching, calculating.

When he sat back panting for breath she said quietly, "You do not ask me why I left Briarcliffe, my lord, but I will answer. I wanted to go to London, to seek my husband. Mr. Simmons only sought to help me." Cassandra paused, remembering the kind gentleman who was now dead. "If not for his generosity, he would not have died."

Her speech amused the marquess. "So, at last, you've turned up a woman. You're in heat for a man, and you've been on the hunt. Well, well, I did wonder."

The marquess looked upon his daughter-in-law with contempt. "So, you think I've kept you here against my son's desire. Then hear me well. Nicholas picked you for his bride to *spite* me. Don't fancy that passion had a part in it. You were his pawn, his broad jest, the plain gentry bride that fulfilled the word but not the spirit of his father's demands."

He leaned forward in his chair, lips drawn back from his toothless gums in a grin. The gray of his eyes seemed swallowed up by the pithy pupils as he strained forward. "I should know; the blood in Nicholas's veins is mine."

A flush stained Cassandra's complexion as the caution that usually ruled her tongue evaporated. It was an argument of long standing between them, and nothing could stop the anger and hurt that came rushing out over her lips in a torrent of words. "You've no right to speak to me like that! I was fifteen when Nicholas married me, but I had the heart and soul of a woman. Had you not forced Nicholas from Briarcliffe in the middle of the night, he would have taken me with him. You despise me because Nicholas found me worthy of his love and because I—I will always love him!"

Her words tumbled to a halt as Cassandra realized

the insulting things she'd said, but the marquess seemed not to have taken offense.

"Love?" he returned, genuinely surprised by her outburst. "What damned foolish talk is this? You speak of love. God's death! Women haven't the sense of hens."

A cold smile edged into the nobleman's expression. "You know nothing of love. As for Nicholas, he's too like me to indulge in sentimentality. Lust, aye! Bought him his first whore when he was just thirteen. But he's a streak of weakness in him, his own pleasures rule. He would gamble and drink my coffers dry if I let him. I warned him two years ago that the title was his by law but I'd see the money and estates handed over to his cousin Dermont if he didn't settle down and marry."

The marquess nodded at his secretary. "To back up my words I sent for him. He's coarse and country-mannered, but even a rude barn will give shelter in a storm. Threatened Nicholas with the signing of papers if he did not produce a suitable bride in a month's time."

Cassandra gave the secretary a quick glance, but Kendal appeared not to take notice.

The marquess did notice the look and snorted. "You'll not start on Dermont, girl. Sheep's eyes ain't in his line. Dirty muslin is more his dish, upstairs tumbling the likes of Cora is to the country boy's tastes. He'd as soon tup a ewe as ride a lady. Am I right, Dermont?"

The old man cackled with laughter as Cassandra quickly lowered her head to keep from meeting the young man's eyes. This was no business of hers, she told herself. All she wanted was to win free of Briarcliffe and the marquess. In a calm voice she said, "You claim you forced your son into marriage. That may be so. But you did not choose his bride. Nicholas chose me. You have no right to hold me against my will." She stared at the marquess, trying not to hate him but finding little in her heart but anger and fear and a desire to best the man who sought to destroy her. "I will go to Nicholas one day. You'll not prevent it." She said the words slowly, in a bold declaration of defiance.

The marquess's smile grew a little broader. "I've no doubt of it. Perhaps I shall send you myself, when you've served my needs. You would like London in summer. 'Tis warm and noisome but a treat for rural eyes. There's just one matter to be settled first." His expression grew suddenly grim. "Who fathered the bastard growing in your belly, girl?"

"Wh-what?" Cassandra's voice began low, then evaporated completely.

The marquess pressed the question. "Is it Simmons's bastard? Well, girl, do you know?"

Cassandra's gaze darted from Dermont to the marquess as she unconsciously fingered the sapphire and emerald ring that rode the third finger of her left hand. "There's no child, there can't be. I—"

Suddenly, a remembered voice cut into the pattern of her thoughts. *If 'tis a boy, name him Merlyn.* Those had been the gypsy's last words to her.

Cassandra paled. It wasn't possible! He could not have known—how could he? Or were the memories that tormented her with guilt not all that she carried with her as a result of that night? She knew nothing of such matters. She had had no mother to confide in. Was it possible?

"Having trouble remembering your brat's sire?" the marquess suggested in faintly derisive tones.

Cassandra felt the marquess's gaze penetrate her. It seared through flesh, seeking to bare her soul, but she resisted the urge to look away. He must never know her guilty secret.

She thrust away the memory of Merlyn Ross, calling to mind the sneering image of the gaoler Dowerty. It was an effective antidote. A shudder of nausea swept through her as she imagined his lips pressed to hers. "If I am with child, I know the sire. He was a prisoner in Newgate."

Contrary to her expectations, the marquess did not question the story. Instead, he said, "What happened to this lusty fellow?"

Taken aback, Cassandra stammered, "He—he was hanged, my lord."

The trembling speech made the marquess smile. So, his information had been correct. He gave Dermont an impassive glance. When he and his secretary had set out for London, he was convinced that Cassandra would be found there. It was simple luck that they had found her so quickly. No, perhaps not. He was ever a thorough man. Such attention to detail had made him send Dermont to Newgate in the first place and then again, after she had been recovered, with a coin purse. The results were most enlightening and saved him from indecision now.

The old man's smile broadened. The scheme that had

been working in his head since his interview with the physician who tended his daughter-in-law after her return to Briarcliffe at last seemed possible.

His eyes shining with malicious delight, the marquess motioned Cassandra to him. "I should thank you, my dear, for you will give me the means to best my ungrateful son."

He leaned forward, grasping the arms of his chair. "'Tis a grandson I need. Aye! An heir. And you'll give me one, Lady Cassandra."

"My lord!" both Cassandra and Dermont began simultaneously, to be cut off by an impatient movement of the marquess's hand.

"I know what you think, and you're a pair of fools," the marquess said coldly. "You would remind me that the child will be a bastard."

A cackle of glee shook his bony chest. "Damme! All men are bastards. And all women, bless them, are sluts. You think I care who put the seed in her belly? God's blood! It serves the jest to know a murderer's by-blow will bear the title that should be Nicholas's. Nicholas might have taken Dermont to court, but against a direct descendant of the line he'll have no recourse. To see my son's face when I tell him, that alone will keep these old bones aboveground a year longer."

Cassandra drew back from the icy gleam of the marquess's eyes, feeling as if she'd strayed into a treacherous bog that had begun to suck her in. The marquess must be mad. "Perhaps the physician is in error," she flung at him. "What if I carry no child within me?"

The marquess's features muddied with color. "You'd best be breeding, lady. Nicholas thought he'd bested me with his sham of a marriage. Now I've a plan which will see him brought low."

"It's mad!" Cassandra whispered through dry lips.

The marquess shook his head as if she were simple. "I've set the course. You're to bear me a grandson. If you're not breeding, you soon must be. I don't know why I didn't think of it before." He ignored her gasp of outrage. "It's of no matter to me whose brat you whelp, so long as the secret's kept. Afterward, you may go to the devil any way it pleases you. I may even send you to Nicholas myself. See, then, if he wants you to warm his bed."

"No!" The word was said low, but it brought momentary silence to the room.

The marquess regarded the young woman before him. She had no pretense to beauty, but she'd always displayed a self-possession he was unable to defeat. In cooler moments he'd admired it. Now he saw her willfulness as a bar to his desires and he knew just how to crush her young spirit.

"What will you do if I show you the door this moment? Will you run to my son with the tale of a gypsy's rape? Oh yes, Lady Cassandra, I know how you came by the ring you wear. The turnkeys of Newgate were no less eager for my gold than for the gypsy's. You will do as I say because you have no choice."

All the amusement drained from his voice as he added, "You may remain and bear your child in the luxury my wealth can provide. Or do you hope your father will take you back? Nicholas told me about his fancy for guineas. Is there enough value in the gypsy's ring to buy yourself a corner of the family hearth?"

Cassandra turned deathly white under the battering ram of his tongue, and the marquess paused. The physician had assured him that she was healthy, but a fit of hysterics might ruin everything. "I need a grandson, healthy and well," he said in a temporizing tone meant to reassure her. "You've nothing to fear in remaining here."

Not expecting a reply, he signaled to his secretary. "Call those lackeys. Lady Cassandra needs her rest. And you, my dear," he said, turning his crystal gaze on her once more. "You will send word when you've made up your mind to be sensible."

White moonlight terraced and cratered with shadows the snow mantling the grounds of Briarcliffe. The heavy fleece-lined cloak around her shoulders warmed her, but Cassandra could not stop shivering as a powerful blast of wind flung itself against the house and the windows rattled. The mournful howling had awakened her and now she could not sleep.

No, that was not right. It was a nightmare that had awakened her. She preferred the numbing cold of the stone floor beneath her satin-slippered feet to the terrors that followed her into the warm bed.

"Oh, Nicholas!" she whispered to the night. "Why did you never come back for me?"

So long ago it seemed, another world, another life, the day Nicholas Briarcliffe came into her life.

It had been cold that day, too, she remembered. The wind whipping from the southern coast of Devonshire had tugged at the old shapeless gown she had worn.

It was her turn to accompany her father to market day in the village. She did not want to go, but he would not listen. The youngest of three motherless children, she had always been the first to receive the attentions of her father.

The thought thinned Cassandra's generous mouth. The attentions of Jack Charlton were something a child could well live without. Charlton was an old and once-respected name, but a succession of bad political judgments had robbed them of their wealth and influence by the end of the last century. Now there was little to remind the Charltons of what they had once been.

Her father had been drinking for days; it was his usual habit. Only periodically did he rise from his stupor, and then his household went in fear. And she, for reasons she could only label as headstrong and stubborn, had never learned to curb her tongue and so received more than her share of his wrath. Perhaps, she thought for the hundredth time, that was why her father acted as he did that day.

If only he had not lost that fifth hand of cards at the fairgrounds. The loss so early in the day had been unendurable, turning his thoughts to ways of raising funds. The conclusion was to offer for sale his youngest daughter.

A churning began in Cassandra's middle as the shame of that day moved within her.

He made her stand among the sheep and cattle pens

as the red-faced auctioneer called out her name. The crowd gawked. The sale of a wife or daughter was not illegal but a rare sight, nonetheless. Yet their embarrassment quickly gave way to a gleeful relish to see one of the quality made a spectacle of.

She did not cry. She did not believe it was happening, not even when the jeering bids began to rise. Her father was drunk, she told herself, she would not be sold.

She did not notice the carriage that pulled into the town square or the emergence of its occupant. A sudden cry brought her gaze up in time to see her father stagger and fall before the blow from a gentleman's gloved fist. A moment later she stared down from the block into the leaf-green eyes of the most beautiful man she had ever seen.

Cassandra shook her head at the memory. Until a few short hours ago she had thought only Nicholas knew of her humiliation. Shame surged through her. Nicholas's thoughtlessness made it so much harder for her to think of facing the marquess again. Why had he told the marquess? Did he not understand what he'd done in giving his father so powerful a weapon? Even if it was in explanation of why he had offered a poor young gentry girl marriage, he must have known his father would find a moment to use it against her.

Cassandra put her hand to her damp forehead. "Go away!" she whispered fiercely as a dizzy swirling weakness curled up about her. It was not the first time she had felt sick in recent weeks, but she had blamed it on her anxiety to be quit of Briarcliffe. Until today.

There would be a child. The physician had been sent for again and her condition reconfirmed that very afternoon.

Sweat formed on her upper lip as she leaned her head against the massive carved post of her bed. It wasn't right! It shouldn't be! It was too cruel a joke that she bore the life of Merlyn Ross within her.

Involuntarily, her eyes sought out the ring on her left hand. Shaped for a man's large hand, the ring was too heavy for her delicate finger. The pale glare reflected from the snow shone in eerie radiance against the gray gritstone of the window casement, dulling the ring's gold mounting, but the jewels caught fire in the cold light, answering the icy glow with brilliant emerald and sapphire flame.

Cassandra moved her head from side to side, the lush fall of her hair sliding forward to hide the ring from her sight. She had not been able to lay it aside as a wiser person would have done. He had asked her to wear it, as the last request of a condemned man. She could not say no. Yet she must forget. Merlyn Ross was dead.

"Oh, Lord!" she whispered brokenly. Had there been a day, an hour's sanity in which she might have sorted out her feelings of bemusement and fear, she might have saved herself from him.

"I was bewitched!" she cried in defiance of the image of the gypsy's long strong body that invaded her mind, enveloping her body in the heat of response. It held her weak and trembling, a tangible reminder of the power he had wielded, wielded still. She had not been strong enough to deny him anything, not even the victory of her pleasure at his hands.

But the memories would not lie still; they beckoned, lured her to remember.

He had not been content with the mere surrender of her body. After the first hard thrusting invasion he had not left her. His hands had gently, tenderly roamed her body, finding again the throbbing secret places that made her ache with a hunger she now knew existed and wordlessly begged him to fill. And the words, the torrent of words that had poured from him. He had called her beautiful, lovely, his love. The astonishment of that was with her still. But the hardest to bear was the memory of the morning.

She had not seen him mount the gallows steps. She had remained behind while the gaoler and the minister went with him. His sad, infinitely tender smile was her last memory of him, that and his fierce last kiss.

"How lonely he must have been," she murmured to herself as tears pricked her eyes. To have offered love to a stranger in hopes that he would not be forgotten. He would never know that his desire would be met. She bore his babe within her. Merlyn Ross could never be forgotten.

What of me? Cassandra wondered desperately. Love. So simple a word. Yet she had never known its power in her life.

She had lied to herself. Though Nicholas's actions seemed to her those of both a savior and a saint, she knew he did not love her. She was the one who loved. He had acted out of chivalry, giving her the protection of his name and position. Perhaps the marquess was right in believing that she had served a need. But she had hoped that her love would be returned in time when Nicholas had bathed awhile in the glow of her own ardor. But now she would not blame him if he would despise her for her night in Newgate. If so, then her days of dreaming were at an end.

A shiver blew across the surface of her skin. She had no illusions about the marquess. He wanted her child; if it were a boy he would seek to make him his own.

"I won't let him!" she vowed softly. She was trapped for now. She must bide her time until her child was born.

A tentative smile spread across her delicate features. *Her child.* The idea, so frightening and impossible a few hours ago, now brimmed with promise. She would bide her time until the child was born and then she would know what to do.

For the first time in two months Cassandra drew a deep sigh of relief. No child of hers would ever know a moment of its life without love. And perhaps this would be the someone in her life who would love her in return.

Chapter Five

August, 1755

A SQUEAL OF DELIGHT REACHED INTO A SHRIEK, PIERCING the long hallways of Briarcliffe. A moment later the noise of the buzzing crowd erupted into laughter. In the upper reaches of the house the baby in his mother's arms cringed. A dark nipple slipped from his pursed lips and one tiny fist clutched the tender warm flesh of his mother's breast as a wail of fright turned his delicate features bright red.

"Hush, hush, little love," Cassandra soothed, cradling her son and brushing her milky nipple against his petal-soft cheek. Immediately, the child accepted the security of her flesh and his hiccupy sobs again became the suckling sounds of contentment.

"Ye should be below, entertaining the marquess's guests, instead of baring yer breasts like a common slut."

Hannah, Cassandra's maid, stood nearby, arms folded across her skinny chest. "You're fair to bursting out of your gown like a brood sow. 'Tisn't proper for a noblewoman to suckle her babes."

Cassandra looked up, her full lips thinned to a stubborn line. Hannah was Briarcliffe's housekeeper whom the marquess had commanded to be his daughter-in-law's lady's maid during her months of pregnancy, but Cassandra knew the woman's main purpose was to spy upon her. "The marquess's guests are no concern of mine."

"Whose, then, I'm asking. If not for the babe in your arms, we'd be left in peace." Hannah's pinched features soured in consternation. "All the work getting ready for the ball this night, it's all on account of the christening on the morrow."

The reminder stiffened Cassandra's features. "The ball has nothing to do with me. I'd have no part in any of the festivities and neither would my son, could I but help it." She cradled her child a little tighter. "He's *my* son. Whatever else, that can't change."

"Best not let the marquess hear ye." Hannah unfolded her arms and placed them on her hips, jerking her head toward the door. "To hear His Lordship tell it, he sired the babe himself. Only that ain't the truth, is it?" A gleam of mischief came into her eyes. "Look at his head of black hair. How's a body to believe 'twas sired by a Briarcliffe? Golden heads, that's all they plant in a woman's belly. The marquess plowed many a local field in his day and every one of the babes grew a head of hair the color of the king's gold." A flush crept slowly into her thin features. "'Twas a time when the marquess could talk a woman out of her petticoats before she— But then, you know of such things. 'Twas a gypsy, they say.''

Cassandra looked away from the woman's malicious smirk. Kendal and Hannah were the only two members of the staff who shared the secret of her son's natural father. That secret was one more reason she did not want to return to the fete below. Someone had asked why Nicholas was not present for his son's christening, and she had not known what to answer.

She caught her lower lip between her teeth, recalling the knowing looks and snickers among the noble gathering below when the marquess explained to his guests how his daughter-in-law had made a brief journey to London to visit her neglectful husband and only returned when things had been put to rights. They seemed to find her a subject for ridicule. Several bold gentlemen passed her chair after the dinner hour to offer their respective services should she feel "neglected" again. One obese gentleman dressed in pink brocade suggested that since she had produced an heir her duty to her husband was done entirely and pinched her sharply on the shoulder.

Anger pinked her cheeks again as she remembered the moment. Her son's ravenous appetite had saved her any more such insults, and she had no intention of returning to them. "Tell the marquess I feel unwell and am unable to return to his banquet."

"I'll tell him," Hannah replied sourly, "but I doubt he'll hear of it. Come tomorrow your bastard's to be christened heir to Briarcliffe. You'll have precious little say in his life after that."

Cassandra did not raise her head until the woman had gone. Six weeks earlier she had given birth to a son, and she had not slept a full night since for fear he would be taken from her.

"Be easy, Adam," she whispered, bending to kiss the small head at her breast. "No one will take you from me. I won't allow it."

In answer to his mother's gentle tone, the baby sighed and released her nipple. As his head lolled away from her breast, a milky stain marbled his smiling lips.

Cassandra watched, entranced, as one sable-lashed lid opened briefly and an eye winked into view. It had not ceased to be a wonder to her, the deep startling blue of his eyes. The burning color of those eyes was not the famous mirror-bright Briarcliffe gaze but held the deep fiery blue of sapphires.

As she gazed lovingly on the small dark head with its tiny features and lips sweetly pouted, she frowned. She could no longer remember the features of her child's father. Sable-black hair, an eyepatch, and a wicked emerald gaze: they were her only memories of her ravisher. How sad, she thought. Her son would never know his father.

For a moment an absurd longing seized her. It was a desire developed somewhere in the middle months of her confinement, and in her loneliness she had given it full rein. A natural need, she reminded herself, but one of impossibility. The desire embarrassed her. How could she want such a thing? The father of her child was a common criminal, hanged for a crime of which she had no knowledge. He was a wicked man. But in moments like these, with none to look upon her soul but herself, she was taken with the shameful desire to see the gypsy once more, to tell him that he had a son, something of himself left behind in the world.

She winced as another familiar feeling swelled within her. In all the months, long after his features had blurred in memory, she could not still the leap of her pulse at the reminder of Merlyn Ross's touch. He had earned the condemnation of the courts and ruined her life. Yet, on that night ten months before, in his company, she had learned the secret lure of desire.

Cassandra closed her eyes against the remembered warmth of his kiss. "No!" she whispered fiercely. If the memory of a single night could so beguile her, how much better would be the passion shared with one she loved. This madness in her blood was nothing more than the longing of a woman who knew the possibilities of desire. The real Merlyn Ross would be detestable in her sight today.

Laughter from below drifted once more into her hearing as she bent and kissed her son's moist brow before hoisting him to her shoulder to gently pat a burp from him. "You're growing, my fine lad," she murmured proudly. To her motherly satisfaction, the warm weight of his body seemed to increase daily.

She rose from the chair in her sitting room and crossed into the nursery which adjoined her bedroom. As she bent to place the child on his stomach on the feather mattress a rill of misgiving touched her. She had not even been consulted about the name to be given her child. Tenderly she pulled the blankets over him and began a slow massaging of his small back. She did not know what name the marquess planned to give the child. It did not matter. She would claim her motherly rights. He would be called Adam.

"Lady Cassandra?"

The whispered call interrupted Cassandra's thoughts and she raised her eyes. Kendal Dermont stood at the door, his pure white jabot shining brightly against the somber brown velvet of his coat. His waistcoat was beige silk embroidered with white thread, but his white stockings and black leather shoes proclaimed him a superior servant.

"Mr. Dermont!" she admonished softly, a finger to her lips for silence.

"You're to come to the great hall at once, Lady Cassandra. The marquess requires it." Kendal was careful that his tone was quiet, but he did not immediately back away. His eyes had missed nothing, including the gaping open of the lady's gown as she bent over the crib. Beneath the low-cut bodice, the full creamy roundness of her breasts was briefly exposed to his view.

Cassandra stood up and pretended not to notice the look in his eyes as she rearranged her bodice, but a direct order from the marquess could not be so easily ignored. She knew it was better not to test his uncharacteristic goodwill that had begun with Adam's birth, at least until she knew what he intended for her future. "Tell His Lordship I shall come down in a few moments."

"Told you the marquess would have his way," Hannah jeered as she stepped into the room. With a wave of her bony hand she shooed Kendal away and then motioned Cassandra to turn around. "Take a deep breath and hold it," she ordered as she began lacing up the back of the ball gown. "Lord, you're near popping out of this gown. No wonder Kendal was hanging back. Got a eyeful, he did. And him always the first to call you a reedy bit of muslin. But you showed him a pair of melons would shame a farmer's daughter. You looking to birth another bastard, you've made a friend."

For months Cassandra had ignored the woman's crude remarks. Now her fingers curled into fists until the emerald and sapphire ring on her left hand bit into the flesh of her palm. She turned on the older woman, rage smoldering in the dark velvet of her eyes.

"How dare you call my son that filthy name! Get out of my sight before I repeat your slander to the marquess!"

The speech astonished the servant. Her mouth fell open and then her gaze became twinkling sly. " 'Twas like that, was it? Could've told the marquess the minute I spied that melting look in your eye when you gazed on the boy 'twas no common rape planted the seed."

She cackled with laughter. "You're a sly puss, playing so meek and mild a body wouldn't think butter would melt on your tongue. No one's guessed how you loved every minute of lying with your gypsy lover."

Cassandra choked on her fury. It had never occurred to her that a woman's natural inclination should have been to hate the spawn of rape. Yet it was clear for all to see that she loved the child beyond all reason.

She glanced at the woman and knew that nothing would be gained by another word. Instead, she raised her chin and passed into the hall.

When she reached the top of the staircase into the great hall, music swelled up toward her as if in greeting. The melody entered her thoughts and she paused, one small hand tightened on the top banister until the knuckles whitened. Music Master Simmons had been particularly fond of the elder Bach.

No. She gave her head a small shake. She must not remember old sorrows and regrets tonight. Too much anguish lay in a past that could not be changed. Indefinable urges surged through her, stiffening her spine. She did not care what the company below thought of her, but she must be strong and fearless for Adam's sake. "I'll not be fodder for their spiteful tongues," she whispered to herself.

She descended the staircase, aware of nothing so much as a vast annoyance for the noisy company below whose volume drowned out the beautiful music. Beneath the huge blazing chandeliers the assembly shimmered in rich colors of scarlet, blue, yellow, and plum the hall appeared as a huge aviary of tropical birds in exotic plumage.

The rich, throaty feminine voice caught her attention first and then Cassandra spied the woman. She was seated at the foot of the staircase surrounded by a half dozen admirers. Her gown was a cool rich green, and above the low neckline her pale, beautifully rounded bosom and shoulders rose as if emerging from a jade sea. Here was the most exotic bird of them all, Cassandra found herself thinking, regarding the lovely woman whose red hair had been powdered to a pale pink. In a sudden rush of envy, she wished she were the woman in the bright gown, for then she would not feel quite so foolish or awkward.

Cassandra glanced at a nearby mirror and the reflection of herself in the tight fitted gown with its wide paniers. Here was no exotic creature. The beautifully made gown of heavy gold satin seemed to bleed her face of color. At her throat and hanging from her ears were the brilliant Briarcliffe diamonds that the marquess insisted she wear, but they were cold and heavy, like a prisoner's collar about her slender neck. The image reflected back was of a small, white-faced girl overwhelmed by the brilliant cloth. With a sigh she looked away, giving her full concentration to descending the stairway.

When she reached the bottom step, she looked to see that the marquess did, indeed, require a word with her. He stood staring at her from the middle of the room, balanced on a pair of gold-handled walking canes. A full-bottomed wig framed his face in masses of gray curls, while diamonds winked in the rows of white silk ruffles spilling from his shirtfront. More precious gems decorated his fingers. From his head to his red-heeled shoes, he was every inch a nobleman, but that was not what made her eyes widen as she neared him. He was smiling, a genuine smile of pleasure.

"Gawking ain't the way of nobility, lady," the marquess snapped, his clear eyes twinkling like the diamonds in his jabot. He lifted the lorgnette attached to his coat with a ribbon to gauge the effect of the gown he had selected for the mother of his new grandson and found it wanting. "God's blood! Put you in the most expensive material on the Continent and still you defy me! You wear the gleam of gold like a shroud."

Cassandra made no comment on the observation she had just made herself. She was tired and worried and could not pretend a joy she had forgotten how to feel.

"Hannah! Where's that blasted woman?" The marquess looked around as if expecting to find the maid standing in the shadow of one of the hothouse palms that ringed the room. It seemed to make no difference to him that his guests had halted their conversations in order to better listen in on his.

"Damme! Lady Cassandra, you look like death!" The marquess teetered dangerously on his canes. "I'll have no puling woman on my hands. A lusty Briarcliffe boy, 'tis what you've bred and what I intend to raise!"

Reading mortification on her face he continued in the same raised tones, "You're surrounded by Briarcliffes; the sooner you realize nothing else matters beside that, the better off you'll be. Come the morning the newest one, Dominic Shelby Briarcliffe, will greet the world."

Cassandra looked from the marquess to those nearest her and saw the suppressed smiles before they turned away. "Perhaps it would be better if I retire with my son," she suggested in a tight voice, ignoring the name the marquess had just given the child. Dominic was the marquess's first name and one she would never condescend to use.

"You'll not. You're to stay here and smile prettily at my guests." The marquess lifted one cane to shake it at her. "I won't pretend to understand it, but you've caught the eye of the Duke of Moreston. Wants you to come to visit him at Thorton Place." He winked at her and leaned near, whispering, "I said you'd have your head once you birthed my grandson. 'Tis said Moreston's a stallion. He'll calm the fret in your blood."

Cassandra lowered her eyes to shield her contempt for the suggestion from his sight. The Duke of Moreston was the man who had left a faint purple bruise on her right shoulder. Instead, she said, "There'll be many guests tomorrow, and if I am weary my son will fret. Therefore, allow me to bid you good night, my lord."

The marquess's silvery gaze narrowed. "You've taken on more than you should. Birthing a babe the size of Dominic has taken the starch out of you. That's why I've sent for a proper wet nurse. Come the morrow, she'll suckle Dominic."

"A wet nurse?" Cassandra questioned. "But you promised—"

"I've changed my mind," the marquess cut in. "Dominic needs the rich country cream of a buxom maid, not the thin blue milk of a gentry lass. Moreston's returning to London directly upon his departure from Briarcliffe. You deserve a reward for the service you've done me. I've promised you a trip to London. I'm not an unreasonable man."

Cassandra felt as if a ghostly hand had touched her and she shivered. "I—I don't want to go, not yet," she whispered under the watchful eyes of the company. "My son will let no other hold him but me. He cries the moment Hannah touches him, even to change his linen."

The marquess waved this away. " 'Twill soon be put right. Dominic—call him by his Christian name, lady—

must learn to command himself. He's to be a marquess."

Before she could gather sufficient ammunition to argue, he turned away, leaving her to accept the snickers and murmurs of his guests as best she could.

For a moment Cassandra stood her ground, chin lifted defiantly against anyone who might dare to approach her. But the time for confrontation had passed and she realized that no one would approach her. Indeed, no one seemed to notice that she remained in the hall. Too quickly the notion was dispelled as a voice sounded at her elbow.

"Ah, m'dear. Thought you'd flown. Told the marquess it don't seem fair, hiding you away after a quick look-see."

With an inaudible sigh, Cassandra turned to face the Duke of Moreston. His plain round face was even ruddier than she remembered, clashing violently with his pink habit, and when he spoke again she knew why. The warm stale vapors of wine and tobacco brushed her face as he slurred, "Care t'dance? The wre-wretched minuet makes a dammed fine figure."

Searching desperately for a way of putting him off under the watchful eyes of the marquess, she said, "A breath of fresh air would suit me more at present, Your Grace. Do you not find the company unpleasantly warm?"

The duke rocked back on his heels, expelling an immoderate chuckle. "Damme! You're a rare treat, madame. A turn about the gardens . . . fresh air . . . a little private chat . . . seclusion." He reached out and gave her elbow a painful pinch that made Cassandra want to tread on his instep. "L-lead the way, m'dear."

This idea appealed to her even less than the first and she automatically cast her eyes about in hopes of finding a familiar face, but none of the brilliant company was known to her. And then she saw the newcomer.

He was at the opposite end of the hall, but she felt his gaze touch her as palpably as if his hand had fallen on her arm. As he approached she became aware of many things. He wore his gray wig in the complicated French style called the Solitare. Two rows of curls rode each ear and the long back curls were looped and tied with a black silk ribbon, the ends of which had been brought around over his white cravat and tied in a bow under his chin. His silk stockings and red-heeled shoes with silver buckles labeled him an aristocrat.

It wasn't only his dress that caught her eye. True, he wore severe black, softened only at wrists and jabot by a delicate fall of pristine lace. Against the backdrop of color and glittering jewels, he looked like a raven among peacocks, self-possessed and predatory. But it was his one-eyed stare that captured her attention.

For one wild moment Cassandra did not breathe. He was familiar, tantalizingly so. Her eyes flew to the black silk ribbon that slashed across his brow at an angle. There must be other men who wore eyepatches, she told herself. There were other tall men who moved with such easy grace. It was the impression of height and darkness and power that made her think of . . .

Ridiculous, romantic, foolish, delirious, all those names and more she attached to the emotion quaking through her in the brief moments before he was standing before her. She did not know him, and yet . . .

"Merlyn?" she whispered incredulously.

The stranger moved sharply, as if stung by the sound of her voice, and then he lowered his head slightly so that she could look fully into his face. His complexion was made fashionable by a dusting of rice powder and rouge, and a satin beauty patch road the ridge of his right cheekbone. He wore a patch, yes, but the single eye gazing down at her was not green but blue, the brilliant blue of sapphire.

With a slight bow he took her small hand in his firm grasp and brought it to his lips. *"Enchanté,* madame," he intoned in a deep voice with just a hint of the French accent. "The Comte de Valure extends his apologies for arriving late. But then, one may sometimes presume upon old acquaintance to beg pardon."

"Comte," Cassandra acknowledged uneasily. Who was he? She did not know him, certainly. And yet he addressed her as if they were old friends.

"I say, Comte, Lady Briarcliffe and I were j-just going for a stroll. Too dashed much of a crush in here."

The Frenchman gave the duke the briefest of glances before saying, "Forgive me, Your Grace, but it appears to me that Lady Briarcliffe is more in need of a goblet of champagne. I believe I see a footman over there." He pointed in the general direction of the thick of the crowd.

Cassandra saw the duke's frown turn to consternation and inserted smoothly, "Oh yes, I should love a

glass above all else. Please, Your Grace. If you would."
To the last she added a shy smile.

"Your obedient servant," the Duke of Moreston
murmured reluctantly. He turned away, his eyes squint-
ed and his gait unsteady, and lurched toward the
middle of the room.

The sinking feeling in Cassandra's middle took a
sudden upward spiral as her gaze rose abruptly to meet
the comte's once more. He was looking at her as if
studying her likeness against a long absence. So intense
was his gaze that she knew she should be insulted, yet
there was nothing suggestive in the look upon his stern
features. Still, she felt compelled to speak and break
the silence. "You have the advantage of me, monsieur.
I don't recall our meeting, and it's impossible that I
might have forgotten it."

A cryptic smile curved his firm mouth. "You flatter
me, madame. There is no need. We have not, I think,
met before. But I sensed your—dilemma." With a nod
of his elegantly dressed head he indicated the path
taken by the duke.

"Oh, I see," Cassandra said softly. "Then I must
thank you, monsieur. The gallantry of your country-
men is well known." She turned immediately away,
aware once more of the marquess's eyes on her, this
time in disapproval.

The touch of the Frenchman's hand on her arm made
her gasp and it fell away immediately. "Pardon, madame. I startled you. I mean no disrespect. There is a
matter, a delicate matter, of which I must speak."

Cassandra did not look up at him, not wanting to see

the same smirking flirtatious look that had been on the florid duke's features. "I think not," she said coolly and took another step.

"Are you not at all interested in word from you husband?"

Cassandra turned back to him so quickly she nearly collided with him, for he moved toward her at the same instant. For a moment she was close enough to see the shadow of a beard beneath his smooth cheek and the tangy odor of vetiver made her nostrils quiver. "Nicholas? You have word for me from Nicholas?" she asked faintly, her honey-dark eyes rising to meet the single blue eye gazing down at her.

"Perhaps madame would like to discuss this in more privacy?" the Frenchman suggested, his low tone a warning in itself.

"Yes, of course," Cassandra replied enthusiastically. *At last,* her heart sang, word from Nicholas. And tonight, of all nights, she needed the reassurance that he cared. "The parlor," she suggested, hardly able to keep the smile out of her voice.

"*Certainement*, madame," he replied, but there was a frown between his brows as he followed her out of the hall.

The paneled walls of the room appeared more intimate and friendly then the formal hall, but Cassandra felt strangely disquieted when the comte closed the doors behind himself and turned to her. For a moment neither of them spoke and, once again, Cassandra was aware of his intense scrutiny. This time she gave her unease voice. "Have I trod upon my hem and torn it, monsieur?"

He blinked as his gaze shifted from a stare to polite perusal. "Forgive me, madame, but you *are* the real Lady Briarcliffe?"

"What?" Cassandra responded in surprise.

With an elegant gesture the comte withdrew a jeweled snuffbox from his coat pocket and flicked open the lid. As he helped himself to a tiny pinch of the tobacco his eyes did not leave her face. "I phrased that badly," he said blandly. "I'm afraid Nicholas led me to expect someone quite . . . different."

Cassandra accepted this statement with a tiny shrug. "I was a child of fifteen when I wed, monsieur. Perhaps Nicholas's memories have not aged with me."

"Perhaps," the comte replied in a noncommittal voice.

Stung by the doubt in his answer, Cassandra took a more aggressive tack. "How well do you know my husband?"

The comte smiled now and replaced the snuffbox in his pocket. "I left him at four o'clock in the morning three nights ago. He held a promising hand of cards, two kings and two jacks and a deuce, if I recall. I had offered to act as his emissary for the christening to take place tomorrow."

"He knows? I—I mean, he knows we expected him," Cassandra stammered, trying desperately to recover from her surprise at learning that Nicholas was openly admitting the birth of her child. Too late, she sensed a trap closing about her.

"Did you expect him?" the comte inquired politely.

"Of course," Cassandra snapped back, her every sense alert for further revelations.

The comte looked away, his gaze following the contours of the room as he said, "That makes my position difficult. For, you see, I am informed that the child to be acknowledged as the marquess's grandson and new heir is a bastard."

He glanced sharply at her to find her eyes dilated with fear. *"Oui*, madame. Nicholas believes you are an impostor hired by his father to bear him an illegitimate heir. It would be so simple, would it not? His real wife is not known by any of the marquess's circle. In truth, most believed till now that the rumor of Nicholas's marriage was false or else the bride so ugly and stupid . . . But then, one could hardly credit Nicholas Briarcliffe with making such a match. It's to your credit that you are not ugly or stupid. The alternative is to assume that you are his wife and a willing partner in this scheme to strip my friend of his rightful inheritance."

Cassandra stared at him, stunned by the accusation. "You—you're despicable! Your accusations loathsome! Nicholas never sent you to spread such lies."

The Frenchman's gaze moved to her left hand that rose instinctively to her throat. "Where is your wedding band, madame?"

"What?" Cassandra gasped.

"The ring you wear. The configuration of emerald and sapphire is most unusual, certainly, but it's not a wedding band. The gift of an admirer, perhaps?"

Cassandra took a deep breath and squared her shoulders, staring her contempt for the man she had so recently hoped would be a friend. "You're either mad or a fool. Nicholas would have no traffic with you in

90

either case. Address your slander to the marquess, if you dare. I'm leaving."

"*Non,* madame," the comte said softly and reached out to take her by the shoulders. If he felt her cringe in fear he did not react. "Stay a moment. It's your husband's belief that your adulterous behavior was a plot to make a beggar of him. Is this not so?"

Instantly there flashed through her mind memories of the dank foul odor of Newgate, the slime and filth and rats, the terror of the dark, and the ugly leering features of the gaoler. "If only you knew," she whispered.

The plaintive note in her voice seemed to touch the Frenchman, for his hands, once hard on her shoulders, gentled till they cupped them in a warm caress. "Have I misjudged you? Is there some explanation I can carry back to your husband that will explain this farce?"

Cassandra shook her head, struggling against the tears that stung her eyes.

The comte's hand moved on her shoulders, shaking her slightly. "This will not serve, madame. I need reasons. What would you say to your husband, were he here?"

Cassandra raised her dark honey eyes to his face, forgetting for the moment that he was a stranger, perhaps an enemy. "I would say, 'Why, Nicholas, did you never return for me? I waited two years, till desperation drove me to seek you.'" Her voice faltered, but her gaze never moved from the face of the man before her. "'You ask me for my wedding band. I sold it a year ago to pay for coach fare that was to bring me to London, to you, Nicholas. But it bought me, instead, the death of a friend and a nightmare journey through Newgate Prison.'"

Some unreadable emotion flickered in the comte's face. "You were in Newgate?"

Cassandra stiffened, the spell of the moment broken. "That amuses you, monsieur?"

The comte did not rise to the bait. "When were you there?"

Cassandra's expression hardened as she decided that he wanted her complete humiliation. "Would you have the very hour? The month was October, the hours numbered twenty-two. I counted each and every one in terror for my life."

The answer drew the man's black brows into a thoughtful frown. "Why did you not seek your husband's help?"

A thread of hysterical laughter erupted from Cassandra. His interrogation was worse than the marquess's had been. "Don't you think I would have, could I have remembered my own name? Lord! The tragedy of that journey. The coach was attacked and overturned. I was thrown free and must have injured my head. I remembered nothing until the early hours of the next morning. By then, I had spent a night in Newgate." She looked away from him. "Rescue, when it came, was too late."

Swallowing the bitter bile of memory, she again accosted him with an angry gaze. "I had no part in the marquess's scheme. The child I bore was the fruit of a Newgate rape."

The comte dropped his hands from her arms, his mouth compressed into a thin line, and Cassandra felt the thrill of confounding an enemy. "Does my frankness embarrass you? Then I must beg your pardon, for I fear I shall begin to scream the walls down unless you leave me this instant."

"I'm afraid I must agree." The marquess stood in the half-open door, his glacial gaze taking in Cassandra's tear-ravaged face and the comte's look of consternation. "Cassandra, my dear. The guests begin to inquire after you. One of the servants heard voices . . ." He let the sentence trail as his eyes narrowed dangerously on the comte. "My daughter-in-law is unaccustomed to the attentions of worldly admirers, Comte," he said coldly. "To lure her away for a tête-à-tête was ungallant."

The comte gave the older man a sardonic smile as he bowed slightly. "In defense of the lady, I must tell you she has acted with the greatest circumspection. And now," he added, turning back to Cassandra, "I will leave you in the capable hands of your father-in-law, Lady Briarcliffe. Our interview was most enlightening."

"What did he want?" the marquess demanded when the Frenchman had gone. "Damme! To be closeted with the Comte de Valure is the utmost folly. Your reputation could be ruined."

"Yes, you're right, of course," Cassandra voiced faintly, managing a weak but scornful laugh. Her reputation could not be in any greater danger than it had been for months.

Annoyed by her answer, the marquess struck his cane on the floor. "Moreston's asking for you again. Told him you must have gone into the garden ahead of him. The great bloody fool's out there thrashing about calling for you. You're to go and find him and accept his invitation to accompany him to London."

Cassandra turned to her father-in-law, a strange smile upon her pale face. "If I should accept the duke's invitation, it would only be because I want to go and see Nicholas."

"If you reach London, my lady, you may seek anyone you wish," the marquess agreed pleasantly.

It was not the answer Cassandra expected, and the realization of it frightened her. "You say 'if,' not 'when.' Don't you expect me to reach London?"

The marquess shrugged away her question. "I care not whether you see my son. I've sent word to him of what I intend. Dominic will inherit. Nicholas gets nothing!"

"Was that not reckless, my lord? Why, I could—" Cassandra began, only to fall silent under his icy stare.

"You could what? Tell Nicholas what he already knows, that the child is not his? You won't," he said smugly. "Dominic will be in my care. If my plans are ruined there'll be no reason for me to keep your fatherless whelp. You'll do nothing. Stupid girl. You never learn." He turned away, leaning heavily on his canes.

"Please!" Cassandra ran after him, catching his sleeve at the door so that he turned his head to look at her. "You'll swear not to harm my son if I keep silent?"

The marquess looked down on the tiny girl, using all his command not to sweep her back with a brutal blow of his cane. "Dominic has nothing to fear from me," he said slowly as his colorless gaze fell frigid as snow upon her. "But you, Lady Cassandra, you had best go upstairs at once. I see now that you are not well. Perhaps 'tis more than fatigue. Perhaps 'tis a chill or a fever. You'd best take care. Fevers have carried away many a young mother."

He means to be rid of me!

The thought rose instantly in her mind. It did not seem possible that he could so brutally and callously deprive her of her son, yet it would put an end to the only uncertain element in his plot. It came to her quickly, in a flash, that she must get away and take Adam with her. But first, she must confound her enemy.

Cassandra closed her eyes and pressed a fist to her forehead, swaying slightly as if she might faint. "Perhaps you are right. I am so tired. I need complete peace. Yes, that's it," she said, letting her voice die away as she moved slowly toward the door.

The marquess watched her go. For an ugly moment he had believed she would see through his thinly veiled excuse to be rid of her. But she was like all weak beings, allowing a tiny fright to overshadow deeper concerns. One way or another, he must rid himself of the only unaccountable in his scheme to best Nicholas. Only she could swear in a court of law that the child she bore was a bastard. The marquess smiled. With his silly little daughter-in-law out of the way, nothing would prevent his plot from succeeding.

Cassandra did not draw breath until she had closed the door to her sitting room. As she lifted her hand from the latch she heard the scrape of the key in the lock. More annoyed than alarmed, she realized she had been followed and locked in. It would be Hannah's doing, of course. An instant later dread washed over her. Adam!

She ran and flung open the connecting door between the rooms, halting just in time in the shadow of the doorway to see the hall door to her son's room being pulled shut by Hannah. A moment later the lock clicked into place.

Cassandra took a deep breath and rushed to the bassinet. When she saw the beloved outline of Adam's dark head against the pale sheets, her heart turned over in relief. In the brief interval between the door's closing and the sight she wondered if the marquess had deliberately distracted her while one of his servants slipped in and made off with the boy.

"Not if he couldn't feed him," Cassandra murmured and hugged herself with joy. That was it! He told her he'd hired a wet nurse, but she wasn't due until morning. The marquess was not so mad as to risk his grandson's health even for a night. Until then only she could give Adam the nourishment he demanded.

She bent and touched the soft black curls over one small ear as she whispered, "We must flee, Adam. We must find a way."

Every sense was alive in her, the tiniest movement would have caught her eye. The sight that met her vision as she turned from the crib brought her up with a small cry of dismay. Standing near her was a tall shadow outlined by the open window. For one wild instant she thought she would be killed, stabbed, or strangled by the marquess's assassin. Even as she gathered breath to scream, the figure moved, straightened, and came toward her, and the scream died unborn in her throat.

"Comte!" she whispered faintly.

"Do not fear me, madame. I came only to see your child. Have you incurred the marquess's wrath on my . . . ?" He fell suddenly quiet as footsteps sounded in the hallway.

In one fluid movement the comte reached into his pocket and withdrew a pistol. For a long moment he stood motionless in the dark until the footsteps retreated. Only then did he move to the door, whispering an oath. He turned to Cassandra. "You realize we are locked in?"

Cassandra nodded slowly, aware now that this man could not have come into the room by any normal means. She turned her head to stare at the open window.

"*Oui.* Your nurse was most accommodating." A pleasant low chuckle came from him. As he retraced his steps across the room Cassandra realized that he had exchanged his black silk coat for a chamois riding jacket and his dancing pumps for boots.

"I am prepared for travel," he continued in his low soft voice. He walked past her, bent over the sleeping boy, and, to Cassandra's astonished ears, she thought she heard him coo.

"Your son?" he inquired. At Cassandra's nod he came to stand before her. Gently cupping her chin, he turned her face to the faint light from the next room.

She heard him suck in a quick breath before he ran a gentle finger over the lush fullness of her lower lip. "You're lovely, madame. I envy the man you love."

For a long moment there was nothing but the sound of their breathing in the room as Cassandra studied the painted pale face with a black patch on its right cheek. She nearly laughed. This man no more resembled Merlyn Ross than the marquess did. Yet she felt no more fear of him than she had of the other, and she knew she'd found an ally.

"You would flee the marquess?" he asked at last.

"Yes," Cassandra whispered. "And if you will help me, you'll earn a small fortune. I can pay you well," she lied desperately, hoping he would be as much in need of cash as most aristocrats were rumored to be.

The tall man before her seemed to consider this before he said, "If I take you away, it's a promise you won't be bothered by the marquess."

Cassandra realized he had come to a decision when he turned and reached down to pick up her child. "You must do as I say with no questions asked."

Cassandra nodded once, watching fearfully as he wrapped a blanket about her child. "Go and fetch your cloak; the night will be a long one and there will be no warm hearths until we reach our destination."

Cassandra did as she was bid, rejecting the idea of changing clothes as he had done. It would take precious minutes to remove the corsets and lacings, time they could not spare. When she came back into the nursery, he had taken the sheet from her bed and was making knots in the corners. Before her astonished eyes, he fashioned a sling and put Adam into it.

"Come here," he directed and slipped it over her head, so that the baby hung suspended on her back. Reaching around her, he tied the ends about her waist. Next he took a handkerchief from his pocket and wound it quickly about her wrists, binding them together.

"What're you doing?' she protested faintly as he bent and picked her up, an action that brought her close to his warm body, so that the exotic aroma of vetiver teased her nose a second time.

"No questions, madame. You promised." He set her on the window casement and climbed up after her. Only then did Cassandra notice the heavy rope ladder attached to the stone.

"I climbed in this way when I was told the marquess had left orders with your nursemaid that your son was not to be disturbed," he explained as he reached out and placed her bound arms about his neck. "Take a deep breath and hold it, *chérie.*"

Before Cassandra could say a word, he swung a leg over onto the first rung of the rope ladder and pulled her to the edge of the casement with his left arm. She could not repress a whimper of fear that he would drop her, but his grip was surprisingly firm. Well-tempered muscles bunched and rippled in the arm encircling her waist as she slipped over the edge of the sill. Squeezing her eyes shut, she whispered hoarsely, "Do not drop me. Please, please, not with the child."

"And lose my promised fortune?" he replied cheerfully in her ear as he began a careful descent of the ropes.

Cassandra felt herself being lowered, suspended by

her arms like a millstone about the neck of a stranger, and for the first time in more than a year genuine amusement moved in her. She was being helped to steal her own son by a man whose motives she could not imagine. What began as a choked sob turned inexplicably into laughter. How vexed the marquess would be when he learned of her escape!

Chapter Six

THE NIGHT AIR DRAGGED PLAYFULLY AT HER SKIRT, BIL-
lowing it to heights that displayed her trim ankles and
shapely calfs, as Cassandra pressed her face against the
Frenchman's hard flat chest to keep out of sight of the
lazily tilting ground far below. With each step he took
she swung a little away, but the steel band of his arm
kept her from jarring against him.

The minutes seemed to drag by as she listened to his
deep but even breathing. The additional burden of
herself and her son made the man's movements awkward, yet he neither groaned nor complained. Finally,
she felt the jolt as he planted a foot on the ground. For
an instant he stood perfectly still, breathing hard and
seemingly unaware of the burden looped around his
neck. Feeling ridiculous because her feet did not touch
the earth, Cassandra wiggled uncomfortably.

"Ma petite madame s'impatiente," he said softly,
teasing her for her impatience. Strong hands encircled
her waist and then she was lifted so that the weight was

taken from her arms and she could remove them from his neck.

He held her a moment, as if enjoying touching her, and the contact plucked a familiar chord within Cassandra yet again. It was dark, too dark to view clearly his features, but for an instant she was sharply aware of the breadth of his shoulders that stretched his leather jerkin and of the powerful hands warmly clasped about her waist. She knew she should not allow this, but his touch was oddly gentle and it forestalled her protest. Before she could be certain why, she was set down.

Sensing what her next action would be, the stranger put a silencing finger to her lips. "Not a word, *chérie.*"

His quiet tone held no note of urgency or anxiousness, but it killed her desire to speak. When he took Adam from her back she expected him to hand the boy to her. Instead, he secured the child firmly but with an easy assuredness in the crook of his left arm. "It's easier for me," he said simply as he reached out to untie her hands. "Come, madame. We must be quick."

The pace he set struck every other thought from Cassandra's mind as they hurried across the open grounds behind the house. The earth which looked so soft and smoothly green in the summer sunshine was in reality pocked with ankle-turning holes and boulders. The lush grasses spattered her with dew and green-thorned weeds caught and puckered the hem of her beautiful gown as she struggled to keep up with the long legs beside her. The night breeze tugged at the small lace cap upon her head and finally plucked it away, together with most of the pins that held her thick brown hair coiled in place. Hair streamed in a silky flood down over her shoulders and into her eyes, but the hard hand at her elbow forced to keep apace until the shadow of trees fell across their path.

When the comte paused, Cassandra swept the hair from her eyes and looked back over her shoulder. In the distance the gritstone walls of Briarcliffe thrust a dark solid shadow against the night. Behind that forbidding exterior the marquess was still entertaining, completely unaware of his daughter-in-law's flight.

Cassandra felt a prickling delight at her situation. It was an absurd, deliberately foolish delight. She was risking her life and that of her son with a man she'd known less than an hour. "You've promised to see me to London. Don't forget the reward," she whispered in hopes of hearing a reassuring response.

A sharp "Sh!" was her only answer and the prickling changed to gooseflesh, but Cassandra realized she had come too far to turn back. When he motioned her before him she obeyed after a backward glance at her child. Adam, at least, knew nothing of her fears and lay curled in trusting sleep. It occurred to her that he had never before done so in the arms of a stranger.

A few minutes later they stepped onto the stony road. The sky seemed bright when compared with the darker canopy of the trees, and Cassandra raised her eyes to the stars, like diamonds in the blue velvet.

"*Oui*. A night for lovers." The Frenchman's voice sounded quite near in the stillness. "Have you a lover, madame?"

Color flooding her cheeks, Cassandra turned an angry stare on the tall, dark man beside her. "Perhaps I've risked earning your contempt by fleeing in this manner, but do not mistake my intention. My only wish is to reach London and Nicholas."

"Ah!" he cried lightly, amusement uppermost as he gently bounced the baby in his arms. "Your virtue is safe, madame."

Cassandra turned away from the smirking man, cross with herself for having even answered his impudence.

A whistled phrase issued from his lips, and a moment later Cassandra heard the bump and stumble of a carriage on the lane. Soon a small private coach appeared on the road ahead, round and shiny black, looking like a giant beetle drawn by a pair of horses.

The coachman's face was shielded by his hat, but she had the impression that he smiled as he leaned down from his perch and said, "There ye be, guv'nor. And with a lady, I see!"

"London-bound we are, Sharp," Cassandra heard her companion say as he snatched open the carriage door. With a hand on her elbow, he lifted her up before him and then hoisted himself up into the carriage and shut the door. Quickly and easily he shifted his bulk into the seat opposite her despite the vehicle's lurch as it moved down the lane.

Adam had not made a sound until now. The rhythm of his breathing changed and he gave a fretful cry.

"Your *enfant* stirs," the Frenchman observed.

Cassandra reached out her arms in the dark. "Please let me hold him. I can hardly be accused of not keeping pace in the coach."

For a moment she thought the request would be denied her. Even as her gaze searched the dark for the shape of her son, the babe roused himself to full wakefulness with a piercing wail. "My son," she repeated with calm authority and was rewarded with the weight of her child.

She heard the Frenchman stir and then the scrape of flint and tinder. An instant later, a tiny flame began to grow on the wick of the lantern he had balanced on his knee. Gradually the flame grew higher and wider until the interior of the coach was fully lit.

"Voilà! That is better," he said cheerfully as he hung it on its peg.

Cassandra blinked twice against the harsh yellow light before her gaze settled on the face of the stranger opposite her. The hairs of his wig had been picked at by the wind and a fine sheen of perspiration had removed much of the rice powder, revealing a swarthier complexion than was usual among aristocrats. Faintly alarmed by the one blue eye staring back at her, she dropped her gaze to her son.

"I'd given up the thought of ever seeing you again, Cassie."

The words were spoken in a rich deep voice devoid of accent. The voice startled her so badly she nearly dropped her son. Her head snapped up and she met again the single blue eye watching her. In bewilderment, her gaze slipped over his broad shoulders encased in leather as if in expectation of some change. "Wha—what did you say?"

Her question provoked a smile from the Frenchman and he reached out to tenderly cup her face in his hand. "What is it, Cassie? Don't say you've forgotten me?"

"Don't!" Surprised by his touch, Cassandra jerked away. But he did not stop; he reached out and grasped her firmly by arms just above the elbows and lifted her, child and all, into his lap. Frightened now, Cassandra cried out, but he stopped her voice with his own mouth.

His lips were warm and moist, his breath sweet and hot in her mouth. Encumbered by the child in her arms, Cassandra could raise only one hand to push the man away. His cheek was rough under her fingertips and she thought, absurdly, that he would soon need a shave. Lowering her hand in search of a vulnerable spot, she encountered a strong steady pulse at his throat. She was not dreaming, he was real, as real as the lips trailing down her cheek to her own throat.

"I've missed you so, Cassie," he murmured into the soft curve of her neck.

"No! Please don't!" Cassandra moaned, pushing him away so that the tingling of her skin stopped. She shook her head, staring at the man whose features were not as she remembered but whose kiss recalled an impossibility. It couldn't be! It was not possible! Merlyn Ross was dead!

"Let me go," she begged faintly, feeling an undertow of unreality dragging at her. "You will have your reward, I swear it."

The man laughed, the sound of it as intimate as the touch of his hands at her waist. "There's only one reward I'd accept from you, Cassie, as you well know." He lowered his head, but she turned away and his lips brushed lightly across her cheek. She heard his deep chuckle, tantalizingly familiar, and then his fingers curled about a breast.

"Cassie, look at me."

Cassandra turned her head slightly to bring him full

106

within her view and a shiver licked up her spine. Her mind no longer played her memory false. His face was different, but the voice, and the kiss, they were the same.

"Who are you?" she demanded.

His chuckle, deep and resonant, was unnerving in its confidence. "Your lover, lady," came the silky reply.

"No!" Cassandra twisted to be free. To her surprise, she was immediately lifted and set back on the seat opposite him. Cradling her son tightly, she stared at the man through frightened eyes.

"What do you see?" he asked her quietly.

"A stranger," she whispered.

"What else?" he prompted.

"Nothing more," Cassandra answered and lowered her gaze, wishing fervently to be back in her bedroom at Briarcliffe. Her son struggled in her arms and she thought, no, that she could not wish.

"Why do you not answer with the truth of what you know?" the man continued quietly. "I'm certain you remember."

Cassandra shook her head slightly, not wanting to voice her beliefs, but her eyes were drawn to him once more in wonder.

He sat forward suddenly, his single sapphire eye seeking her golden-brown gaze. "You know who I am, Cassie. Admit it. Do not be deceived by appearances."

Cassandra stared dumbly, too frightened and fascinated to look away. She did not know what to expect when he reached up and quickly switched his patch from one eye to the other, but the reality startled her to speech.

"You haven't lost your eye!"

"You're quick-witted, Cassie. What else do you see?" He bent forward to bring this face on a level with hers. "What is the difference?"

"It's—why, your left eye! It's green!" Cassandra shrank back until the horsehair cushions stopped her.

He snatched off the patch. The flickering flame of the lantern lit his features, but Cassandra saw only the reflection of sapphire flame in one eye and emerald in the other. Reaching up, he removed the wig, revealing the sable-black hair she remembered. A moment later he peeled the patch from his cheek and rubbed off the rouge and powder to display the bronzed face that she remembered against her will.

"Merlyn Ross!" Cassandra gasped. "I thought you dead."

"Did you cry for me, Cassie?" Merlyn asked sweetly as his gaze lowered to her bosom against which her babe lay.

Cassandra shook her head. "It's not possible. The marquess confirmed that you were hanged."

Merlyn smiled as if at a simple child. "I have friends, though I had thought myself abandoned the night we met. A few coins here, a few coins there, what's one body more or less to a gaoler? I was only one of four men to hang that morning. I must assume they substituted some other wretch for me." His gaze shifted from her to the baby. "Never in my life have I been more grateful for the vagaries of life."

Cassandra pulled her son protectively close. "I don't know what you mean."

"Do you not?" Merlyn's gaze went meaningfully

108

from her to the child once more. "Did you call him Merlyn after me?"

Cassandra stared at him, aghast. "The child's not yours!" She scrambled about in her mind frantically for some explanation that would put him off, but the lie great enough to serve would not come. The best she could manage was a weak bluff. "You'd best let us down. 'Tis miles back to Briarcliffe. You'd be far and away before I returned."

It was only when silence stretched out interminably that she wondered if he might throw open the coach door and fling mother and child out. "Oh, say something!" she cried finally, the harshness of her tone echoing in her ears.

Merlyn's face gave no hint of his feelings, but she immediately sensed a difference in his silence and looked up to find him staring at Adam.

Adam had grown momentarily quiet, entertained, no doubt, by the loud voices about him. But now he began sucking noisily on his fist between hungry fretting.

"Feed your son, Cassie," came his calm reply.

"What?" she asked.

To her complete astonishment he leaned forward and unerringly found her breast, which he boldly squeezed. The gesture stung her pride more than any other action he might have made. "You damnable, vile, impudent oaf!" she cried. "I'm no brood sow for marketing at the fair!"

"Tsk, tsk, that's no fit language for a lady," Merlyn admonished through easy laughter. "Only, tell me. Why are you playing wet nurse to the child? Ladies do not usually suckle their own."

Caught between outrage and mortification, Cassandra could not find her voice. He had dared to touch her intimately, without the least hesitation. For the second time in her life she knew the melting fear of physical vulnerability. Then she remembered the only weapon she had. "I am the Marchioness of Briarcliffe. You'd do well to keep that in mind."

Merlyn burst into laughter. "Lord love us, you must do better than that."

"It's true," Cassandra protested. Greatly daring, she added, "If you really knew Nicholas Briarcliffe, you'd know what I say is true."

Merlyn sobered on the moment. "What I know, my sweet liar, is that the grandson the Marquess of Briarcliffe plans to foist off on the beau monde is a fraud."

Cassandra paled visibly. Seeing the effect of his words, he said conciliatingly, "Come, Cassie. You've every right to be angry with me, but, I swear, I did try to find you. My friends did not ask my consent in their plans. I found myself drugged and shipped to France before I could stop them. When I returned, you had left Newgate without a trace." His gaze darkened. "'Tis been hell this year without you. We've lost time, my love, precious time."

"I'm no love of yours," Cassandra cried. "Hear me. I am the wife of Nicholas Briarcliffe. He is my husband these three years."

Merlyn's gaze narrowed. He did not know how to prove her wrong or even why he should. But her tone made him believe that she was not glad for his return from the grave.

The pain of that realization cut deep, deeper than he

thought possible. He sat back carefully, anger working in him. For nearly a year he had searched for her, combing every tavern, public hall, and bawdyhouse in London in hopes of glimpsing her great dark eyes. While she, it seemed, was scheming and intriguing with one of the most notorious old roués in England.

His memories of her could not be reconciled with this new possibility of a calculating woman, but, he reminded himself, he had viewed her through three-quarters of a bottle of brandy and the narrow scope of a noose. Virgin or not, she had had no protector, no future beyond selling herself. His eyes strayed to the babe once more, and a new thought struck him. He'd made her pregnant; perhaps she had done what she did because she needed money to care for the child.

"You've offered me money to escort you to London. How will you pay me?"

"Nicholas will see to it," Cassandra said confidently.

Merlyn shook his head. "That won't do. London's a three- or four-day journey. The marquess will soon learn you are gone. We cannot afford to spend our nights in roadhouses, but we must eat. How will you pay for it?"

Cassandra gnawed the corner of her lower lip and then she remembered. One hand flew up to one ear, but the diamond drop was gone. So, too, was the other. Only then did she realize the cold weight of the Briarcliffe choker was no longer clasped about her throat. "I must have dropped them on the grounds," she murmured to herself.

At her stricken expression Merlyn's lips twisted in mockery. "My lady should take greater care with her jewels. The night often conceals a thief." With practiced ease he stuck two long fingers into his waistcoat and withdrew her diamond choker. "Is this what you're looking for?"

Cassandra stared at him in amazement. "But how—? You stole them!" she accused.

"Of course. What else would you expect from a thief?" Merlyn returned in good humor.

"Thief? But you never touched . . ." Cassandra faltered. It came to her quickly, the light touches of his fingers when they stood in her bedroom and, later, when he'd kissed her and she'd been pressed tightly against him. Still, it did not seem possible that he could remove the jewels without her knowing it. "Who are you?" she demanded.

Merlyn's mouth widened into a grin. "I'm the Comte de Valure, just as you saw. To be honest, it's one of my better disguises. I'm a thief by trade. A jewel thief."

Cassandra considered this, less appalled than she expected to be. "That's why you were in Newgate?"

Merlyn shook his head scornfully. "Hardly! I've never been caught. I was condemned for the murder of a young woman whose bed I'd just quit."

Cassandra's spirits plummeted. "You murdered a woman?"

A grimness tightened Merlyn's mouth. "Does it spoil your appreciation of our night together to think you bedded with a murderer?'

A tremor shook Cassandra as she jerked her head in denial. "Yes—no! It changes nothing!" she cried.

Merlyn gazed at her, into her honey-brown eyes bright with tears and a soft mouth that trembled in fear, and a strange sensation flowed through him. He realized with a heightening of the feeling that he was blushing!

For more than thirty-two years he had used his wit and callousness as a weapon and shield against the world. He'd forgotten there were still vulnerable souls abroad. He reached into the pouch near his seat and withdrew a silver flask. "Drink a little of this brandy. You're shivering."

Cassandra took the bottle and put it to her lips. The liquid warmth spread quickly from her mouth to her belly as she swallowed a small mouthful. "Thank you," she murmured.

Merlyn watched her cheeks flush with color, not knowing what to say. When she handed the bottle back to him he took it without a word.

"You have my jewels. Will you take us to London?" she asked, more determined than ever to reach the safety of Nicholas's arms.

"You'd best settle the lad, he'll soon make himself sick with crying," Merlyn suggested. His grin revealed a set of surprisingly healthy teeth. "Don't play the coy maid on my account."

The maddening tone of his voice scraped her raw nerves and Cassandra snapped back, "You can hardly imagine that I would—would—"

"I don't see that you've much choice," he returned, still in good humor.

Cassandra debated a moment, gnawing her lower lip in indecision. It was a mistake. Merlyn moved with such speed she had no chance to evade him. He lunged forward suddenly, reaching around her, and tugged loose her lacings. Hard strong fingers separated her gown and grazed the sensitive flesh of her spine, leaving her gown hanging from her shoulders.

"Feed him, confound it!" he muttered.

Cassandra lowered her eyes from his face, not wanting to see its violent strength. Taking a deep breath, she reached up to slip her right shoulder free of the gown. A shiver that had nothing to do with the coolness of the night traveled across her bare skin as she carefully pulled her arm free, exposing a fully rounded breast. It was all the encouragement Adam needed. One tiny hand, pink and wriggly as a starfish, came up to grasp at her bosom as his small mouth began rooting hungrily.

Only when Adam's wails gave way to coos of contentment did she look up again at Merlyn, a cold, forbidding anger in her dark eyes. To her amazement, she saw that he had turned his head away. Her eyes moved over him. She had forgotten that there was a beauty in his rugged features and how his hair lay in ebony curls at his temples and nape. Against the stark whiteness of his shirt, his skin was bronze. And how large he was. The coach was so small their knees touched. All that she had forgotten.

But there were other things she had not forgotten, things that had brought instant recognition. She shivered, remembering the hands that moments before had held her close and the lips that had claimed hers with such assuredness. What did he want of her? She choked down her fear and looked down at Adam. Whatever it was, she would have to meet it. Behind her lay certain separation from her son, perhaps even death. Ahead lay . . .

Merlyn did not lift his gaze until he was certain both child and mother were engrossed in one another. The deep red and gold highlights in the mahogany mane framing her shoulders were richer than he remembered, beckoning him to run his fingers through the silky strands tangled by the wind, but he did not touch her. Instead, he contented himself with looks. He could not believe he had found her, not quite, though he had held her against him, felt her breath on his cheek, heard her dearly remembered voice. How could he not look upon her in wonder after a year's fruitless search for her? Her lips were pouted now and a small frown marred the smooth expanse of her brow. Her thoughts were troubled ones.

"So, too, are mine," he murmured softly as his eyes fell with new intensity on the child sucking impatiently at his mother's breast. The pearly luster of her naked breast reminded him of the kiss they had shared and he tore his gaze away.

His gaze went back to her face, its gentle contours a familiar companion of his dreams. For a year he had searched for her, hoping against all odds that she might be found. To stumble upon her tonight with a child in her arms, that was one thing he had not made plans against.

The thought brought a deep scowl to Merlyn's features. A scant week ago he had chanced to meet Nick Briarcliffe in one of the many gaming halls of London. He had been drowning the bitter anger of another night's fruitless search for Cassie. Perhaps that had attracted Briarcliffe, for he quickly learned that their moods matched. Sullen and angry, Briarcliffe let slip that the wife he'd never bedded had given birth to a child and that his father intended to set the bastard up as his new heir.

His own suggestion that Nick steal the boy was a bad joke, meant to make light of another man's woes. When Briarcliffe nodded and asked him to find a suitable man to do the job, he'd replied that a discreet inquiry might be better. For a hundred pounds he offered to go to Briarcliffe as Nick's spy.

Merlyn grunted softly. He was nearly always in need of funds. To offer his services as a spy seemed a small thing at that moment. The results were no business of his. Until now.

Again his gaze moved over the babe. The black silky curls and lashes were vivid swathes of color against his dewy fresh skin. A child. His child.

Now he noticed another sight that made a smile stretch his features. It winked at him from the third finger on her left hand, the finger he had placed it on himself. His talisman, his emerald and sapphire ring.

Merlyn reached instinctively to touch it but drew back when she flinched. He looked at her in surprise. "You would rather not admit that I am alive. That makes me curious. Why should you wish your child's father dead?"

He paused, watching with no satisfaction the confirmation of his statement in her blush. His voice was harsher when he continued. "If you believe I care that you entered into a plot to fleece Nick Briarcliffe of his inheritance, you're wrong. I'm acquainted with the hardship of a life without funds or protection. And I've learned how to change that. You see before you Merlyn

116

Ross. Yet an hour earlier I was the Comte de Valure in your eyes. Give a man a velvet coat, hide his dark locks with a wig, and he takes the form of a nobleman. The world accepts it. Arrogance, like manners, can be learned. An accent is the skill of the lowliest thespian. I'm a thief because it pleases me to be so."

The smile he gave her was both cocky and tender, and Cassandra felt an unwanted urge to smile back but did not.

"Perhaps we're more alike than you'd care to admit. Our victims are the nobility, those who can well afford to lose what they have through no effort of their own. I frightened you needlessly a moment ago when I might have told you the truth. I killed no one. You see, with honesty, we could deal well together, Cassie."

He leaned forward and plucked his ring from her finger with a touch so light she would not have realized it had she not seen him do it. "But you would pretend that you're a marchioness, and I am happy enough in your company to oblige you in making a fool of yourself. But know this, Cassie. When all is said and done, you belong to me." So saying, he dropped the ring back into her lap.

Cassandra said nothing. The shell of calm she had used to buffer the shocks of the night was shattered. He thought her a schemer and a fraud, a woman who had sold her child for money. Closing her eyes, she willed away the vision of Merlyn Ross. If he had been welcome in her dreams, he was not in reality.

Yet before them lay London and all the hours and days between.

Chapter Seven

CASSANDRA STIRRED UNDER THE PLEASANT SENSATION OF a kiss. The gentle tug of teeth on her lower lip drew a shivery sigh of pleasure from her. Her eyelids fluttered but refused to open. It was a dream, of course, but one that she was reluctant to give up. To be surrounded by a cocoon of love, enfolded in protecting arms that sent ripples of desire through her, had been a dream often repeated in the last months. The difference this time lay in the intensity of her response. When warm palms traced the outline of her naked breasts, communicating the sweet sensation of desire, she arched herself against the pressure as her nipples hardened. Her breath quickened as warm caressing lips closed over hers once more.

The deep chuckle in her ear was another new facet of the dream, and for a moment Cassandra stiffened. Then she was being lifted and laid on her back. The odor of leather and the sway of a coach surprised her, but before she could wonder at these additions she was caught against the hard expanse of a naked male breast. The sweet firm warmth of his body overlay hers. Stroking and kissing, he seemed to envelop her vibrant flesh in a need as urgent as her own. The spicy scent of vetiver blended with the earthy exotic perfumes of their bodies as Cassandra experienced the lingering touch of his tongue in the hot silky hollow of her mouth. Flesh and spirit blended, absorbed and distilled into a single essence.

Blazing above the pulsating, shimmering, swelling, peaking beauty of their union was her lover's gaze, the glorious, magical, transculent flames of emerald and sapphire.

Oh yes! her heart cried. *There's such magic in your touch. This is love . . . is what I seek and cannot find!*

The carriage swung wide to avoid a boulder in the road and Cassandra was jarred awake. Eyes wide in surprise, she met the gaze of Merlyn Ross. So intense was his blue-green stare that, flushing, she lowered her eyes to her gown. She was fully clothed, but that was not entirely reassuring. She was lying within the circle of his arm, his chest a pillow for her head. Had he kissed her, or was it all a dream?

Number 20 on St. George's Street at Hanover Square was ablaze with lights when the coach carrying Merlyn and Cassandra rolled into the London avenue.

"It seems your husband is entertaining," Merlyn voiced in irritation when their coach had halted on the opposite side of the square.

Cassandra stirred, brushing the sleep from her eyes

with one small hand. "Ooh," she breathed as every muscle in her body protested movement, reluctant to pull away from the broad chest that offered her a comfortable pillow each night as she slept. In spite of this intimacy, they had spoken little after the first night, the meals they shared in wayside taverns the only respite from the punishing ride of the coach.

For a moment she lay still, enjoying the warmth that enfolded her, but when his statement played back through her thoughts she bolted upright. "We've reached London? So soon?"

Merlyn smiled and adjusted Adam, who slept in his left arm just as she had in his right. "Do you know you're beautiful when you've just awakened, Cassie? Were your dreams so sweet?"

Cassandra turned away from his knowing smile, feeling the color bloom in her face. She could almost believe he had read her thoughts. Looking out the window, she saw the broad facade of the great town house which boasted three full stories of red brick, a dozen front windows, and a hooded doorway of new design.

"Nick lives in grand style, don't you agree?" Merlyn prompted.

Cassandra turned back to him and then her head swung again to the window. "Nicholas lives here?" Suddenly uncertain of herself, she edged back from the window until she was in the shadow. "I had no idea," she exclaimed softly.

"No idea at all, Marchioness?" Merlyn returned in mock surprise. "I find that odd, yes indeed. You boast to be the wife of the man who owns that house."

Cassandra gave him a quick, angry look. The spell between them was broken. How could it be otherwise? "I never said I had been to Nicholas's London residence." She leaned forward to look out again. "Perhaps you should leave us here to find our own time to enter. If my husband is entertaining, he certainly would not wish me to be seen by his guests in my present condition."

"Not at all," Merlyn returned calmly and reached to unlatch the coach door. "If your husband is half as eager as you believe him to be to feast his eyes on you, then your ruined gown and unbound hair will only serve to augment his pity."

"He'll think me the rudest sort of beggar," Cassandra protested, looking down on the soiled, wrinkled mess that had once been a ball gown. Days earlier she had shed the impossible whalebone paniers over which the gold silk had been draped, and several of her petticoats had been sacrificed as Adam's diapers. "I have some pride."

"That I'm beginning to believe," Merlyn answered brusquely. "But you will understand that I am eager to collect the reward due me. And, of course, to see you to the safety of your loving spouse's arms." Merlyn pushed her gently to the open doorway. "After you, Marchioness. I will care for little Adam."

Cassandra hesitated, a knot of fear growing in her middle. She had dreamed a thousand times of what it would be like to walk into Nicholas's home, to find him seated at his dinner, or alone in his library with a brandy and a book. Never had she imagined that their reunion would take place within the view of strangers.

A hand, warm and compelling, came up and rested on the bare skin of her slender neck. "You don't have to do it, Cassie. I'll believe that you were married if it will make you happy. But come away now. Come with me."

Cassandra turned her head so that his face came into view. He again wore the disguise of the comte, yet the wig, patch, and fresh powder could not hide from her eyes the disturbingly masculine lines of his true features. His gaze made her teeter on the brink. The deep sapphire eye seemed to speak what he could not, forming the thoughts on the surface of her heart.

Stay with me. This man you call husband is the stranger. Could he love you as well as I? Remember our night together, my words of love. Remember my kiss. One word. One glance will save you from what lies before you.

Cassandra turned her eyes away from his compelling gaze, her emotions a turmoil of fear, panic, repulsion . . . and desire. Even now, she thought desperately as she recorded her body's response to the warmth of his voice and his touch. Even now, in sight of her goal, so dearly sought and so dearly paid for, she could hear a faint voice in her mind urging her to relent, to go with the enigmatic stranger beside her who made her dream such dreams as perhaps no woman had ever had.

"I can't," she whispered so softly that he did not hear her. What she felt for Merlyn, born in the brief hours of a single night, could not sweep away the hope of true love that had made her life bearable these three years. She knew nearly nothing of him or even if he could be trusted. He was an escaped prisoner, a thief. What more she could not imagine. It was no life for a child. "I can't," she said louder, shaking off his hand. "I have a husband. It is not a lie. And there's Adam. He needs the protection of a decent man."

Merlyn recoiled from her as if she had spat on him. She did not see the look of hurt and humiliation her words had caused, and too quickly it was gone. *She did not want him.* The thought thundered through his head, thickening his pulse with pain. He who had loved and searched and longed for her for nearly a year had been rejected out of hand, and for what? A debauched wretch who claimed the title of marquess.

The heavy pounding of his heart shook him. Until the night she had shared his cell at Newgate he had never known the meaning of the word *love*. And yet he was certain that because of it, she had left his side with the seed of his life taking root within her. Yet now she would deny him as not good enough for his own son.

His gaze switched to Adam, his expression grim. The child's cap of black hair and dark blue eyes were as true examples of his claim as any that could be offered. Did she expect Briarcliffe to simply accept the babe, knowing he was another man's handiwork?

His mask of indifference changed to rage. Cassie did not want him. But his son, no other man would claim Adam as his.

Merlyn snatched the latch and the door swung open. Then he turned to her, his face only inches from hers as he said, "Go, Cassie, and be damned. You've whored for me. I'll not begrudge your husband his turn. But you'll not take my son with you!"

A hand in the small of her back propelled Cassandra

out into the cobblestone street. In disbelief, she heard Merlyn cry "Drive on!" and the carriage door slam shut behind her. Even as she gained her balance and turned toward it, the coach lurched forward to the crack of the coachman's whip and began rolling down the street.

"No! Wait! Don't!" Cassandra cried, a feeling of unreality so strong in her that she could not believe that the coach was gaining speed, leaving her running behind. The thundering of her heart overshadowed her running footsteps, and then, incredibly, the coach made a swing into a narrow dark lane and was gone.

"Oh, God!" she whispered in the eerie quiet after the coach was out of sight. He'd stolen her child!

She did not see the rider cantering through the square nor hear him until his surprised shout startled her as he came too quickly upon her in the dark. A splash of muddy water kicked up by the passing horse dampened her stockings, and for the first time she realized that it was raining, a cold misty drizzle too fine to hear.

"You! Girl!" the rider called after her as he slowed his mount. "What do you think you're about?"

Afraid that he might stop her, she turned and ran toward the Briarcliffe house. Now more than ever she needed Nicholas's help and protection. She had the presence of mind to know she'd be turned away from the front door and ran toward the terrace instead. After a moment she found the gate in the wrought-iron fence that guarded the grounds.

The quiet of the street with its elegantly fronted houses contrasted sharply with the traffic at the rear of the garden. Here the steamy heat from the kitchen hung in the air like earthbound clouds, reflecting the kitchen fires and lighting the yard.

Cassandra stepped around a topiary shrub trimmed to the shape of an elephant and caught at the sleeve of a passing maid. "I must speak with Lord Nicholas Briarcliffe," she said quickly. "This is his residence?"

The maid, sweat steaming from beneath her starched cap, gave the unknown woman a cursory glance that said plainly she had no time for nonsense. "We'll 'ave no beggars 'ere. His Lordship's express orders. Now, off with ye. There's a musical evenin' inside and dinner to do."

Cassandra dashed the tears from her eyes, determined to enter. All she could think of was the sound of Merlyn's voice as he had shoved her from the coach. *You'll not take my son!* But Adam wasn't his, he was hers, and the thought of losing the only certain thing in her life made her furiously bold. "I'm Lady Briarcliffe. You'd best show me indoors, my girl, before I cause such a scene you'll wish you'd thought better of it." And she took a menacing step toward the maid.

The speech was magical in its effect. Within minutes Cassandra was seated in the butler's pantry with a cup of tea at her elbow while the master of the house was being apprised of her arrival. She barely tasted the warm liquid sliding down her dry throat. Had it been broth or even dishwater she would not have discerned it. Every taut nerve of her body hummed with the knowledge that she was, at last, within the walls that housed Nicholas.

She had no inkling to warn her, to give her a hairsbreadth of grace in which to prepare. One moment there was only the cheerful chatter from the kitchen beyond. The next moment the door crashed open. Heart thumping wildly, Cassandra rose to her feet to face him.

He was tall, taller by more than an inch than Merlyn, but the once-rapierlike physique had thickened, straining the buttons of his waistcoat beneath his wide-skirted coat of pink silk. But Cassandra was undismayed until her loving gaze rose to his face. His perfect features, too, had changed. The same aquiline nose sliced the halves of his face and golden brows winged upward toward the perfect white cap of his powdered hair. But the aching beauty was gone, distorted by the first stages of gout. His mouth was the next difference she noticed. The thin upper lip was lifted back from his teeth in a grimace that had nothing to do with friendliness, and the full lower, deeply clefted, now seemed too thick for beauty. Then she saw his eyes, and a chill as sharp as a Derbyshire winter pierced her through. The pale green was frozen ice, the pupils like twin birds of prey trapped within.

"You are—?" he asked imperiously as the predatory gaze swung from her tearstained face to her ravaged finery.

Cassandra opened her mouth, but the sound was strangled by the strange workings of her throat. This was the moment she had been waiting for, and yet she could think of no beginning.

"I presume you're one of Sadie's girls." He wrinkled his nose and pulled a scented handkerchief from his coatsleeve to hold to it. "Lord! You smell of the water closet. Sadie will pay for this presumption. She knows I can't tolerate a filthy trollop."

As he came near she caught the unmistakable odor of attar of roses. It surprised her into remembering the odor of vetiver oil that clung to Merlyn in spite of their long journey, and the feminine scent of her husband's garments disconcerted her. When he reached out and took her chin in his slim fingers, she could not repress a shiver.

Nicholas smiled at the young woman's shudder. Good, he thought, she knows her place. "Well, open your bodice, chit. Let me see the goods Sadie would fob off on me. Percy will be in later. He's a fancy for soiled goods."

"I'm no trollop," Cassandra began, "I—"

"Silence!" he demanded and struck her across the mouth with his open hand. "You're a dirty, ill-favored little slut," he bit out.

Stunned, Cassandra did not even hear the string of obscenities he then tossed at her. He did not recognize her! And yet she knew him, adorned with all the artifices of patch and powder and coarseness that dissipated living had wrought.

When his anger was spent Nicholas looked on the girl's pale face in utter surprise. "God's death! Don't tell me you're one of those who's just come up with the carrier?"

"What?" Cassandra asked faintly, but he continued, not hearing her.

"Percy can't abide a green miss. Drawing red gold is not at all his style." Nicholas let his hand slide from her chin to the slim column of her neck. "I, on the other hand, am most disposed toward instructing new petite doves."

"Please!" Cassandra protested and moved back, not wanting the touch of his hand on her. "Surely you remember me. I am Cassandra, your lady wife."

Nicholas's arm fell to his side. "What jest is this?" A dark scowl lowered his golden brows. "Who put you up to it?" He ran the tip of his red tongue over his lower lip. "Was it Percy? That would be like him, the rotter! Even the gazettes are touting the news, though they dare not name names. But it sticks in my throat—and God's death if I don't use ill the man who's dared do this!"

The lightning-quick flex of his fingers on her throat surprised Cassandra in its strength. His black pupils expanded. "Who paid you to come here? Who knows that the cartoons of the noble cuckold the gazettes are plying on the street are about me?" His grip tightened until Cassandra could no longer draw breath.

Frantic, she pulled at his fingers, but they were like bands of steel. He leaned nearer, crushing her windpipe, his handsome face livid in rage. "Who told you? Who are you?"

Almost in surprise he realized that the ugly red blotches springing up in the young woman's complexion were caused by his fingers. Just as abruptly, he released her and she staggered against the butler's table. "Answer me!"

Tears swelled and coursed in hot streaks down Cassandra's face as she fought the black dizziness of fainting. "Please . . . believe me. I am . . . Cass."

"Nonsense," Nicholas declared, taking a step toward her and raising his hand again. "What fool would not expect me to remember the green chit I made my wife? God knows, if I hadn't been in such a rage over my father's threat, I'd never had shackled myself to her." His eyes went indifferently over the young woman before him again. "You have her size, though I suspect she's grown, as girls are wont to do. Percy didn't think of that, did he? And your coloring's all wrong. The chit had mousy hair and no bosom to speak of."

He reached out and caught a handful of her hair. The gleaming dark masses falling about her shoulders gave her an innocence he decided he liked and his tone warmed with the male timbre of desire. "But you, my girl, you're curved enough to entice a man. With a bath and a decent gown, you'd do quite nicely." He reached down with both hands and drew her to her feet by the shoulders with no further thought of the fact that he had nearly choked her to death a moment before. "Tell Percy I'm diverted. And you, my dear, may come back tomorrow night."

"It was a cold day, November," Cassandra began in a calm voice that belied the heavy hammering of her heart. "You wore a blue riding coat and your carriage bore the Briarcliffe crest. It was market day in Hatherleigh. You paid my father twenty guineas for me. He could not believe it, neither could I. The wedding took place in Bideford because you said it was unseemly that we should travel all the way to Derbyshire still unwed."

Her eyes never left his face as she spoke and so she saw the brief glimmer of recognition in his eyes before it was swamped by rage. Blood darkened his complexion beneath the rouge and powder, and Cassandra knew with sickening clarity what would follow. She swung away when the second blow came. It hurt all the same. The flat of his palm missed her cheek but caught her on the ear and the world rang.

"My father!" the nobleman roared. "He put you up to this! None but he shares the secret of my bride."

She saw the narrowing of his pale eyes, so like those of a bird of prey, and fear spilled through her veins like icy water. With a cry of terror, she swung away and flung herself at the door, but he was quicker. He grabbed her by the arm when she dodged him and twisted it behind her back in a hold that tore a cry of excruciating pain from her.

"You won't get away, after all, my dear," he said in her ear. "I've no use for a wife, understand me, no use at all."

Cassandra's plea for mercy was drowned out by the crash of the tea table she reached for to steady herself, and he immediately clasped a hand over her mouth. "You should have let me think you were one of Percy's jests," Nicholas said, dragging her backward from the door. "My father and I have no illusions about how we'd use one another given the chance." He gave her arm a vicious tug that nearly pulled it from the socket.

The crisp knock on the door startled both of them, but Nicholas recovered first. "Go away! This is private business."

"Begging your pardon, sir," came the embarrassed reply through the door. "There's an message just come from the Comte de Valure. 'Tis said it's urgent."

Cassandra's relief was so great she nearly swooned.

"Ask him!" she cried. "Ask the comte to identify me. He brought me to London. He has my child."

"Child?" Nicholas released her with a little shove, then spun her around with a hand on her shoulder. "What child?"

"My child," Cassandra repeated. Too late she realized that this was the last bit of information she should have given him.

"The bastard my father would fob off on the world?" His look of amazement eased into sparkling mischief. "Now, that *is* news. Harrison," he called to his butler on the other side of the door, "have the housekeeper tell the messenger to wait. You are to remain by this door."

When he turned back to Cassandra he was smiling. "That's right, my dear. Perhaps you are the wife I married and who thought to cuckold me. By God!" he crowed in delight. "This is too good. Did the old bastard get you with child himself?"

Cassandra shrank back from his quicksilver gaze, but Nicholas did not mind. "Wouldn't have thought that possible," he mused mildly, "yet it would be like him if he could still perform. But he's made a strategic error in sending you to me. If he thought I'd be forced to recognize my wife he's a greater fool than he thinks I am.

"I have no wife," Nicholas said distinctly, his gaze as frigid as sleet on Cassandra. "My father may claim what he likes, but I have no wife." His eyes shifted to her left hand, and a mocking smile lifted his upper lip. "He didn't even think to have a wedding band copied for you."

Cassandra followed with her eyes his gaze. Her left hand was empty. She'd pocketed Merlyn's ring, unable to wear it in his presence. "I sold it to reach you."

An elegant shrug lifted Nicholas's shoulders. "A poor lie, but not easily disproved. That will take de Valure, I believe."

"You will send for the comte?" Cassandra asked, and a tremor of hope shivered through her. Immediately the hope died. He would not come. He had her child and cared nothing for what might happen to her.

Nicholas gave her a hard look. "There's something I do not know, I suppose. No matter. De Valure is my friend, as you shall see. In the meantime, my dear, I must persuade you to remain in my company."

When he reached for her, Cassandra cried out in fear. It took both her husband and the butler to get her up the backstairs from the first floor to an attic room where she kicked and screamed till she was exhausted.

"An excellent wine, Nick. My compliments." Merlyn swirled the glass stem between his fingers, idly watching as the candelabra flames slipped in and out of the ruby liquid. It was nearly three in the morning. He and his host had been drinking since midnight. The empty bottles they had shared lay on the table before them.

Nicholas pulled at the fragile Brussels lace below his cuff. He wore it long, nearly to his fingertips, to cover what he considered to be his only flaw. His hands were thick and square, with puffy palms and short, stubby fingers. His favorite mistress said they were the hands of a common laborer.

Nicholas's long-lidded gaze swung to the comte's

hands. The fingers were long, with blunted tips and wide, flat palms. Not precisely a gentleman's hands either, but more shapely than his own. Nicholas made a mental note to probe the comte's past. It was a reflex thought for him. Anyone worthy to be considered a rival was watched and probed until his weaknesses emerged. And right now the comte knew more about his weaknesses than he did about the comte's, a dangerous, untenable situation.

"I am eager to learn of your trip," Nicholas suggested after draining his glass.

Merlyn relaxed. The game was under way. "I went to Derby and met Lady Briarcliffe, as you wished me to. I salute your taste, for she is enchanting." Nick's quick look made Merlyn smile. "The *enfant* is a black-haired *petit*. I would say the father is a handsome devil. I would say, also, that it is definitely not you, *mon ami.*"

The Frenchman's laughter did nothing to improve Nicholas's temper and he roared to his feet. "Who is he, that's what I'd like to know!" He turned on his guest, eyes narrowed. "Did she succumb to your charms, Comte, or are the lady's morals too suspect for even your tastes?"

Merlyn shrugged in apology. "As to that, I did not have the opportunity to press the lady in any great way. She was surrounded by the marquess, a sallow-faced secretary, and a dragon named Hannah. I will say I found her pleasant to behold. You could have done much worse, Nick. Why did you not bring her to London?"

"I married to spoil my father's will," Nicholas stated matter-of-factly and resumed his chair after reaching for another bottle. "Love nor liking had no part in it. In fact, I nearly ruined myself, so great was the rage in which I went in search of a wife. You might as well hear the story, as I'm certain the frightened little wretch died the first year." And so he repeated in little sympathy and a great deal of anger the story of his marriage.

"You brought her at the fair?" Merlyn asked in astonishment. "As one buys a cow or a clutch of hens?"

Nicholas sneered at the other man's squeamish tone. "I'd have done worse things to stop my father. As it was, Father was no more eager than I to gazette my marriage. I said nothing and he could not find it advantageous to mention it either, until now."

Nicholas looked away, pretending to uncork a bottle as he carefully chose his next words. "The damnable thing is, I'm convinced the girl died of consumption or whatever. Father wrote me about her nearly two years ago. He'd kept her under a close watch at Briarcliffe that year and said she was ailing." Nicholas's face was grim as he continued. "I didn't know whether to damn her to die or hope she lived to be a millstone about the old bastard's neck."

He laughed suddenly, the sound of it setting the chandelier to tinkling. "What's so rich, my friend, is this. A stray tabby wandered into my home this evening, claiming to be my wife. 'Don't you recognize me?' she whispers like some stage stumpet." His brittle gaze cut to his guest's face. "You'll enjoy the next line, Comte. She said she came to London with you."

Merlyn was surprised Cassandra had been so foolish as to mention their association, but long years of living a life of duplicity had taught him to mask his emotion. *"Moi?* But I am flattered. Is she beautiful, this *petite actrice* who knows my name?"

Satisfied by his guest's easy answer, Nicholas poured the fourth bottle of port. "Too short in the carriage and too delicate for my tastes, but she'll make a tasty morsel for some lusty fellow. I was forced to strike her when she got saucy, and you won't believe how quickly she bruised. She's abovestairs. Would you like to see her?" he inquired, pausing in the midst of pouring.

"Moi? Do I appear eager for cuddling an armful?" Merlyn protested. "No, I must decline. Another night, of course . . ." He waited for perhaps three heartbeats before adding, "What will you do with this impostor? She comes from the marquess, of course."

"Of course," Nicholas returned easily. He did not care what de Valure thought. There would be ways to handle such a man if need be. There were rumors about him. A few questions put to the right ears . . . "I cannot send her back to my father in defeat. That would only give him another chance to use the girl against me. What do you suggest, Comte?"

Merlyn made a pyramid of his fingertips and rested his chin on them for a moment. "I would place the girl in a situation where she would find ample distractions, enough to make her forget my name and yours."

"Mother Tess?" Nicholas suggested.

Merlyn shrugged. "Perhaps. But neither you nor I must be connected with it. I have associates who must not hear a breath of scandal in regard to my name."

This bit of news curved Nicholas's mouth. Just as he suspected, the Frenchman had a vulnerable place.

Later he would discover just what it was. "You have a plan?"

"Oui." Merlyn's smile was boyish. "I know a man whose services prove useful to me from time to time. He goes by the name of Jack. The hour is late, but if the coin is right he can be roused on short notice."

"Tonight?" Nicholas looked genuinely surprised.

"Are you not in need of swift action?"

Nicholas shrugged. "She's a comely piece. What matter a day or two of delay?"

For the first time Merlyn felt a rill of fear race up his spine. The thought of Nick Briarcliffe touching Cassie in any way made him furious. Already he longed to rush upstairs and survey her bruises, but he dared not even express an interest.

Damn you, Cassie! he thought through impotent anger. *Little scheming, lying fool, didn't you know you couldn't fool the husband?*

Aloud, he said, "I only wonder, if the marquess knows she's here, might he not choose this moment to find you, ah, in harmonious life with your wife?"

"Good God!" Nicholas sprang to his feet. "So that's it!" He struck the table with a fist. "He sent her here to be discovered under my roof. No doubt he will arrive in the morning with a parcel of his cronies to find her ensconced in my house. Comte, I thank you. For a lying little bitch I nearly fell into my father's trap. Send for your man. I'll welcome him on any terms he makes."

Merlyn rose lazily to his feet. "Jack is not easily aroused with a summons. I, myself, feel in need of the night air. For a friend, I will journey to collect Old Jack. An hour, shall we say?"

Chapter Eight

CASSANDRA FINISHED THE LAST KNOT IN THE ROPE SHE had fashioned from the old bedding she had found in the trunks scattered about the attic. The only light, from a small arch window six feet off the floor, made the pale semicircle of light in which she frantically worked. Her breath came in quick shallow gasps of fright and her hands smeared the rope with flecks of blood from the cuts she had received when she pried the trunks open.

She tried not to think of what might be happening below. Inside her there was only a dull ache. Surely, she thought numbly, the pain should be a greater. Even now she could hardly believe the moments following Nicholas's entrance into the room. She had expected aid and succor, but he had not recognized her. He claimed he had no wife. And the pain, the pain he had inflicted on her made her body throb and her head ache worse than the beating she'd received in Newgate.

Nicholas did not, would never, love her. Cassandra

felt a queer lurch of her heart and her hands momentarily stopped working. Shame and anger roiled in her, heaving suddenly to the surface with an intensity that made her moan under its onslaught. Nicholas hated and despised her. He would not even admit that he knew her. But she had seen the moment of recognition, and the disgust in his face that came with it. The marquess was right. Nicholas had used her, made her a victim of his scheme, and then abandoned her when he changed his mind. All this time, while she had been waiting, hoping, and fashioning beautiful dreams of their future life together, he had been hoping that she was dead. There was no love. There never had been. Only on her side. Like all the times before.

"How could I have been so stupid?" she whispered brokenly, her fingers clenching tightly to stop their trembling. It was all a joke, a great huge joke which she had taken for reality. The man belowstairs was as blackhearted as any Newgate denizen. Like a wormy apple, his core was rotted and poisoned.

Trepidation and fear quaked through her, but she quickly squashed the disabling emotions before they completely swamped her. Nicholas would be back, she had no doubt. Before that, she must escape.

Cassandra found a heavy shoe and, standing on a trunk with her hands wrapped in cloth, she broke the window's glass and began picking the pieces free from the molding. Adam. He was the only thing of her own she had ever possessed, and all the pent-up love she had carried within her the eighteen years of her life was his. But first she must find him.

The scraping of the key in the lock came as she

hoisted herself headfirst over the edge of the sill. She had thrown her cloth rope outside onto the roof and was halfway out when the attic door creaked open. Squirming wildly, she thought she would slip through before someone spied her, but a moment later she was grabbed by the hips and pulled back into the dark.

"Don't touch me!" she cried, struggling like a wild animal against the arms encased in coarse linen that engulfed her. But the man was stronger and he clamped a hand tightly across her mouth as his other arm dragged her from the trunk and into his embrace.

"Quiet, chit, and ye'll ne'er be harmed. Scream and ye'll be killed," a rough country voice said against her ear.

The man did not wait for her reply but forced a kerchief into her mouth when she opened it to scream. A second one he used to secure the first, effectively gagging her.

"That'll do the trick," he said in a good-natured voice. "Best rest easy, girl. Jack's got hisself a job to do."

He released her and quickly knelt. Seizing the opportunity, Cassandra kicked out wildly at the figure in the dark and caught him under the chin. He muffled an oath and caught her foot. "Be still, you little slut, or I'll bash yer head in!" he muttered furiously as he bound her ankles together with still another kerchief. "Old Jack means ye no harm. We're goin' on a little trip."

"You're certain you know what's to be done?" Cassandra jerked her head up to find Nicholas standing in the doorway, a silver candlestick in his right hand.

139

"Aye, guv'nor. Ye've nary a worry. The comte told me ye had a bit o' petticoat goods for Mother Tess to be delivered."

Cassandra's gaze switched to the shadowy face of her captor at the mention of the comte's name and she tried to put a world of questions into her frightened stare, but he did not look at her. He was tall and stoop-shouldered, with long greasy ropes of grizzled hair and a beard. A patch covered his right eye, and the left was red and runny. Yet her heart lurched in instinctive recognition. Almost at once she discounted it. He wouldn't be so foolish. It was her fevered imaginings.

She tried to laugh at her foolishness, but the cotton stuck to the roof of her mouth and she began to choke. Then, miraculously, the gag was torn from her mouth.

"Quiet, now, or I'll throttle ye," she heard her captor say as he braced her between his knees and pushed her head forward to ease her nausea. Leaning over her, he growled in her ear, "Play the victim, you wretched little bitch, or we both may die."

"There, now, I'm ready," he said, rising to his feet and jerking her to hers. "I'll be taking me wages, gov'nor." And he held out his hand to the man in the doorway.

"Outside," Nicholas replied and turned and started down the narrow steps.

Cassandra was lifted and thrown over Old Jack's shoulder. Every jarring step brought her closer to freedom, but she took her captor's advice and kicked and twisted and made his progress as difficult as possible.

When they reached the kitchen door only the butler was there to greet them.

"See this man to the hack in the alley," Nicholas directed. He had pulled his jabot loose and it hung open from his shirt, revealing fine golden hairs, but Cassandra closed her eyes to this. He was a devil, just as his father was.

Old Jack paused on the threshold. "What am I to tell Mother Tess?"

Nicholas shuddered, remembering how close he had come to falling into his father's trap. It would be best if he stayed clear of the girl entirely. "The girl's hers to instruct as it pleases her." His smile was chilling as he added, "As I've had some experience with her, I'd say she deals well with pain. She'll be a special pleasure to certain clients."

Before she could protest, Cassandra was dumped from Jack's shoulder to her feet and his hand closed her mouth. "Ye'll keep yer mouth shut, if ye've good sense," he warned. "Ye hearin' me?"

A little shake brought her eyes up to the bearded man's face and a terrified nod was extracted from her. Immediately he bent and untied her feet.

"Me coins," Old Jack said, once more holding out his hand.

Nicholas handed him a small purse, surprised by the smoothness of the thief's palms. They were not at all what he expected. This was noticed in passing, but later, when he had retired with the pink of dawn, Nicholas was to remember and wonder.

A heavy hand pushed Cassandra into the alley off the

kitchen. When Old Jack reached out to open the hack's low door, she ducked under his hand and would have run. But he was quicker, grabbing her by the collar. He scooped her up and dumped her into the cab without any regard for her safety.

Only when the vehicle was lumbering down the narrow passage did he turn to her, his red eye blazing. "Damn you, Cassie!"

The plodding clip-clop of the horse's hooves on the brick pavement was at odds with the galloping pace of Cassandra's heart. "Merlyn?" she whispered between doubt and relief.

"Certainly," Merlyn returned coldly, "and you nearly gave me away!"

"Can't you beg for more speed?" Cassandra replied, her voice rising in irritation against his unfriendly tone.

Turning his head, he gave her a withering glance. "Had I not held you back, you'd have fled pell-mell down the street, all heels and petticoat hems. Briarcliffe is no fool, for all his indolent air. When it suits him, he's a quick and deadly enemy." He allowed a moment to pass before he added, "But then, you've learned that much, have you not?"

Cassandra looked away from the even stare of his single eye. "He didn't even recognize me. I thought he cared for me a little."

Merlyn saw the spasm of pain cross her face, and it roused in him a fierce jealousy. *The man would have destroyed her, yet she pines for Briarcliffe,* he thought in a heaving rage as he spied the shadow of the bruise on her face. When he spoke, his voice was colder than ever. "Nick cares not a fig's worth for anything but his own desires. You think he did not recognize you? I beg to differ. But you were in his path and he meant to strike you aside, like a mongrel dog."

Cassandra turned her face back to him, but all she saw was the austere lines of his profile. "But I am his wife!"

Cassandra thought she heard him mutter an oath before he grabbed her by the shoulders and effortlessly dragged her into his lap. He brought her so close she could feel the hairs of his false beard on her face. "Every look, every word you utter, makes me want to shake you till your teeth rattle. Then I remember you as you were in Newgate, and the notion is replaced by an equally strong desire. But I must submit to neither, must I?"

Cassandra stared at his shadow-sculptured face and murmured, "No."

It was more than she should have dared. He jerked her against his chest as a hard kiss stopped her mouth.

It was as before; at the touch of his mouth everything else disappeared. There was only the warm pressure of his lips and then the gentle flick of his tongue into the moist valley behind her lower lip that made her gasp. She was melting, her limbs becoming softly pliant in his hard embrace. She did not want this, this warm dissolving that made her forget, forget so many things, but neither could she break his spell.

When he suddenly broke their contact, shoving her back into her seat with his hands on her arms, she was left bereft, lips parted and eyes half closed.

"Damn you!" Merlyn muttered savagely, holding her still. "I understand now what I should have realized before. Oh, yes, you play very well the role of ingenue. But you know, damn you! You know what it is to heat a man's blood. You lift your head so appealingly and say, 'Pray, do not hurt me,' knowing a man will want to taste the sweet nectar of your lips. Well, no more," he bit out, his voice lowering in warning. "If you dare ply your wiles on me, you'll pay the full price. For tuppence I'd take you now and—" Merlyn caught himself in time and released her.

When his dark head moved away, Cassandra sucked in a trembly breath, the strange warmth that had flooded her ebbing away. "I don't want your help," she flung at him. "I want Adam. What have you done with him?"

Merlyn's expression turned faintly mocking. "So poor of heart? If you would outwit Nicholas Briarcliffe, you'll have need of my talents."

"What talents?" Cassandra retorted, heedless of the narrowing of his sapphire gaze. "I've no need of thieves and rascals. If not for you, Adam and I would be safe."

"Would you, now?" Merlyn replied, his ironic voice at its most dangerous. "And where would that be? The dungeon of Briarcliffe? Or do you believe Nicholas will change his mind and welcome you home with a babe at your breast?" Merlyn saw her cringe at the mention of her husband, but he could not stop the angry words.

He seemed to grow larger in the confining space, filling up every corner of the private coach. "You are certain to be caught, Cassie, in one trap or another. At best you'll suffer least at my hands. At worst . . ." He shrugged. "The worst you cannot imagine. But that will change if you leave my side."

The words were said fiercely, as if in challenge, and Cassandra understood that she would be made to honor some new bargain between them. The knowledge trembled through her, and she closed her eyes to blot out the desire she saw in his stern masculine face.

Merlyn studied her a long moment without comment. She seemed unaware of the danger lurking nearby. The rough gin-blurred voices of the lane in which they had turned echoed in the narrow corridor between the dun-colored houses of the district. She would have no experience with the kind of life that inhabited the lane, the sort that would slit a throat for the sake of a pair of silk stockings or a lace handkerchief. No, she could only stare up at him with her sherry-colored gaze, as intoxicating as any distiller's brew.

Innocent, he thought yet again as he pressed the itchy whiskers of his disguise back into place, and the idea angered him anew. He did not want her innocence. Whatever idiot's dreams he had fashioned that night in Newgate were smashed when she chose Briarcliffe over himself. Yet he craved her company and her body, freely given as before. Nothing else mattered—except his son.

"Enough of this nonsense," he muttered as the hackney halted in the lane. "Come."

Cassandra's wrist was caught in a firm grasp, but she didn't protest when he stepped out and pulled her after him. He alone knew where Adam was and must be followed. "Even into hell," she whispered to herself.

Mud ran thickly in the street and splashed in over the sides of her shoes, cold and sticky, when she stepped down. From Tom Thumb's Public House on the corner the smells of hot rum and cinnamon vied with fried sausage and potatoes. The melding of odors made her stomach churn, and Cassandra clapped a hand over her nose and mouth as Merlyn pulled her into a nearby alley.

Here a new stench rose up to meet her nose and sting her eyes as she was led past the refuse of chamber pots and cleared tables. A dozen dark doorways, some no higher than four feet, passed her view as she was relentlessly dragged along behind the huge cloaked figure of Old Jack.

Thief. Accused murderer. The appellations sped through her mind, reminding Cassandra of the dark deeds to which Merlyn had confessed. It suddenly occurred to her that such a man might be leading her from the street so that no one would hear her cries of help as he encircled her neck and throttled her. The thought instantly took root in possibility, frightening her to action.

"No! No! Let me go!" She tried to jerk her arm free from his grasp, but the momentum of his larger body pulled her two or three steps before he swung around to her.

"What flight of fancy is this?" Merlyn thundered. In the perfect light of day these side streets were treacherous to traverse. In the dark, with a vocal bit of muslin in tow, he might as well have hired a band to herald his arrival for all pickpockets and cutthroats abroad.

Cassandra dug in her heels in the mud, more

confident now that he had stopped. "Release me now, or I'll scream. I swear I'll scream fit to rouse the dead."

"God in heaven!" Merlyn muttered and gave her arm a tug that sent her stumbling into his waiting arms. One scoop of his powerful arms lifted her into his embrace. He hadn't meant to touch her again, not until the safety of his destination had been reached, but she struggled so helplessly, her soft warm weight invitingly rubbing against him, that Merlyn forgot his resolution. He was furious with her for being young and enticing, and for having spurned him for a man who cared nothing for her. There came a sudden need in him to possess, to master the passion she roused against his will. No attempt was made to beguile or seduce her, only his pleasure was served in the crushing violence of their lips.

Cassandra did not struggle. She did not even whimper. She'd learned much of men in her few hours in Merlyn's company, most of it to do with passion. This knowledge served her now and a feeling of power triumphed over her fear. Merlyn had a weakness. He wanted her, desired her even against his will. Her death was the last thing on his mind. Laughter curved her mouth beneath his and then bubbled out of her throat and into the night.

Merlyn dropped her back onto her feet as though she'd suddenly bitten him. "Mistress, one of us is mad!" he uttered coarsely before swinging around and stalking off.

Cassandra watched his dark silhouette for perhaps three steps before racing after him, her skirts lifted against the filth.

When he turned and stopped at one dark entryway, she paused several paces behind, feeling suddenly shy. What if he decided to leave her behind? The throbbing of her lips answered quickly enough and she stepped near him, so close she could reach out and touch his arm, but she did not.

Merlyn's knock was a hard rhythmic tattoo. Immediately there was a scraping noise as a bolt was drawn and then the door opened a crack, pouring yellow candlelight into the gloom of the alley.

"It's Merlyn, Meg," he whispered and then turned to Cassandra with a motion of his arm. "Inside, you little fool!"

Cassandra stepped over the threshold into a poorly lit room furnished with a rough board table and two chairs.

"'Ere, what's this?" their hostess cried. Six inches above Cassandra's own five feet, a pretty auburn-haired woman stood behind the door. With hands on hips, her full bosom was forced to the brink above the lacing of her low-cut bodice. Her eyes, an astonishing China blue, went in slow consideration over Cassandra, ending at her muddy skirts before rising with contempt to her face again.

"There's a good girl, Meg," Merlyn said in his best Drury Lane voice as he slammed the door shut behind him. "Meg, my love, meet Lady Cas—ah, Cassie."

Meg's eyes flashed once more over Cassandra in rapier-sharp appraisal.

Cassandra noted the hostility in surprise but forced a polite smile to her lips as she acknowledged calmly, "Meg."

Ignoring the greeting, Meg turned to Merlyn. "I didn't count on *her*."

"Your diction's slipping, Meg," Merlyn said as he slipped his cloak from his shoulders and began removing his beard and wig. "You'll get only maids' and tarts' roles if you do not polish your speech. Cassie may prove helpful there." He took out a kerchief and rubbed at the greasy makeup that had made his eye red and runny-looking. "After all, you'll be providing a home for her these next few days."

"What?" both women voiced in unison, neither pleased by the idea.

Merlyn sent a hopeful glance at the table where places for two had been laid. "Dinner so late? You're a treasure, Meg, a pure treasure. 'Tis why I thought of you."

Meg bristled under the velvet of his tone, but her milky white complexion pinked to strawberries in the cream just the same. "You're a devil, Merlyn, and that's a fact. Expecting a girl to house your new whore as well as your bastard."

"Adam's here?" Cassandra cried, and her tender breasts engorged with milk at the mention of his name. "You have my son?"

Meg's considering gaze went once more over the tiny young girl. Then her eyes shot up to meet Merlyn's wicked grin. "You're a bloody fine one, stealing from the cradle."

Merlyn's smile deepened as he reached out and wrapped an arm about Meg's neat waist. "Jealous, my love? I remember it was you who threw me over."

"Aye, that's a fact," Meg said, snuggling suggestively

149

in Merlyn's embrace. "But there's been none to equal you." Her gaze went back to Cassandra. "But then, you know what it is for the likes of Merlyn to fill yer bed."

Cassandra did not answer that. "I want my son, now."

"It's really hers?" Meg asked Merlyn.

"Aye, that's a fact," Merlyn returned in a perfect imitation of the woman's accent.

"And yours, that a blind man could see. Them eyes. Cor! They give me a turn when he first popped them open. Them's Merlyn's eyes, I said to meself. Curly black lashes and all."

"Some think he's the exact replica of me," Cassandra offered through stiff lips.

Neither of them answered her. Merlyn removed his arm from Meg's waist and started toward the table. "Cassie stands in need of shelter. There're bound to be inquiries about her, and I can't house her in a likely place." He added quickly when he saw the stubborn jut of Meg's chin, "You know I'd never put you in danger, Meg."

Meg gave him a glance that had enough heat in it to scorch a lesser being, but Merlyn stood it easily. "Aye. I give you your due. You've never hurt me, and few can claim that honor. But one pert word from *her*"—and she jerked her thumb at Cassandra—"and it's the toe of me boot to the pair of you."

"Now that that's decided," Merlyn said, rubbing his hands together and hoisting a leg over the back of a chair at the table, "I for one am in need of sustenance.

Squab pie?" he inquired politely as he held out a platter of crisp pastries to Cassandra.

"I want my son." Cassandra remained still, her gaze moving uneasily between the two.

"Come. He's sleeping upstairs," Meg answered and moved toward the back of the room, where there was a narrow stairway. Following quickly on the woman's heels, Cassandra climbed the steep worn steps to find herself in an even narrower passageway.

"He's in here," Meg said as she lifted the latch on the first door on the hall.

The shutters had been left open and the moonlight, reflecting from low clouds, clearly lit the room. Cassandra saw him almost at once, the black curly head rested on a straw mattress under the window. As she raced to bend over him, to touch him and make certain that he was breathing, she murmured a silent prayer of thanksgiving.

"'Tis a fine lad you've got. Him and me, we were friends right off. Merlyn said I was to care for the babe like me own." Meg moved to the bed to watch curiously as the young mother lightly stroked her child's silky curls. "A fine lad," she repeated and, looking for something to say, added, "Had one meself, once."

"You?" Looking up, Cassandra knew she'd said the wrong thing, for Meg's expression was rigid, the soft blue eyes steely. "I only meant that—"

"I know what you meant, dear." Meg shrugged, the stiffness easing from her, but her gaze was dangerously bright. "I'm not the motherly type. Still, I miss the little tyke. The consumption took him two winters past."

She leaned over Cassandra's shoulder to the sleeping boy. "My John had the look of your son, same black tuft of hair and long frame."

Cassandra met Meg's eyes across the foot's space, but she refrained from asking the question uppermost in her mind. "I'm sorry about your John," she said quietly.

Surprise flared and then subsided in Meg's gaze, as if she'd underestimated her prey. Chuckling under her breath, she walked back to the door. "I'll leave you to see to the tyke while I see to his sire."

Merlyn was licking his fingers free of a second pastry as Meg's trim ankles appeared on the stairs. A grin wedged his face as he called cheerfully, "Did you tuck in both our guests?"

Meg impatiently tossed back an auburn curl from her shoulder. "You're slipping, Merlyn, me dear. They're a parcel of trouble you'll not soon be rid of."

Merlyn's mouth hardened as his uncompromising stare met hers. "Adam's my son. I've claimed him."

"Touchy, ain't we?" Meg exclaimed slyly. "You never were one to show your feelings before, Merlyn. Makes me wonder if you've fallen in love with that little baggage."

Merlyn shrugged, a faint derisive look in his eye. "Don't press me, Meg. I fancy the idea of a son of my own."

"But if you don't fancy the girl, why bear the burden of her troubles?" Meg asked in a matter-of-fact tone.

Merlyn replied to this by taking a long pull on his pint of ale. He had just asked himself that question. When he'd left Cassie in Hanover Square he'd told himself he was well rid of her. Yet he'd traveled no more than two blocks when he'd decided to send that message to Briarcliffe. He'd suspected she'd soon need his help, and he'd been right.

When he set his mug aside he said, "Though it's no business of yours, I'll tell you why I'm protecting them. Nearly a year ago I paid a Newgate gaoler for an evening with the girl." He raised his single blue eye to Meg's smirking face. "I see you begin to understand too much. The girl's no tart, and I should know. I found her pleasant company and wanted to set her up as my mistress, but she was to marry. God knows how the man managed to keep his hands off her, but he had, so he knew the boy was not his. Tonight I removed them from his home."

It was not quite the truth, but Merlyn suspected the melodramatic aspects of the story would so engage Meg that she would not think to look for loopholes in his tale.

"Ooh, the poor thing," Meg cooed, all soft sympathy. Then quickly her expression altered, becoming as stern as her open wantonness would allow. "If she'd wanted to come with you, you'd not have had to strike her. I saw that bruise on her cheek. It's not above a few hours old."

Exasperation colored Merlyn's voice. "I didn't touch her. That's her husband's work." He rose slowly to his feet, bracing himself with his hands on the table, a grim expression on his face. "I've brought her here for her protection and my amusement. When the amusement dims she'll be left to look to her own."

Meg gave him stare for stare. "Cruel, that's what you

are! Looking no farther than to scratch your itch. Poor wee thing. Just a child herself, suckling a babe, and you'd have her on her back half the night, besides. If that's not cold-blooded, I'd like to know!"

"Hush! Both of you!" Cassandra admonished from the head of the stairs. "It's little enough to ask that you allow Adam his sleep."

"Come down here," Merlyn demanded in a low but carrying voice. "What nonsense have you been spreading? Meg, here, thinks I've done nothing but beat you."

At Cassandra's startled glance, Meg blushed nearly as dark as her fiery hair. "Meg must know something of the hardship of dealing with a man of your ilk. Is that ale? I should like a glass," Cassandra said coolly and descended the stairs.

Cassandra could have said nothing better to set Meg more firmly in her camp. "Like ale, do you, deary? You're quality. 'Is that ale? I should like a glass,'" Meg parroted perfectly. "You've a lovely voice, Cassie. You'll not mind if I practice?"

"Certainly not," Cassandra replied, carefully avoiding Merlyn's gaze. She did not feel comfortable in the company of either of them, but, clearly, Meg was the better ally. Merlyn had yet to make it plain what he expected of her in return for his protection. She would do what she must, but she would not go meekly or humiliate herself with tearful pleadings. She knew the worst he was capable of, and, contrary to her peace of mind, the knowledge was not wholly unpleasant.

Merlyn watched Cassie daintily sip the mug of ale Meg set before her. He said nothing as her sharp white teeth sank into the tender crisp crust of a squab pie, but he gave in to an impatient yawn when she reached for a second piece. She was stalling, and she knew he knew it. If she ate till her belly ached it would make no difference. He was ready to claim his first payment.

Meg stood between the pair, her eyes on first one and then the other. The high color of defiance rode the girl's cheeks, while Merlyn's easy manner meant that he was in a most unpredictable mood. That was the puzzle, Meg decided. She couldn't determine what the girl's feelings were for Merlyn nor his for her. She'd borne the man a son, yet Cassie seemed curiously virginal, reluctant, and deplorably ignorant of the art of flirtation.

Meg's avid gaze swung back to Merlyn and she could hardly suppress a sigh at the sight of him. A year or better, that's what it was since she'd last seen him. And bedded him? Meg ticked off the time with growing restlessness. Three, maybe four years. Acutely aware of him as a disturbingly virile male, she nearly bent to taste the warm spicy skin of his neck exposed by his open collar. Meg smirked as her eyes cut to the younger woman. *That* would make her take notice.

The workings of her mind led her far into speculation of another kind. The broad shoulders, the easy smile on lips with the brand of passion in them when he chose, these were enticements she remembered well. His raven-black hair, loosely queued, revealed his strong gypsy-dark profile which her fingers itched to trace.

Again Meg's blue gaze turned speculatively to Cassie. She was small and neat, like fine china, but her narrow waist and generous bosom were assets a man would find appealing. What would it take to win Merlyn away from her?

Meg began to clear the table, saying solicitously, "Any soul can see you're fair worn through, Cassie. You go on up and see to your babe. Merlyn and I can finish up."

Cassandra glanced at Merlyn, who had not even looked up. For reasons she did not probe, a sinking feeling of disappointment settled in her. She had been girding her emotions for a battle that would not now occur. "Yes, of course." She rose quickly to her feet, too quickly, she realized when the taunting sound of Merlyn's laughter rolled through the room.

"Don't flee, little dove. I don't as a rule polish off a fine meal by eating little birds like you." Meg's throaty chuckle drew a muttered profanity from Merlyn which Cassandra did not quite catch. He stood and reached out and his long lean fingers encircled her wrist. "Come, Cassie. I seem to remember a certain pledge, a bargain of price was to be struck between us."

His fingers tightened and Cassandra wondered why she did not twist away. Instead, she allowed herself to be drawn along the table until nothing stood between them. His sapphire eye, wiped free of its gooey make-up, was holding her still, confining her against her will, and she could not resist. Then, suddenly, he was standing so near she could see nothing but the pulse beating at the open throat of his rough shirt. The feeling of stifling heat rose through her, blocking her breath and finally moving her to turn away.

"Don't." He said it softly, but the sound reverberated through Cassandra's body, setting every nerve to stinging awareness of his nearness. When the fingers of his other hand settled on her neck the tingling increased. They slid up to cup her chin and then slid down, pushing aside the heavy silk curtain of her hair. "Don't turn away, Cassie. You know what I want. I'll have my payment for this night's work."

Cassandra jerked her arm free as she took a step back. "To protect Adam I'd bed a dozen men, if necessary," she flung at him. "But you'll get no more than you take. If you've forgotten, I'm a married woman!"

Merlyn stared at her, a dangerous glitter brightening his eye. "You're no more married to any man than you are to me!" He took a quick step forward and, grabbing her by the waist, pulled her hard against his long length. His face was only inches from hers as he said. "I could, so easily, make you forget your husband was ever born."

Cassandra shuddered, the intolerable feel of his strong warmth nearly suffocating her. She was hot, yet she shivered as if from the cold. "Were you capable of making me forget a single thing, I would beg you give me repose from any knowledge of you!"

For the space of a dozen heartbeats they faced one another, and Cassandra counted the moments. The coiled violence that seemed so intimate a part of him was writhing just beneath the surface. She felt it in the convulsive hold of the hands on her waist and neck and in the unblinking gaze fixed on her.

"Well, now," Merlyn said softly, as if to shout would bring the roof down upon them. "I'd thought to tenderly bed the mother of my son. But you, it seems, prefer the role of whore. Fair enough, my little Cassie. Fair enough."

The first rending of her gown came as so much of a surprise that Cassandra did not immediately react. It was the second rip, the shredding of the only garment she owned, that loosened the numbing dread that held her still. She swung her palm full and flat across his cheek, but he did not cease tearing the bodice from her. Frantic, she reached out and grabbed blindly, catching the ribbon of the patch that slashed his brow. It came away in her fingers. With a roar of surprise from him, she was suddenly released.

"You ignorant, reckless chit!" Merlyn cried, one hand racing up to shield the eye that had been covered.

Horrified by her action, Cassandra pressed the patch into his other hand, choking out, "Oh! I'm sorry! I didn't mean—"

Meg, who had been watching them with all the eagerness of a spectator at a Covent Garden theater, now stepped between them. "The pair of you are a sight." Her gaze took in Cassandra, then Merlyn, who had deftly replaced his patch. "She fears the touch of your hand, Merlyn. Ask her if it's because of the memory of the pain she suffered in birthing your babe."

Merlyn's head jerked up, the thought a new one for him. He'd never considered what Cassie had endured in giving life to Adam. "Is it true?" he asked in almost foolish surprise.

Cassandra stopped the impulse to allay his doubts. It was a small straw to clutch at, but it was all she had. "It's true. The doctor said . . . he said . . ." She lowered her eyes in seeming modesty but actually because she was afraid he would read *liar* in her gaze. "He said I should advise my—my husband to curtail his conjugal rights for at least six months."

Merlyn's jaw fell slack, but almost at once his features hardened in suspicion. "Why did you not say so before?"

Cassandra took a deep breath. He was not an easy man to fool. She raised her head and looked him straight in the eye. "I had forgotten. The caution did not seem necessary at the time. Most husbands allow several months of peace to the matter of the marriage bed after a birth."

"Aye. 'Tis so," Meg added quickly, seeing at last a chance to entice Merlyn to her bed. If Cassie didn't want his embrace, he'd soon turn elsewhere. "I've been a mother, I know. What do I have to gain by lying for the girl?"

"I don't know," Merlyn said evenly, but his eyes never left Cassandra's face. He was in over his head in matters of which he knew little, and it cut his pride to the quick to admit it. "If I leave now I may never return."

Cassandra said nothing, but the thick slow beating of her heart painfully skipped a pace. As she stared at him, he made a sudden impatient move as if to sweep a thought aside and turned on his heel and walked out into the night.

Cassandra looked about her, almost in surprise, to find Meg's bright blue gaze on her. "Do you think he'll come back?" she asked.

"Does it matter, deary?" Meg returned.

159

Chapter Nine

"FIE ON ALL THE DEMONS THAT BE!" MEG CALLED
dramatically as she swept into the tiny parlor of her
home in the alley off Lewknor Lane. Still in her powder
and paint after an evening's performance at the theater
where she had landed a bit part, she looked quite the
elegant lady as Cassandra's genteel tones tripped lightly
from her lips. With a second dramatic gesture, she
swirled one edge of the cape she wore up over a
shoulder. It was a borrowed stage prop of royal-blue
velvet, rubbed shiny in places after years of quick
changes, but that did not affect the flattering picture
Meg presented to her audience of one.

"You look lovely, Meg," Cassandra said as she laid
aside the knife with which she was peeling potatoes.

Meg arched a brow. "Come, Cassie, you must have
had a handsome wardrobe, being gentry and all."

After two weeks in Meg's company Cassandra knew
well that the woman's curiosity would not be satisfied
until some tidbit had been extracted. "No. My family

had little besides a few dusty portraits and a bit of rocky ground."

"Still, you had enough to be dowered," Meg suggested helpfully, but Cassandra shook her head. "Nothing went with me into my marriage."

"A love match!" Meg cried delightedly, her eyes rolling back in her head in a manner that regularly earned her a scolding from the theater director. "Was your husband tall and handsome as anything?"

The remark caught Cassandra off guard and she replied without thinking. "I thought him the kindest, most beautiful man on earth." The description hardly applied to the rage-distorted face of her husband that rose quickly to mind. That image drew a trace of a shiver across her sensitive skin and gooseflesh sprang up. "I was wrong," she finished quietly.

"Poor wee soul. It gives a girl a turn to learn she's not what the butcher ordered." Meg gave her a sideways glance. "I mean, Merlyn did say your husband never bedded you.

"Of course, 'tis none of my business," Meg continued, seeing the girl's expression change and close against her. "Our Merlyn's an odd sort, don't you agree? He's a loner, thinks too much. Why, once, after a particularly bad review of his new play, he sat right beneath this very roof and drank Blue Ruin till he couldn't unlock his jaw. Took more than two quarts to put him under," she said, admiration strong in her voice.

Cassandra knew Merlyn had been an actor. Meg had told her he was not a leading man—his deep voice and eyepatch made him too wicked a figure to play heroes—

161

but was a respected villain of some renown. *When he's not stealing jewels or people,* Cassandra reminded herself. He was like a many-faceted gem in the ring he'd given her, reflecting different colors and patterns, never the same twice. Instinctively, her hand rose to touch the ring pinned inside the neck of her gown, but she stilled the impulse. Meg saw too much for her comfort.

"A fortnight and Merlyn's not come back," Meg commented as she loosened the frog closing at her neck and slipped the cloak from her shoulders. "Aren't you worried?"

"No." Cassandra's tone was indifferent, but as each sunset gave way to another night she wondered with new intensity how she would manage now left to her own devices. It was that fear that had prompted her to ask Meg to find a job for her. "Did you have any luck?"

"Hardly a whisker's worth," Meg answered, accustomed to the daily question. She made an impatient sweeping gesture with a hand. "You're not exactly the type to take up the trade." She glanced once again at her guest to see if Cassandra had understood her meaning. "Well, then, what's left? Don't suppose you'd agree to ply the needle for a living, not with your gentry and all?"

"I'm not too proud to eat," Cassandra answered.

Meg gave her a surprised look. "Then there is one thing I heard today. The Company Players are looking for a new seamstress. The last ran off with a stagehand. There's a mort of mending, some sewing, dressing players, and that sort of thing," she warned. "You'd not be coddled. Not a fig's worth of consideration. If you were too slow or your work was poor, out you'd go."

Cassie lifted the skirts of the purple grosgrain gown Meg had given her to replace the one Merlyn had torn to shreds. By cleverly cutting around the soiled and worn spots, she had refitted it to her much smaller frame. Nothing could be done about the unflattering color. "Perhaps I could show this as an example of my work."

"I suppose," Meg said doubtfully. "But, for gawd's sake, do pull that switch of dark hair from your face. 'Tis not a sin to be plain, but you'd make a study of it. Maybe I can do something with powder and pomade. There's nary a bit of color in you, except when you're in the company of Merlyn Ross."

Cassandra ignored the last comment. The work was menial but not degrading. Best of all, no one would ever think to look for her in the wardrobe corner of a theater. "What are the wages, Meg? I mean to repay you for the meals we've shared."

Meg's eyes rounded in disbelief. Did the girl really think she had been the grand provider for the three mouths beneath her roof? Had she no idea of the cost of the cheese and bread and cream they'd greedily consumed? If not for the regular arrival of the butcher's boy and the dairyman's runner, they would have starved, for Meg had yet to see a coin for her acting. It didn't require a guess to name their benefactor. Still, if the girl wanted to pay . . . "Three guineas a quarter," she announced.

"Is that fair?"

"Lord love us!" Meg cried with unladylike vigor.

"Gentlemen dole out tuppence for an evening's pleasure."

"Then why have there been no others to take the job?"

"Merlyn was wrong, you're no fool," Meg answered with an approving nod of her head. "There's many what would jump at the chance, and provide other services as well. And that's the trouble. The director's wife is a jealous fat old bawd who once trod the boards herself. She fancies her husband will have trouble keeping his hands off any baggage above twelve years, and she's right." Meg gave Cassandra a meaningful look. "Just so you know, deary. Still, they won't have any frights among the company and there's bound to be many a fancy piece trying her luck—director's wife or no. Perhaps, if we pin up your hair with a few bodkins, pomade your lips lightly, and—"

Meg raised her eyes to the ceiling as a gusty cry from above interrupted her. "Your little Adam has first choice, as usual, but then you're to come straight back to me. It comes to me there's a certain crimson velveteen gown . . ."

Meg was still murmuring to herself when Cassandra sped up the stairs to her son.

"One more deep breath, Cassie. It must be a snug fit," Meg commented as she took another tug on the lacing that closed the back of the crimson velvet gown. "Aye, that's it. You've a surprisingly narrow waist for a girl who's birthed a babe. And you've hips to match them generous curves above."

Too nervous to answer, Cassandra continued to pull

Meg's boar-bristle brush through her heavy mahogany mane which hung over one shoulder. It had taken them all the evening before to refashion the velvet gown Meg found in her attic. Luckily, it was a smaller size than the grosgrain, requiring only a few tucks and the raising of the hem.

"You go to the theater first thing this morning," Meg said. "That way I can stay with Adam. Back by noon, mind. If I'm late for rehearsals, I'll be out on my ear."

Meg stood back to judge her work. "Turn around, then, and let's have a look."

Cassandra slowly turned, looking over one shoulder and then the other to try to catch the effect.

Meg reached out to adjust the lace at the top of the bodice cut low to reveal the outline of breasts and shoulders. She patted it and flicked it with her fingers before yanking it out altogether. "Don't need it. Spoils the look."

Cassandra's mouth primmed as she stared down at the daring expanse. "What about the director's suspicious wife?"

Meg glanced at the decolletage and shrugged. "Was a time when me breasts were as firm and high. Ten years ago I had all the lads dancing about me skirts, begging for a kiss. Sweet Meg, that's what they called me. Then our Merlyn came along. Oh, he wasn't so lovely as the rest, but he has a way about him that makes a girl forget there ever was another man."

The wistful words made Cassandra unaccountably angry and she snapped, "Don't call him our Merlyn as if we shared joint ownership of the man. We'll likely never see him again."

Meg gave the younger woman a speculative glance. "You'll see him, and when you're least expecting it."

Cassandra smoothed the velvet over her hips, pretending indifference as she said, "Have you seen him, Meg?"

"No. And don't think I wouldn't tell you if I had." Meg lifted her chin, her eyes sparkling between half-closed lids. "Was I keeping company with 'your' Merlyn, I'd make certain you knew."

Cassandra's puckered brow smoothed. "I don't see why."

"Don't you, now?" Meg returned, a smile slipping naturally into place. "Then it's not my part to teach you. Still, I've never seen a woman yet could walk away from one of his smiles. You'll forgive him his temper. The gown was ruined before he touched it. Besides, he's generous when the mood suits him. You'll have a dozen gowns to replace that one, mind my word. Now, don't pucker up like a prune, you'll need to be sweet as syrup this morning."

Cassandra stood perfectly still while Meg applied various artifices to her face, darkening her lids with kohl and pinking her cheeks and lips with rouge.

"Now let's have a look at you," Meg said at last and went to drag out the cracked full-length mirror she kept covered in one corner.

Cassandra stood before the glass and stared. It was not the reflection that looked back most days. Her brows were arched in bold surprise, her ruby lips pouted in consideration. The swell of her shoulders and breasts above the deep crimson gown seemed much creamier and more lustrous in contrast. It was as if

Meg had erased her own ordinary features and re-placed them with a beauty's likeness.

"I feel quite new, as if you've made me over inside and out." Cassandra laughed, and even the sound of it seemed richer, more important. "The ugly duckling is now a swan."

"I prefer to believe," a masculine voice said, "the mademoiselle was always a swan who only now sees the full possibility of her beauty."

Startled by the rich voice with just a hint of a French accent, Cassandra and Meg turned to find a gentleman lounging in their doorway. He wore a tricornered hat over his wig, and his blue velvet coat was cut away in the newest fashion to reveal bias-cut breeches that displayed slim hips and powerfully muscled thighs.

"Cor!" Meg cooed, forgetting her genteel accent in the full amazement of seeing so richly dressed a gentle-man.

Cassandra only stared at the rouged features of the gentleman with a black silk patch and a single eye full of wicked emerald laughter, and her heart leaped in her breast.

Meg, realizing the gentleman must have sought her door for a purpose, favored him with a saucy feminine smile in full appreciation of his masculinity and her best imitation of Cassandra's cultured tones. "Do come in, m'lord. You're most welcome."

The tall stranger had to bend to enter. Sweeping his hat from his head, he made the ladies a pretty bow of acknowledgment. *"Enchanté."* He turned to Meg. "The lovely mademoiselle will understand if I say I must speak with Cassie alone?" He appeared to pull a gold coin from thin air and offered it to her. "For wine, good wine," he suggested.

"Cassie? Why, you sly puss!" Meg cried, shaking a finger at the younger woman. "You never let on you knew a soul in London, and here's a handsome Frenchy come for you." Not waiting for a reply, Meg took the coin he offered, bit it quickly, and then dropped it into the bodice of her gown.

"Wine it is, bread and cheese, too, if you'd like. I'll be only . . . well." Her gaze swung to Cassie, who'd said not a word. "I've an errand to run on the next block. Perhaps an hour?" she suggested and received the man's quick nod. "Be *nice* to the gentleman, Cassie," she said with emphasis as she swept past her and out the doorway.

"Merlyn Ross!" Cassandra accused stiffly when Meg was gone.

Merlyn shrugged, an irritated look breezing across his features as he said in his natural voice, "You're the only soul I've ever known could spy me out so quickly." He threw his hat on the table and took two purposeful strides toward her. "Why is that, do you think?"

The question in his deep voice sounded with unnerving intimacy in Cassandra's ears and she glanced at him uneasily through her lashes. "Why do you always wear your eyepatch? I find it detracts from your disguise."

Merlyn reached up and snatched it off with a smile. "You don't seem able to keep your eyes from me, that's true." His voice was very low, yet it reverberated through the room. "You called out my name the night of the christening ball, remember? But perhaps it's not

168

so strange. 'Tis only fair that my image should remain with you when yours haunts me."

Cassandra turned away from his mesmerizing stare. Despite her unreasoning joy to see him she would not give up easily her accumulated grievances, not the least of which was his long absence. How dare he stroll back into her life looking more . . . more . . . She gave him a brief glance. Magnificent. It was the only word to describe him. Even in the paint and powder of a dandy he was absolutely the most uncompromisingly masculine creature she'd ever encountered. An unwonted breathlessness overcame her at the thought, and that reaction annoyed her further. "Two weeks without your company convinced us that you were not coming back." She turned fully to him, her chin lifted in challenge. "We've done well without you. Beginning today, I earn my own way."

This news clearly startled him. "Earn your way?" His eyes swept over her and then halted at the lovely display at her neckline. "Surely Meg has not convinced you to ply the harlot's trade?"

Cassandra gave in to the childish impulse to stamp her foot as quick temper flared through her. "You're a beast!" The retort sounded trite and petty, even to her own ears, and the notion was confirmed by his laughter.

"Oh, I see. Meg's prompting you for the stage. God's death, you'll have them tossing rotten fruit before the end of the first act."

"Go away!" she hissed at him. "I do not want you in my life."

Merlyn seemed not to hear the dismissal, for he

pulled out a chair and seated himself, careful to spread the full skirts of his elegant coat. "You've not asked me who I am today. Or you do remember? You've met Jack Commoner the condemned prisoner, Old Jack the childnabber. Meg must have told you of Merlyn Ross the actor. Sit, lady, this stiff posture misbecomes you nearly as much as that gown."

"What's wrong with this gown?" Cassandra asked before she could catch herself and was submitted a second time to his humiliating laughter.

"Not a woman alive can bear to be criticized. Look at you, all starch and indignation. Yes, if you will have it, you've a pretty look, but I prefer your Newgate garb." His darkening gaze made Cassandra's breath suddenly hard to manage, but he did not comment upon it. "Where was I? Oh yes. You will remember the Comte de Valure."

"What evil has this comte come to perpetrate?" Cassandra asked saucily, knowing she trod thin ice but not caring for the moment if it gained her back a little of her poise.

Merlyn smiled sweetly at her. "He's stolen a king's ransom in jewels and needs a place to hide them."

"What?" She had not truly believed he would admit to yet another villainy.

"Do not bray, Cassie. It ruins the effect of your attire. Surely you didn't think I'd come to play benefactor to a small child and his mother?"

The mockery was not lost on her, and Cassandra colored up. "I'd believe any evil to which you confessed," she answered bitterly. "So, now that I've seen you, I must bid you good day. I'll not keep stolen property."

Cassandra moved to the door and opened it for him, but Merlyn did not move. "Don't you wish to know the message I have for you?"

Cassandra hesitated, her dark honey eyes full of suspicion. "What message could you have for me?" When he did not reply, she took a reluctant step and then another toward him, too human to resist.

"That's my Cassie," Merlyn said, patting the chair next to his own. "You will appreciate this far better than I since I've been busy providing for you since last we met."

"You? Providing?" Cassandra sat on the edge of her chair, in warning that she would leave on an instant. "I'm not so gullible as to believe that, not when I've seen Meg dealing with the butcher's boy myself."

"Your ignorance is remarkably obtuse. I find it extraordinary that you recognize me in disguise so quickly. No," he cautioned when she opened her mouth. "I know what you'll say. I told you once before that most of life is an illusion. But then, I have that message to deliver," he continued calmly. "Actually, two. The first is that we must leave London. Immediately. Do sit down," he directed, grabbing her by the arm when she popped up from her chair and tugging her back down. "You've no need to concern yourself over a job you'll never have. We leave at nightfall. In the meantime . . ."

He released her and sat back folding his arms across his chest. "You'd be amazed at the things I've done this past fortnight. Oh yes, I had dinner with Nick Briarcliffe, but I must disappoint you. He did not ask after your health," he said smoothly, ignoring her gasp. "Last evening I spent at Watier's with Sir Edward Strickland. His young wife has just given birth. The physician pronounced good health for the child and a quick healing for the mother but prescribed an extended period of—shall we say celibacy—on the parents' part."

Dreaded anticipation pulled at Cassandra even before he spoke his next words, but she could neither silence him nor flee, for he held her pinned with his emerald eye.

"Having been dealt a similar hand, I was all fine commiseration. Told him it was my experience that a man with a mistress who'd given birth needed a second in order to survive the six-month abstinence." Merlyn's smile twitched, as if the memory gave him pain. "I do not, on the ordinary, mind giving amusement to a man. I think I carried it off rather well. Strickland laughed uproariously, saying he'd never heard a better solution. Yet he suggested that I keep better tabs on the first mistress, because it sounded to him as if she were playing me false. I laughed with him, to be friendly, and asked him just what was the normal period of absence from the marriage bed. You see, I had to admit there was no babe, only a joke to please him."

Nothing in Merlyn's manner suggested that he was joking now. Cassandra opened her mouth, but no sound came from her suddenly dry throat.

"A month," Merlyn finished. His voice was cool, but Cassandra felt the heat of his blue-green gaze on the sensitive skin above her low-cut bodice. "A month," he repeated with all the gravity of a sentencing.

She didn't know which of them moved first. The idea of flight was uppermost in her mind, but she thought she detected a sudden tensing in him that warned her he was about to act. She was halfway to her feet when one hand clasped her elbow and spun her around so that his other arm could encircle her waist. She meant to scream, but something stopped her. His gaze was no longer cool and sardonic but shockingly alive, like twin flames of emerald and sapphire. Surrounded by the heat of his body which communicated itself to her through his clothes and hers, she knew her last effort to avoid the inevitable was gone.

"I wanted you that first night, in the coach as we left Briarcliffe," he said softly. "But I waited. I wanted you the night I brought you here. Curse Meg for taking your part against me. I would not be here now but for a quirk of circumstance. 'Tis justice, madame, that you can find no tongue to give me further lies."

Cassandra choked on her voice, halfway between laughter and a sob. He smiled so tenderly she was almost certain he felt sorry for her. His hand moved, touched her face to draw back a strand of hair that had found its way onto her brow, and then traced a feather-light pattern from her cheek to the corner of her mouth.

She shuddered, torn between fear and the exquisite heat that scorched her skin at his touch. It was like the warm flooding of brandy through her veins, melting and soothing, offering false courage for the acceptance of that touch and much more.

When he lowered his head and his lips settled on hers it was almost a relief. It broke the hypnotic spell of his fingertips and replaced it with a stronger, less frightening feeling. Kisses were common enough, she told herself. It was the other, the touching, the stroking, the sensual caress that made her ache to arch her back and rub herself against him. The wicked desire to purr in pleasure: that was what she abhorred.

Merlyn raised his head, eager to see her face which so perfectly reflected her feelings. "You are so beautiful," he said quietly.

Cassandra turned her head slightly away, unable to endure the look of desire gleaming between the thick tangle of his sable-black lashes. He was too close, and the nearness made her want to touch the planes of his face with her lips, to feel his kisses on her mouth and be content, no, intoxicated by their effect. Hers was not the fear of a victim for her conqueror. It was the fear of an addict who looks upon her weakness, at the lure held out, irresistible and tantalizing and undeniable. The knowledge made her tremble. She did not love him, but she did desire him.

"Let me go," she said faintly, looking up. "This must not be. I am a mar—"

"Enough!" The hand that had stroked her so gently encircled her neck, the fingers tightening just until her words stopped. Gone was the look of the cajoling lover. In its place was the fierce look of a man who would brook nothing to obtain that which he desired. "You will remind me, madame, of that which is best forgotten. We will speak no more of it. Ever."

His fingers shot roughly through her hair and forced her head back as he bent to kiss her. It was different, hot and heavy with a passion he no longer tried to govern. When he released her mouth his breath came quick and hard in her ear. "Give me what I desire, Cassie. We've no need of holy words said over us. You belong to me. Yield to me!"

With a whimper of despair, Cassandra's resistance collapsed and she lay softly within his embrace. What use were denials when she could feel his hardened desire pressing against her middle? All that was left to her was to keep her own body from exacting a moment of delight.

She soon learned that passive surrender was not what he demanded. His kiss deepened, the drugging sweetness now overlaid with the impatience of anger. But its power was the same, carrying her back where she would rather not have gone, to the night when she had surrendered herself to his magic and been left with the deep craving for it ever since.

"Love me, Cassie." His deep musical voice was hardly more than a sigh. "Open yourself to me. Make your flesh pliant. Give of yourself to me."

"I—can't," Cassandra answered in a ragged voice, but she knew it was only half true. Her flesh was blossoming, opening under his touch. She hardly noticed when he lifted her into his arms and carried her up the narrow stairs. She had never been in Meg's bedroom. She saw only a flash of pink satin curtain and ruby carpet before a mattress gave under her weight.

She did not argue but watched in utter calmness as he

divested himself of his finery and wig. How much more did the sable black of his own hair suit him, she decided, no longer aware of anything but him. The strong bronzed body that emerged from the silk and velvet coverings was hard and smooth, like the polished surface of fine wood. His masculine perfection took her breath away. She could not remember knowing the shape of him before. The broad chest, the taut muscles of his belly, the firm cables of his thighs: they were all new, and yet achingly familiar. Suddenly the desire consumed her to touch that fine hard warmth, to know again what she had forgotten yet could not forget.

Merlyn reached for her only to drag her from the bed. His fingers worked feverishly, undoing all Meg's hard work as pins and laces were loosened, and then Cassandra stood before him in her glorious nakedness. He held his breath, taking in every detail of her slim body from firm, full breasts with taut, darkened nipples to the still slender waist and tantalizing dark triangle between her creamy thighs. Desire flooded him anew, and the need to cast a spell over her with his possession so that she would never again be able to deny him. Sweeping her up in his embrace, his body followed hers into the inviting softness of the bed.

Lowering her to her back, he began tracing with his lips the form of her womanly body. There was a pleasant ripeness to her hips, and the mysterious fluid her breasts delivered up to his seeking mouth tasted of exotic sweetness. The tender assault of his mouth and tongue continued, pausing and searching out her most vulnerable places, tasting and teasing until Cassandra moaned and trembled, caught in the silken web of his desire and hers.

"Ask me, Cassie," he urged. "Beg me to love you. Say it!"

Cassandra shivered at the order. Her body was aflame, consumed in the need to belong to his, but she gathered her strength in a final desperate attempt to resist the admission. The strong dark face above hers, erased of its rice-powder pallor by a fine sheen of sweat, held no lover's softness; no fine sensitive words of love flowed from the wide mobile lips. There was only the magnetic blue-green gaze of a wizard.

Merlyn knew the struggle taking place within her. Her flesh under his hand was vibrant to his touch. The warm inner softness of her body was open and ready for him. The taste of her desire was on his tongue. He told himself that the words did not matter. She wanted him: that was all that mattered. He could bear to live a little longer without the victory of hearing her surrender.

Cassandra lost the battle when he entered her. She arched her back, lifting her hips for him, and he slid deep within.

"Yes, Cassie, wrap your legs about me. 'Twill be so good for you. Let me fill you, love you, bury myself within your silken warmth. Only your pleasure—and mine."

She heard his deep dark voice, as soft as velvet in her ear, and knew his victory was shared. She followed its commands until the faint fluttering within her became a vast aching throb. Then the rhythm claimed her.

Yes, a hushed voice encouraged. *The rhythm*. It promised . . . and gave . . . *Ah yes!* Cassandra closed her eyes. *Pleasure!*

The sight of two naked bodies entangled in her sheets gave Meg a turn, but she choked down a cry when she recognized Merlyn's dark head. It took her a moment longer to recognize Cassandra, willingly curled against his longer frame.

"Well, bless me. Didn't think . . ." Meg stopped as it occurred to her to wonder what had happened to her French guest. The clothing scattered about told the story. She smiled in amusement. Merlyn had always had an uncanny way with disguises. She'd not recognized him! But something told her Cassie had.

With the sharp unsentimental vision of a guttersnipe, Meg surveyed Cassandra's slender pale limbs entwined with the dark hard thighs of her lover's and smiled at the dry tears that formed salty slicks on the girl's lovely face. Their lust for one another had been too fiery not to burn itself free. But perhaps Cassandra knew that and feared the consequence. Perhaps she feared being branded so deeply she could never forget this man.

With warmer vision Meg's eyes sought the virile shape of Merlyn partially revealed by the tumbled bedding. His long lean body was the color of polished copper. As she watched he moved, as if startled by a dream, and then his hand reached out and found Cassandra's breast. He turned toward her blindly, rubbing his cheek against her shoulder like a child nuzzling its mother. The gesture surprised Meg. She did not believe, for all his appreciation of a beautiful woman, that he was the kind to be caught in love. If she were right, at least Cassie had a child to keep her company when the man was gone. "Poor wee girl," Meg exclaimed as she shut the door on the pair.

As she passed the second door on the hall, Meg pushed it open to check on Adam. "Sleeping cozy as you'd wish," she said to herself. "Only, you'd best wake up, lad, to the news you'll be sharing your mother with your sire for a spell."

Meg didn't regret the loss of her opportunity to share Merlyn Ross's bed again. She knew she had never had a chance against Cassie. She was just as glad. There were too many handsome young bucks with gold in their pockets in the theater galleries to regret that. For instance, there was that strange young man who'd followed her home just now. With a bit of encouragement, he might be persuaded to come in and help her enjoy the good French wine she had purchased.

On second thought, she dismissed the idea. She was due at the theater in thirty minutes and the director didn't take kindly to a tipsy cast. But if he came back, she'd not turn him away.

Chapter Ten

CASSANDRA WATCHED, WITHOUT SEEING, THE PACKING OF the trunk laid open at her feet. The bundles of clothing Merlyn had purchased and brought with him for Adam and herself made no impression upon her. A chilly draft sent a shiver wiggling up her spine, but it was an automatic gesture. Her eyes did not move nor did she blink when Meg uttered a curse as she stubbed her toe on the trunk.

"What's the matter with Cassie?" Meg murmured out of the side of her mouth as she picked up the last of the things from the table where Merlyn sat smoking a pipe.

Merlyn shrugged and exhaled a bluish cloud of smoke. "She's frightened of sea travel." His eyes did not meet Meg's disbelieving glance. "Just finish the packing. I spent a small fortune to see Cassie and Adam properly dressed for our journey, and there's not much time before we must catch the coach for Dover."

Meg rounded on him with a string of curses and

Merlyn, his nerves stretched beyond endurance, jumped up from his chair and struck her with the flat of his hand. It was not a hard slap, but the crack of his palm across her face brought Cassandra's eyes up. Her pupils widened and her lips parted as if she would speak, but words failed her. Instead, her hands flew up to cover her eyes and she bent over her lap as great racking sobs shook her shoulders.

"Lord! What'd you do to the poor girl?" Meg exclaimed, forgetting her own pain as she hurried over to put her arms about the smaller woman.

"Nothing," Merlyn said in a flat voice. "Nothing at all." Suddenly he found Meg's house too confining and he grabbed up his coat which was slung over the back of his chair. "I'll be back in an hour. Be ready." A moment later he slammed out the door.

"Here now, Cassie. He's gone. You can tell Meg what's wrong."

Cassandra lifted her face from her hands, appalled by her weakness. "Did he hurt you?" she asked, reaching out to touch Meg's reddened cheek.

Meg looked genuinely surprised. "Hurt me? Lord love us! 'Twould take more than one of Merlyn's love taps to hurt me. Is that what frightened you? I had it coming. What with his temper roaring fit to boil over, I knew when I pushed him I might be scalded. Thing is, why's he in a rage? I came back early enough to know he was pleased with your company this morning. What happened?"

Cassandra caught her breath in a hiccupy sob and tears sparkled in the tips of her dark spiky lashes. The last flicker of hope that it wasn't true had died when she gave up to his magician's touch. She could no longer deny it. She was falling in love with Merlyn Ross. But he had not stayed to hear that confession. He had risen and dressed and would have left her without even waking her had she not called out to him. She should have let him go; then she would not have heard the words that broke her heart.

"He hates me, Meg! And I, fool that I am, can't find it in my heart to hate him back for what he's done to me! I wish I were dead!"

The intensity of that feeling was shared by Merlyn, but not for the reasons Cassandra believed. Moving through the underworld company of Lewknor Lane, Merlyn gave no notice to the many greedy eyes following him. Most took one look at the madness that lay like a fiery mantle about him and moved aside. The one unfortunate who took a chance on Merlyn's preoccupation to lift his coatskirt received a fist full in the face for that miscalculation. A moment later, Merlyn disappeared behind the doors of the Fox and Hound Tavern.

The tavern was full, but its portly proprietor greeted his new guest with a greasy smile and a rough shout for a barmaid.

"Care for a private room, guv'nor?" the owner inquired hopefully, eyeing the velvet coat and red-heeled shoes.

"Just a table and a bottle of Blue Ruin," Merlyn answered. "And be quick. I've matters requiring a clear head."

The owner of the Fox and Hound knew better than to

inquire just how his customer expected the lethal gin to clear his head. Going back behind the bar, he said to the girl who would serve the table, "Keep an eye on the quality, Polly. His kind is the first to give trouble. That wicked patch over one eye, could be Gentleman Jem, the smuggler, himself."

An hour later Merlyn found that half a bottle of raw gin did not improve his thinking but it did make easier the venting of his emotions.

"She says she hates me. Hates me! The father of her son!"

The plump barmaid astride Merlyn's knee nodded her blond head and smiled prettily. She didn't know what the fine gentleman was saying and didn't much care as long as it ended with them in bed abovestairs and the transfer of a few of the coins she could feel bulging in his money belt.

Merlyn felt her small dirty hand reach for his purse, tucked in his pocket, but did not stop her. The hand went first between his sprawled legs, groping for evidence that he was ready to climb the stairs, and, not finding it, moved surreptitiously to the purse before returning to the business at hand.

Merlyn felt nothing close to desire for the dirty girl rubbing herself against him. The pert pink-crested breasts she teased him with after unlacing her bodice left him curiously unmoved. He did not want that kind of release. He wanted to put his fist through the wall, to explode and shatter every building for miles around. And all because of a lying, scheming deceiver he could not forget.

Only when Cassie lay in his arms could he be certain

that she lived for him as he did for her. In those moments she could deny him nothing. Her body acted against her will and met his need with its own. But later, when sanity returned, she despised him twice as much because he had shown her her weakness and made her succumb to it.

At a more insistent tug at his pocket, he looked up and slapped the girl's hand away.

"Aw! What'd ye do that for?" Polly bawled at him and then remembered she'd best not displease him before he'd had his pleasure. Quickly her small round arms went out and about his neck and she brought her painted lips down hard on his.

The kiss did not affect Merlyn. Other than a refusal to allow her tongue entry into his mouth, he neither responded nor turned aside. When at last she dragged her mouth away, a frown on her brow, he was as puzzled as she. He stared at her. He'd bedded dozens like her in his life, some wealthy wives of peers, others like Polly; all of them sluts. They all wanted something. He'd found most women knew their desires were more easily wrought by spreading their legs, or promising to do so.

"At least you're honest about it, Polly," he said in a quite different timbre from the smooth bass that was his natural voice. He was drunk. Well, nearly, he decided as he poured another glass. That was his intention. "Women! They're all sluts!"

"Aye! Whorin' bitches, ever' one, God bless 'em!" came the rejoinder from across the room.

"'Ere's to that!" cried another, and boisterous laughter erupted in the tavern.

Merlyn scanned the company. They were dirty and loud, drunk and stinking. Thieves, whores, cheats, and con men, it was a company he knew well. Some were dressed as well as he, others in the meanest rags, but they all shared the common denominator of youth. There wasn't a face above forty in the crowd. The ravages of poverty and filth took a toll in the slums of London far greater than in rural shires. Old age was a seldom-bought commodity. Once he had been a part of this company. But he'd managed to overcome the odds and break the cycle that kept most of them tied to poverty even when wealth was briefly theirs. He'd dared to hold back the impulse to spend every tuppence. And, like seeds, they grew. Whatever Cassie wanted from him he could provide. Why did she hold him in such disdain?

In the moments following their lovemaking she had allowed him to hold her close. She even slept in his arms, as trustingly as she had done in the coach from Derbyshire. He had thought at last there would be an understanding between them. What had happened to destroy it?

He couldn't remember. He would have left her to see to their departure, but then she had awakened and called to him. He had been too eager to kiss her, to see the pleasure return to her eyes when he pleased her, to judge the warning in her eyes. She was unsure of herself, but that did not surprise him. It pleased him to think she had never become used to a man's caresses. It was a delight that made him eager for her. Her reluctance, he had thought, was nothing more than shyness. What had she said about wickedness? He could not remember when her struggles became a fight in earnest. Perhaps he'd said the wrong thing in promising her that with him she would grow accustomed to making love during the day as well as at night.

Merlyn shook his head in irritation and emptied his cup. They said many more things after that. All of it was forgettable but the last. She said she would not be the mistress of a man who was a thief and a liar, a scoundrel and a rogue. It hurt, couldn't she see how her words hurt him?

So he struck back. He told her that Briarcliffe was searching London for her, that he'd come to the Comte de Valure's rooms demanding to know where Jack could be found, for he had discovered that Cassie was not at Mother Tess's.

She'd looked at him then with those great dark eyes, in pained puzzlement like a child who'd been punished for a transgression she did not understand. Then she'd said, "Despite all, he *is* my husband." Why had she insisted upon that even now?

There's Adam. He needs the protection of a decent man.

The memory of her words ripped him like hot tongs, and rage shuddered through Merlyn. He had looked about him in faint contempt, but the urge now died. He was fooling himself. He was still one of them: a thief, a rascal, and a commoner. That was why she scorned him.

In his mind's eye he saw Cassie's frightened gaze, the golden dark honey eyes watching him in fright and distrust and loathing. He knew then all the Blue Ruin in London would not erase it from his mind.

Merlyn stood up so quickly he toppled Polly off his knee onto the floor.

"I'm a fool to save you from the fate you so truly desire," Merlyn roared, seeing through a gin blur not Polly but Cassandra at his feet. "You'd have Nick when it's I who set your blood afire. Well, you'll stay by me awhile, like it or not. You'll stay with me till the day you admit it's my caress you desire. One night you'll beg me. That night I'll make you admit it's I you crave!"

Polly swore at him before she remembered his bulging purse. Looking up through her lashes, she found him staring black as thunderclouds down at her. Not bothering to lower her petticoats which had fallen back from her wide-open legs, she smiled. "Like what ye see, guv'nor? 'Tis cold down 'ere. Why don't ye help me up and we'll retire abovestairs?"

Merlyn dashed a hand across his brow, surprised to realize the hum and scattered laughter of the Fox and Hound had died. All at once he noticed Polly sitting on the floor. He frowned. "Get up, girl. The floor's filthy." Reaching across her, he picked up his hat from the table and moved to the doorway.

Polly screamed invectives at his retreating back, but Merlyn didn't hear them. He'd never yet given up any jewel he'd stolen, and Cassie was the rarest gem of them all. He would keep her until he could exact his revenge.

He paused, weaving slightly on his feet. Revenge for what? Revenge because he'd fallen in love with her and she did not return that love? No, because she detested him. It shamed her to think her body burned for the embrace of a common thief, a lowly gypsy. But she did burn for him as no woman ever had, he thought triumphantly, remembering soft kisses from her tender lips. Until she admitted it, he knew, he'd never be free to forget her. And he wanted to be free now. The bewitching spell of love made him feel and act like a madman.

When the man jostled against him he was ready, not because he saw the two fellows follow him out of the Fox and Hound but because the explosion that had ridden just beneath the surface the evening long had begun to erupt. He put out one long leg and hooked it around the knee of the man who had bumped his shoulder and jerked the dodge from his feet. At the same time he withdrew a small lead-weighted cudgel from his pocket and brought it down with brutal satisfaction on the head of the second man, who was reaching for his purse. He didn't even look back over his shoulder at the havoc he had wreaked.

Make him love her, had she? He'd just see about that!

The public coach was filled to capacity. Six passengers sat inside and six sat outside braving the wind and weather of an autumn squall that had blown in from the coast. The leaden clouds spilled a steady stream of wet cold upon the day, and for the third time in an hour Cassandra wondered about those passengers sitting outside overhead, just behind the coachman.

"'Tis fine weather for ganders," commented one passenger, noting Cassandra's continual gaze toward the roof.

Cassandra looked down into the frankly smiling eyes

of the apple-cheeked woman who sat across from her. Wrapped in a fur-lined cape which matched the dull brown velvet of her traveling gown, she was obviously a lady. Perhaps a squire's wife returning home after a shopping spree in London, Cassandra decided, reading in her open face and unpowdered brown hair the simplicity of country life.

As if she'd read Cassandra's thoughts the woman said, "I'm never one to stand on ceremony. Agnes Watters is me name, but the squire calls me Nessie. That's a fine babe you have. Same black hair and blue eyes as his handsome sire."

The squire's wife nodded pleasantly at Merlyn, who sat by Cassandra's side, and he chuckled in appreciation. "Aye. I'm proud of my little family," he said in a country burr, slipping an arm around Cassandra's waist and drawing her nearer so that from shoulder to knee the heat of his body touched her. "She's a sweet little thing, is my Cassie."

Anger pinked Cassandra's cheeks, but Lady Watters mistook it for passion of another kind. "Like lovebirds you are," she said, smiling. "Reminds me of meself and the squire our first years. Wasn't a thing could keep us apart after sunset. First twelve years, twelve sons to show."

Merlyn heard Cassie's gasp of outrage with satisfaction as his fingers curved up from her waist to touch the underside of one breast. "She's shy yet, but babes will settle her," he returned in good humor.

"'Twas like that with me, too. The squire's a full-blooded man, couldn't keep his hands off me two minutes running. Me mam said marry him before I was breeding more than rumors. 'Tis a smart lass what drags her man to the altar first." She winked at Cassandra.

Under the guise of resettling Adam in her arms, Cassandra jabbed Merlyn sharply in the ribs with her elbow. "Sorry," she murmured unrepentantly, "but 'tis a horrid crush."

Merlyn did not remove his arm. Instead, his hand wandered up and boldly cupped her breast firmly. "Don't fret, my love," he said loudly enough for the other passengers to hear. "Your impatience will be rewarded. I've just enough shillings to ensure us a private bed at the coach inn."

This declaration caused the four other passengers to smother their giggles and chuckles behind their hands.

Cassandra turned to face Merlyn, furious that he'd deliberately embarrassed her. He smiled down at her, an openly provocative grin on his sensual mouth. For an instant, she was seized by the desire to throw an arm about his neck and bring his head down to where she could wipe that smile away with her own lips. The impulse got the better of her. She raised her hand and laid it against his cheek. Quickly he followed her lead, lowering his head to her upturned face. Too late she saw the glint of desire spark the flame in his single blue eye. She could only meet the heat of his parted lips with a tremor that was part surprise, part desire.

She expected to be crushed and cruelly taken advantage of. Instead, his lips were persuasively gentle, resting a moment on hers before his tongue darted through and briefly touched hers in a gesture that curled her toes in their satin slippers.

Merlyn dragged his mouth from hers with the greatest reluctance, aware that not only had she accepted his kiss but she had initiated it. The knowledge surprised him, for she had not spoken to him since he returned drunk and sullen from the Fox and Hound the night before. Gazing down into her lovely flushed face, he was struck by a new thought. He'd never been kind to her, not really, only when he needed to calm her fears.

"Ain't he a card?" Nessie Watters remarked with a knowing nod. "You'll be like me, Cassie, a dozen strong babes to show for the years you spend with your young man."

Cassandra was saved from a reply by Adam, who stretched and began to make hungry noises as he sucked his fist. A moment of dismay kept her from reacting. There were three other passengers in the coach, all of them male.

"Here, Cassie, my love," she heard Merlyn say a moment before his heavy cloak was laid about her shoulders. Underneath the cover she felt him loosening the strings that laced the back of her gown. When that was done, he put one long arm about her shoulders, holding the cloak so that she was shielded from the curious gazes of the other passengers as she fed her child. The gesture touched her, erasing the teasing of moments before, and she glanced up at him with eyes full of gratitude.

Merlyn smiled calmly back at her, but, inside, he was strangely moved. Did so small a thing really please her? Did she not know how much it delighted him to find any excuse to touch her? Then he remembered how trustingly she had behaved in Newgate. She had believed him when he said he would free her. Later, she had believed him when, in the disguise of the comte, he had promised to help her escape the marquess. She believed so much of what he said. Would she believe him if he said he loved her, wanted her to stay with him forever? Or would she remember that he was a common criminal, capable of any and all vices? Merlyn frowned. What had he to lose by trying kindness?

A sharp cry of "Chatham" roused the half-dozing passengers an hour later.

"That'll be me squire waiting on the road!" Nessie Watters said when the coach had rocked to a halt, and she threw open a window to peer out.

The gloom of night had little effect on the spirits of the passengers as they piled out into the road to be eagerly solicited by lantern-bearing boys hired by the nearest half dozen roadway inns. Crys of fresh linen, goose-down ticks, and warm ale mingled with shouts of greetings from friends meeting those passengers leaving the coach.

Merlyn fastened his cloak around Cassandra's chin before he took Adam in his arm and helped her down into the muddy lane.

"There!" he shouted and pointed toward the open door of the nearest inn. With his guiding arm about her shoulders, he hurried them through the rain to the inviting warmth.

Moments later Cassandra stood in a small room at the back of the inn. "'Tis the best we got," the innkeeper volunteered, his eyes moving from her to her escort. "Quality sleeps here. Room's off the road. Ye'll sleep deep as death with none to disturb ye." When he stuck out his hand Merlyn dropped some coins into it.

"Two pints of ale and a warm supper, immediately."

The commanding voice instantly answered the inn-keeper's unspoken question. Quality, absolutely, even though his unpowdered hair and eyepatch gave the man the wicked look of a highwayman. The proof lay in his accent. "Aye, that ye'll be havin'."

When he was gone Cassandra moved to sit before the fireplace, where fresh logs had been coaxed into flame. She held Adam on her lap and removed his outer blanket, which had gotten soaked in the brief traverse from coach to inn. Only then did she notice that Merlyn had not moved from the doorway but stood with his back to her, his head cocked to one side as if listening.

"Is something wrong?" she asked.

Merlyn turned back to the room, a deep cleft between his brows. "The last man to leave the coach, the tall, skinny one with the red wool scarf about his neck, he seemed uncommonly interested in your direction."

Cassandra wrinkled her brow in thought. In truth, she had given little attention to the passengers. "Did he ride above?" At his nod, she smiled. "Perhaps he thought me pretty."

"Perhaps," Merlyn returned in a disbelieving voice. "I'm going below. Come here and lock the door. Open it for no voice but mine."

Reluctantly, Cassandra rose to her feet and laid Adam on the bed. "What if the innkeeper returns with dinner?"

"Tell him to set it in the hall," Merlyn replied flatly. "Lock the door, and don't ask me why."

A moment later he was gone and Cassandra was left to hang their rain-soaked clothing before the fire and nurse her ever-hungry infant. "Your father's a very autocratic man," she said to the child in her arms, and it made her happy to say the thought aloud.

Half an hour later, Merlyn returned.

"Well, did you see him?" Cassandra inquired when they sat down to the meal he had brought with him.

Merlyn sipped his ale and sighed. "He'd gone. Went into town and rented a horse not fifteen minutes after the coach arrived."

"You followed him? Why, you're soaked through!" she voiced in astonishment as she looked closely at his clothes.

"Afraid I'll catch my death?" he asked with a softening of his scowl. "I suppose I should relieve myself of these sodden clothes." He rose immediately to his feet and began undressing.

Cassandra tried to pretend that her dinner plate was fascinating, but his every action seemed to lure her gaze to him. He removed his leather riding coat and unfastened his waistcoat with rapid movements. His stock he unwound and laid over the back of her chair, with jabot and shirt quickly following.

The rational, prudent thing would be to fasten her eyes on the fire, Cassandra told herself. The rational part of her had no say when Merlyn removed his shirt and the firelight's golden glow lit the planes of his torso. Unlike the thick inky mane on his head, silky fine hairs etched a more delicate path down the smooth, muscled wall of his chest. It fanned down from each flat nipple to a fine dark line that pointed to his navel before disappearing into his breeches.

Cassandra licked her lips, feeling a delicious, dizzy warmth of desire flood her loins. She knew she should look away, give him no advantage, but she could only raise overly bright eyes in a flushed face to meet his.

Merlyn stood perfectly still, as surprised by her reaction as she. The admiration in her gaze was innocent of guile or scheme. In spite of everything, she did find him attractive. The knowledge of that power made his belly quiver. If only he could, in good conscience, abandon himself to the pleasure they both desired. But that would be foolish when he expected trouble. "We'd best eat before it gets cold," he said, sitting down quickly in his wet breeches before she saw the telltale signs of his passion.

Cassandra lowered her gaze back to her plate and picked up her fork while humiliation stung her cheeks fiery red. He had rejected her!

Serves me right, she scolded herself. She had gaped at him like any Soho trollop. There was no excuse to be had. Perhaps, for all men said, they wanted a woman only when it suited them. Her head dipped lower. Worse than a trollop, she'd not even waited for his demand to be made. Bewitched, that's what she was. Merlyn, the wizard, had bewitched her beyond even the brazenness of a whore.

"You and Adam may have the bed," Merlyn said when their dinner was finished. "You'll need a good night's sleep. Tomorrow we reach Dover, and our next night will be spent on a packet bound for France."

"And you?" Cassandra questioned softly, uncertain what she wanted his answer to be.

"I'll sit by the fire awhile," he answered easily and reached for the bottle of brandy he had brought up with him.

Cassandra moved to the bedside. After a quick glance over her shoulder to make certain he had turned his face toward the fireplace, she loosened her gown and pulled it over her head. A moment later her petticoats and corset slid to the floor in a heap which she stepped over and climbed into the bed. Only when she sat in the middle of the feather tick removing pins from the lace mobcap that had kept her hair in place did she realize he was now watching her. Slowly, in heady realization of his gaze upon her, she uncoiled the heavy mass of mahogany hair and spread it fanlike over her shoulders.

It was the timeless unconscious feminine gesture of surrender that drove Merlyn to his feet in spite of himself. He did not so much cross the floor as draw near the lure held out to him. Quite unintentionally he found himself standing over her, and she looked up at him, her eyes nearly black in the dim light. Leaning down, he kissed her trembling mouth, which sighed under the touch of his lips. He could not make love to her, he told himself, yet his arms went around her, drawing her softness tight against his naked chest, and he groaned in pleasure. Only the thin layer of her sacque separated them, and then that, too, was gone and they lay back together on the bed.

The whimper of the child beside them claimed Cassandra's attention, and automatically she tensed.

Merlyn felt the change and blessed the breaking of the spell, but the throbbing at the base of his belly proclaimed him a fool as he backed away from her. He did not look at her, though he felt her wide, questioning eyes on his back as he returned to the chair before the fire. A gulp of brandy helped him catch his breath, and then he slumped down in the wing chair.

"Sleep, Cassie, my love," he whispered after a moment when he heard her soft sobbing.

"What? What was that?" Cassandra sat up in bed, only to be caught in a viselike grip that trapped her arms by her sides, stopped her scream, and forced her back against the pillows.

"No words."

It was said low, yet Cassandra knew it was Merlyn's arms which now relaxed about her. Then she heard again a faint echo of the sound that had awakened her, and she turned her head toward the doorway. The latch was being lifted and a stealthy weight applied to the door itself. When it slowly opened, Cassandra knew the only reason she did not cry out was that she was holding her breath.

They were two darker silhouettes against the gloom of the hallway beyond, but Cassandra saw the distinct flash of a metal blade as it caught the dying firelight. They stood silently for so long she nearly called out in anxiety, but Merlyn's weight held her firmly. They were staring at the contents of the room, studying it until they found the bed.

It happened all at once. Both shadows charged the bed and Merlyn rose up to meet them with a cry like a banshee's. Cassandra screamed in sheer terror when the bed slid across the floor under their attack, and, grabbing up Adam, she jumped to the floor on the far side. She heard an unfamiliar oath a half second before the thud of fist on flesh. Whirling around, she saw one of the intruders flying back from Merlyn's crouched form. A moment later she saw the second figure draw his knife.

"This here's the one," the figure said over his shoulder to his companion. "Him first, laddie. Then the girl." He said nothing more, for Merlyn drew a blade from his top boot and sent it flashing across the darkened room to bury itself up to the hilt in the man's chest. The intruder gave a scream of surprise, then toppled forward onto his face.

The second man scrambled to his feet and ran for the door, only to find it blocked by the first of the inn guests to come running at the sound of the furor.

"Outta me way!" he cried shrilly and with his knife slashed a path past the unfortunate young man in nightcap and gown. Merlyn was past the guest in a flash, leaving Cassandra to deal with the stunned gentleman and her crying child.

"What's goin' on here?" demanded the innkeeper, appearing by his bleeding guest's side.

"We were attacked," Cassandra answered, moving her son to her shoulder so that she had a hand free to wrap Merlyn's stock about the man's wound. "He and a companion tried to murder us in our beds," she said, pointing at the dead man sprawled before the fireplace.

The innkeeper looked down at the dead man and then suspiciously at the young woman before him. His eyes missed nothing. The light showed her full breasts straining against her sacque and the narrow waist and curving hips of an extraordinarily comely female form. "'Ow's I to know what them men was doin' in 'ere?" he asked with a speaking glance at her undressed state.

"Because my wife is not in the habit of entertaining men in her nightclothes," Merlyn answered, reappearing in the doorway. His gaze went straight to Cassandra. "Are you all right? Give me Adam. Now, innkeeper," he continued in a deeper, angrier tone. "What do you have to say for yourself?"

"What?" the man barked in surprise.

"If this is a measure of your hospitality, you may be certain the king will hear of it. Law-abiding citizens not safe in their own beds when they've a shilling to call their own."

"That's so," offered the young man whose arm was being bandaged. "I travel this road regularly, and never before in my life have I been attacked practically in my bed." He looked around at the innkeeper. "I could have been robbed, too."

"What d'ye mean?" the innkeeper bristled. "Ye're sayin' they were after yer gold?"

Merlyn put his arm about Cassandra's shoulders. "I am saying that my wife wears a valuable ring. 'Twas my wedding gift to her." He raised her hand to display the emerald and sapphire ring. "Lovely, isn't it? Thieves would find it irresistible. And you, sir, give them warm respite for the evening that they may hunt in your halls in dead of night."

"I done no such thing!" the innkeeper cried, thinking of the ruin that was likely to befall him were news of this to reach the common ear. "They mustta come in the back way. The slut who cooks for me always leaves the latch off." He waved his hands at the crowd in the hallway. "Ye folks go back to yer rooms. I'll cart the body out; then all of ye can get back to the rest ye're paying for."

Merlyn felt Cassandra stiffen when the innkeeper's candle spread its light over the inert form of the dead man, and anxiousness for her safety vied with annoyance that he'd been forced to do murder before her eyes. Would she understand that it was for fear of her life that he'd done it? Or would she hold it against him as one more crime?

When the body had been removed and the door closed, he turned on her. "I swear I never killed a man before this night!"

Cassandra heard this declaration in surprise, seeing in his face an expression she'd never before witnessed there. He was angry, yes, and more than a little defensive, but that was not all. There was a fear in him. It was there in the blue-green gaze beholding her. With a jolt she realized that he must have removed his patch in order to better see the intruders.

"Your patch! Did the innkeeper notice?" she asked, looking around on the floor for the leather string.

Merlyn swore under his breath and took long strides to bring her within reach of his hands that took her shoulders in a painful grip. "Look at me, damn you! Do you think me a murderer?"

Cassandra tried to hold the brilliance of his emerald-sapphire stare, but the colors blended and blurred. "I believe you," she whispered huskily. "You threw yourself upon them without knowing whose battle you fought or why. You might have died."

Merlyn pulled her quickly into his arms, relief bursting through him in a physical shudder. Not only had she given him her confidence, she had praised him. He wanted to tell her that it was not bravery but a gut-wrenching fear for her and Adam's safety that had made him act. Instead, he silently held her until the tremors quaking through her made him remember the chill of the room. "Why, you're cold, my love," he said and reached down to pick her up in his arms. "To bed, Cassie."

"Wait." Cassandra put a hand against his chest to keep her head from sinking naturally against its solid comfort. She dreaded telling him, but she knew she must. "I know—knew the man who died. He was a groom at Briarcliffe. The marquess must have sent them. Oh, Merlyn! He's had us followed!" Her voice quavered and cracked on the last words, the pent-up fright of the past hour falling from her now in tears.

"Hush, love," Merlyn said, cradling her closer as he walked over and sat down next to his sleeping son. He did not put her from his lap but continued to hold her and gently rock her as if she were a child until her shivering subsided.

"I've known for a week that someone followed me. Once I'd made fairly certain that Nick believed the comte had no part in your disappearance, I thought perhaps I dodged mere shadows. I had, in all honesty, forgotten about your father-in-law. He, too, will be searching for you. 'Tis hard to believe his luck, for all that. So, here's what we must do."

Chapter Eleven

THE SHARP SUNLIGHT OF THE AUTUMN AFTERNOON MAGNI-
fied the clear vibrance of the air. Every tree and blade
of grass stood out in sharp relief. Across the meadow,
fields of hay baked to a warm golden brown. The cool
crisp nights had tipped the green of the trees with gilt
and the bramble vines were shot through with scarlet
tongues amongst the green. It was harvest season and
the earth hung heavy and sweet with its ripened
growth. But for the gentle glide of small milky white
clouds in the cerulean sky, the air was still, weighted
with the odors of grass, the sharp-sweet tang of wild
berries, and the faint salty scent of the sea many miles
to the north.

Cassandra breathed deeply, reminded of her home in
Devonshire. In summer the droning of bees, dusted
yellow on their underbellies with pollen, would have
completed the sights and sounds of the day. For a
moment longing for a home, a place of her own, seized
her with an acuteness that made her catch her breath.

"What's wrong, Cassie? Did a fly sting you?" Merlyn inquired, pausing on the roadside.

Cassandra turned to him, tipping her head back to meet his gaze. The sunshine had added a sheen of perspiration to his face and bronzed his cheeks. A few inky black curls, so pure an ebony they shone with bluish highlights in the strong natural light, had slipped from their ribbon and clung to his damp brow and neck. The hawkish nose, heavy brows, and harsh lines of his face prevented him from true handsomeness, but he didn't need it, she thought with an unexpected leap of her pulse, and she hurriedly looked away.

"My feet ache," she said and turned back to the road before them. She'd given up counting the blisters her walking boots had rubbed on her ankles after the first week. Two weeks earlier, they had fled Chatham undetected. They'd waited until the coach was standing in the yard with their luggage aboard before sneaking out the kitchen door. Now they had nothing but the clothes on their backs and endless miles of byways and footpaths behind them. "How much farther must we travel today?"

Merlyn fell into step beside her, making a conscious effort to match his long stride to her smaller, delicate steps. "Another hour should bring us to the outskirts of Trowbridge. We'll rest there for the night."

He looked down at her and smiled. Adam had reached up and grabbed the ruffle of her mobcap and tugged it sideways until it nearly covered one of her eyes. His gurgle of contentment as he crammed the lace into his toothless mouth was echoed in his father's sigh. It was a good day to be alive, Merlyn thought. Never before had he known such contentment. And all because of the slip of a girl with great honey-brown eyes who walked beside him.

Cassandra did not notice his satisfied smirk. She had other matters on her mind. More than once in the days since they'd been on the road she had noticed other women turning their heads as Merlyn passed. She was no longer too naïve to know that their lowered lashes and secretive smiles were invitations for his company. She wondered now if he ever took up one of the more provocative glances he'd received when he went into the villages alone some evenings. It would explain his behavior toward her. In her experience of him he was not a man to deny himself the pleasures he desired. So why, then, had he not taken advantage of the many nights they'd spent in isolation, sleeping along the roadside, to make love to her?

Not that she wanted that, she admonished herself. She was glad to be left alone and dreaded their next encounter. It was only that she couldn't keep from her mind the memory of that night in Chatham when he'd drawn back from her. Not since then had he so much as kissed her. Had she behaved so unforgivably? Or had he grown bored with her when there were so many other desirable women available? The only way to know would be to ask him, and she didn't want to face his aversion a second time.

When the evening sky tinted the night with mauves and golds and deep purples, Merlyn left Cassandra and Adam sitting in an empty thresher's hut. The night had turned midnight-blue when he returned, whistling a tune Cassandra had become accustomed to hearing. It was a bawdy drinking song, the words of which he'd sung for her when she'd inquired. After that, she just enjoyed the melody while trying not to blush as the words filtered into her thoughts.

"Mutton pies, a pair of them, and fresh berry tart," he announced when he appeared in the doorway. "Light a candle, Cassie, my love. This is too good to be nibbled in the dark."

Cassandra's mouth tightened as she reached out to do his bidding. He never allowed her to accompany him into the villages where he went each night to find provisions for them. Suspicion had been growing in her that he did not do so because he knew she would not approve of the methods he used.

"Shouldn't we be running out of shillings soon?" she asked, innocently raising her eyes to his when the candle was lit.

A corner of Merlyn's mouth twitched as he sat down beside her and opened the napkin he carried. "'Twas a spot of luck, our finding this place abandoned. In another few days it'll be filled with workmen." He neatly broke each pie in half and then separated the tart, putting half on her side of the napkin and the larger piece on his. "I've even managed a bottle of ale," he announced proudly as he pulled the bottle from beneath his coat.

"Stolen it, you mean," Cassandra answered, not touching her portion of the fare. "You've stolen everything here, haven't you?" she continued, holding his gaze with an accusatory stare.

"What of it?" Merlyn shrugged carelessly. "I keep you fed. You've no cause for complaint."

Cassandra gnawed her lower lip, looking down at the crisp meat pastry as if it were a purloined ruby necklace he'd set before her. "You've stolen every time? Every meal? For weeks?"

Merlyn looked away, feeling uncomfortable before her incredulous gaze. "Eat your food before it's cold."

"No." Cassandra shook her head, feeling as guilty as if she'd been the thief. "How could you? You knew I'd never agree."

"That's why I didn't tell you. You'd have been needlessly worried about something that does not concern you," Merlyn replied, sticking a quarter of one pie into his mouth.

"Not concern me?" Cassandra repeated in astonishment. "Here I sit night after night, eating ill-gotten goods, and you say 'tis no concern of mine."

Merlyn swallowed his mouthful and reached for the ale. "I say 'tis no concern of yours because it isn't. You had no part in the theft. You never asked me whence came the clothes on your back or how I kept you fed when you shared company with Meg. Why now this missishness over tuppence?"

This effectively silenced her for the moment. It was true. She'd never before questioned his largess. She had assumed his funds were the result of pawning the Briarcliffe diamonds. Her head jerked up. "What became of the necklace and earrings you stole from me?"

Merlyn looked at her in surprise. "What do you suppose?" He shoved a hand into the open neck of his shirt and produced the diamond collar and pendants. "There, my lady. You'll not tax me with that."

Cassandra looked at them in wonder. "Why didn't you sell them if we needed money?"

Merlyn cursed under his breath. "Ignorance! How long do you think it would be before someone recognized them? There aren't many who can afford such baubles. The dealer would show them to young noblemen first. Perhaps Nick Briarcliffe himself would be asked to name a price for his own family's jewels. I've had no time to separate them from their mounts and fashion new ones for them. They're worthless to me."

"You can do that?" Cassandra asked doubtfully.

Merlyn looked up at her, grinning. "I have many talents, my love. You know only a few."

Cassandra ignored this as she pulled his ring from her finger and tossed it in his direction. "That aside, you may take back this ring and sell it. Or is it stolen, too?"

In a violent move Merlyn plucked the emerald and sapphire ring from the matted straw floor and rose to his feet. "I should strike you for that," he said quietly through clenched teeth.

Instinctively, Cassandra raised her hands, remembering the stinging slap he'd delivered to Meg. But that violence did not come. Instead, he grabbed her by one wrist and hauled her to her feet. She heard his quick intake of breath, and then she was pulled roughly toward him and enfolded in an angry embrace a second before his mouth swooped down on hers. It was not a lover's kiss but rather that of an angry man momentarily shaken out of his self-possession.

"Why? Why?" Cassandra whispered shakily when at last his arms relaxed about her.

Merlyn shook his head, equally dazed by the spark of emotion that had roared into full passion at the touch of his lips. "I don't know," he said shortly, dropping his arms from her. "You shouldn't have done that," he said a moment later, his voice flat and dry.

Cassandra gazed at him in full surprise. "Does the ring mean so very much to you?"

Merlyn opened his hand to reveal the ring in his palm. "My father made it. 'Tis the only thing left me of my family."

"Who are you?" Cassandra whispered, eyeing the emerald and sapphire stones that winked at her from his palm like the sacred eyes of some heathen idol.

Merlyn sighed. It was not a night for questions. "What answer would please you? Will it make you like me better if I say I really am a French comte? What if I tell you my mother was a gypsy fortune-teller hanged as a thief? Ha!" he cried bitterly. "That you will believe because it fits your opinion of me ere this. Well, hang her they did, and me, her son, they banished to the workhouse."

There was a derisive edge to his voice as he turned to face her fully. "You keep company with a workhouse child, my lady. A poor gypsy boy raised on charity and kicks, born to hang."

His intention had been to still her curiosity, and he knew he had succeeded when she lowered her head and said nothing more. After a moment he took her face, a pale shadowed oval, in his hands and found her cheeks slick with tears. "What's this, Cassie? Are these tears for the poor mite who watched his mother dance on the gibbet, or for yourself?"

"Oh! Do be silent!" Cassandra cried and put a hand to his lips to still his hard cold voice. "You can be so cruel, Merlyn Ross. In all my life I've never known a crueler man."

Merlyn moved back from her touch, not because he didn't want it but because he knew she was not finished with her questions, and now that they had begun they should be answered. "What do you, my lady, know of cruelty or hardship? You've never known a day without enough in your belly and only the fresh welts from the workmaster's knout to keep you company. You've never cried till there were no more tears and then been made to walk the treadmill for the weakness. You've always been wanted, always housed and fed and cared for."

Cassandra faced him, the meal on the floor between them forgotten. "Do not tax me with that Drury Lane speech. Perhaps it's made another lady's heart soften, but you can have no idea how easily I could fling your words back in your face."

Merlyn felt a strange sensation flow over him as he stared into her huge golden eyes. It wasn't just passion; he'd long ago realized he could win her to him with just a touch. He saw clearly for the first time that there was a wide, incalculably deep chasm between them, and he had not the first inkling how to bridge it.

"What's between us, Cassie?"

Cassandra did not need to ask him what he meant. "Nicholas."

Merlyn snatched the patch from his eye, the better to see her. It was a long, quiet look. "I've never believed until this moment that you truly wed Briarcliffe. I don't believe he loved you, for if he had, he could never have turned away from you. Why, why did you marry him?"

Cassandra looked away from that burning gaze, aware that tears of humiliation were forming. "I had no choice. You say I know nothing of suffering, but I tell you I know enough to curdle a tender heart. That's not an excuse," she challenged, looking up quickly. "I'd do it again to get away from the life I'd known. Perhaps I'd have married any man to end that."

"Was it so bad?" he asked quietly.

Cassandra raised her head to stare over his shoulder into the night. "Have you ever been to a county fair on auction day? Cattle and swine are usually sold. But one fall day three years ago my village fair had for auction an uncommon item. A gentleman in need of funds for the gaming tables put it up for sale. The law makes it legal."

Suddenly Merlyn understood what she was about to say and his heart contracted in sympathy for the shame he saw in her bright eyes. Nicholas had told him the truth, but he had not believed it.

"It was only the last of his many cruelties. I'd learned early in life that any resistance met with the power of my father's knotty hand." Cassandra winced, but the moment passed quickly. "When the Briarcliffe carriage halted before the auction block I thought it must be a golden angel who emerged. Nicholas bought me for a hundred gold sovereigns, and I loved him for it. Lord! I'd have gone with Satan himself had he possessed a hundred sovereigns. So, there you have it. I didn't wonder when my golden knight insisted upon an immediate marriage. But I've learned many things this past year, and all of them prove me to be the grandest fool ever born. So I say to you again: Nicholas stands between us because I'm legally wed." Her chin wobbled, but she kept her eyes wide upon unshed tears. "It's all the pride that's left me."

If she expected sympathy she was disappointed. Merlyn crossed his legs and sat down, reaching for a second piece of pastry. Suddenly he looked up, a full grin on his tan face. "I like you better for telling me that. It's a hard world for the weak. It's harder yet for a woman. You've been harshly used. There's no denying it. But you've come through it, Cassie, with heart and head intact and a fine young son to boot. You're a survivor. That's more than many can say."

The devastating warmth of his smile took away her shame, and like a flower turning its lovely face to the strong bright sun, Cassandra felt her cheeks bloom with color under his flattery. He had not offered her pretty phrases of pity or laughed in her face, and he might have done either. She sat down beside him, her stomach grumbling with the suddenness of her returned appetite.

"There's one thing more," Merlyn said when he'd watched her chew and swallow several mouthfuls. He took her left hand in his and slid the emerald and sapphire ring back on the third finger. "You should know the truth, Cassie, and the truth is, I feel no guilt in having bedded you, for, truly, you're my wife in fact, if not by the letter of the law. You'll wear my ring, and we'll speak no more of thieves and mistresses and adultery." He raised her hand to give it a brief kiss just below his ring and then released it.

Cassandra did not trust her voice for some time. He had called her his wife. Did she wish that were true? Adam, then, would have a father, and she'd be free of the marquess and the threat he brought.

She stole a surreptitious glance at Merlyn as he sat beside her. Inner laughter curved his hard mouth, and the shadows of his powerful shoulders danced a jaunty jig on the ground behind him. In moments like these, she could almost believe he might love her. If only that were so! But Merlyn Ross of the wicked smile and the wizard's gaze of emerald and sapphire was a thief, a man who felt no compunction in relieving other men of their hard-earned goods. Such a man was unpredictable. Such a man could steal her heart, and that would leave her nothing at all.

"I will keep the ring on one condition," she said when the last of the ale was gone. "Tomorrow we both go into town to seek our supper. I'll wager what you will that we can find shelter and supper without stealing them."

Merlyn leaned back on an elbow, a lazy smile hovering on his lips. "A wager always intrigues me. Winner names the prize."

The perfection of the day before was but a memory by noon of the following day. Cold gray rain slanted out of the slate sky, turning the roadway into a slick morass. By three in the afternoon Cassandra could hardly bear to put one foot before the other. Rain weighted her gown, plastered hair to her forehead and cheeks, and ran along the ends to dribble icy rills down the inside of her collar.

Merlyn had tucked Adam inside his coat and buttoned it up so that only the boy's face was visible above the neckline. The babe seemed content with this arrangement. Merlyn's only complaint came when his shirtfront was suddenly covered in a warm flood.

"Damme!" he cried, his expression a composite of surprise and consternation.

"What's wrong?" Cassandra demanded irritably, thinking Merlyn was about to shout at her yet again for treading on his heels.

Merlyn turned to face Cassie, who had been following him and using his tall, broad form as protection. "Madame! Your son has drenched me!" he voiced in indignation.

Cassandra tried not to laugh, but it burst from her. Full rich laughter bent her nearly double and she slipped in the slick mud, lost her footing, and fell squarely on her behind.

Merlyn's lips twitched, a sputter of chuckles escaped, and then he threw back his head and roared. The great noise coming at so close a range frightened Adam into voicing a protest of his own, and though higher than his sire's, his voice promised to be deep and rich in time.

"Serves you right," Merlyn admonished when he had regained his composure. Reassuringly patting the small backside under his coat with one hand, he reached out and pulled Cassandra to her feet with his other.

Cassandra pulled the soggy mobcap from her hair and used it to wipe her face. She did not notice Merlyn's intake of breath at the sight of her. Eyes shining in mirth, the bloom of color bright in her cheeks, her rosy mouth so softly inviting a lover's sample—she was more beautiful in this moment than any woman he'd ever known. And he knew why. A mantle of fear shrouding her from the instant of their first meeting, bleaching her of humor and the youthful glow that should be hers, had fallen away. The ability to laugh made her beautiful. The thought warmed Merlyn. *I shall see that she laughs every day after this,* he silently vowed.

The cart appeared quite suddenly on the lane hemmed in by eight-foot hedgerows. Merlyn pulled Cassandra out of its path before noting that the slow clip-clop of the small pony could be easily outpaced.

"Whoa!" the driver called when he was apace of the two figures on the roadway. "Ye should know better'n to take the path in this weather," the driver scolded them. He set his wide-brimmed hat back from his eyes. "Ye're for town?"

Cassandra took Adam in her arms, tossed Merlyn a speaking glance, and moved forward to greet the farmer with a genteel smile. "As you see, sir, we are afoot and in wretched condition. For ourselves we do not care, but my son is but three months old and I fear he may suffer a congested chest in such weather."

Merlyn rolled his eyes at her speech. It held so piteous a false note that he could barely contain his laughter. To his surprise, his feelings were not shared.

"A wee babe, do ye say? Lord bless! 'Tis no day for a wee one, Josh Tinker's athinkin'. Up ye come, then, lass, and yer babe, too." He pointed at Merlyn. "That be yer man?"

Cassandra looked back over her shoulder as if she'd forgotten Merlyn existed. "Oh, him. Yes, he's with us."

"So," Cassandra whispered under her breath when the three of them were piled into the back of the wagon with Josh Tinker's load.

"It's no proof of the bet," Merlyn answered as he shifted his shoulders in search of a more comfortable resting place among the canvas-covered barrels. "Get me hot rum and a slice of ham for supper; then we'll call the bet won."

The trip by wagon was no quicker than on foot and they were no drier, but Cassandra could not complain when they pulled into the muddy yard of the White Stag Inn. "I think I may be able to walk again tomorrow," she murmured, stepping down, only to find that her bruised hip had stiffened in the hour following her fall and she had to grab Merlyn's arm to steady herself.

"Age before beauty," Merlyn whispered maliciously as he held out his arm to allow her to step ahead.

A moment later a woman appeared in the doorway of the inn, wiping her hands on her long white apron. "At last ye're home, Tinker. And what have we here?"

The woman stepped over the threshold and Cassandra was immediately reminded of a ship under sail. Yards of dark blue linen made up the skirt that covered amply rolling hips, and white ruffles from the tight sleeves that ended at her elbows flared like flags on the yardarms of a ship of the line. There was the look of the brewery about her in the puffy cheeks with raisin eyes.

"You," the woman said, pointing at Merlyn. "Ye're lookin' to earn a wage?"

"Now, missus, ye wouldn't be askin' a man o' me talents to tote barrels o' rum," Merlyn replied, mimicking perfectly her accent.

The woman's eyes screwed up in what Cassandra later learned was an almost permanent squint from nearsightedness. "Who says there's rum in them barrels? Good English ale, that's what we've got."

"And I'm King George's prime minister," Merlyn countered with a chuckle. "A man can sit just so long in a sea of brew without his nose tellin' him whether 'tis English or Indies he's smellin'. Not that I mind. A toddy o' rum comes close to heaven on a day like this."

The woman eyed Merlyn carefully and, liking what she saw, said, "What talents do ye claim—besides a quick tongue?"

Merlyn stepped forward, put his arm about the woman's shoulders, and whispered something in her ear that Cassandra could not hear. The woman cackled gleefully and walloped Merlyn's chest with a great paw of a hand. "Away with ye, ye wicked man! Me Josh wouldn't like it one bit, ye sayin' them things to his wife."

Merlyn winked but dropped his arm from her shoulders. "We won't be tellin' him, then." He gave a very stiff Cassandra a sideways glance and then murmured, "Me wife isn't half pleased herself."

A look of satisfaction spread over the woman's features as she, too, noticed the young woman's posture of disapproval. "She don't look yer type."

"So said my father," Cassandra interjected. Ignoring Merlyn's raised brows, she continued. "That's why we're on the road. Father would not hear of my marriage to a—a cobbler. We're gentry, he insisted. Even when Jack got me with child he barred the door and had my poor love hounded from the door." She offered Merlyn a wide, melting glance. "Only a week ago did Jack return and, together, we've fled."

"Poor little lamb, and poor little tyke. Ye should be ashamed," she scolded Merlyn with a wagging plump finger. "'Tis one thing plyin' your silver tongue on a woman what knows better, but to get a wee slip o' a girl great with child and no vows said—well, that's wicked. That's what it is."

Merlyn bit his lip to keep from smiling as Mrs. Tinker's three chins wobbled indignantly. She was an aged tart if ever he saw one. Traces of the pox bridged her nose and chin. "Don't tax me withal. I've married the girl."

The woman's gaze went to Cassandra's left hand and widened in surprise. "That's a pretty ring ye have there."

"Her father give it to her," Merlyn supplied quickly, annoyed that Cassandra had not had the presence of mind to hide so valuable an article. She had a lot to learn about begging.

"'Tis beginning to rain again," Cassandra hinted gently.

"So it is," Mrs. Tinker exclaimed. "Well, don't just dawdle. Ye need a proper meal and the fire to dry ye out."

Cassandra saw that Merlyn was about to speak and beat him to it. She had promised to win them shelter and food, and she was enjoying herself too much to allow him to win it for her. "We can't, I'm afraid." She looked down, drawing the blanket from Adam's face. "We have no money."

As if on cue, Adam let loose with a wail of woe.

"Poor wee mite," the mother of ten cooed. "O' course ye must come in, if only to warm the babe."

"Well, perhaps for a moment," Cassandra answered, reluctance heavy in her voice. "We must find shelter before dark. It's so difficult with rain hounding us."

"Doing it too brown, my love," Merlyn whispered in her ear as he fell into step beside her.

"It's working," Cassandra retorted with a lift of her chin.

"Hot rum and ham," Merlyn reminded her.

The hot rum appeared almost immediately. "The wee girl's blue to the lips. With a babe to suckle she needs some fire in her blood," Mrs. Tinker explained as she set the tankard of rum down before Cassandra. "Worked ever' time, and I suckled ten." A smaller one she set before Merlyn. "And you, you lusty rascal, she won't needs bother with you this night if there's a bellyful of warm brew to dull yer appetite."

Cassandra switched the mugs when the woman had gone and sat back in her chair before the parlor fire with a saucy smile on her lips.

"You think quite a lot of yourself at the moment," Merlyn said in good humor.

"Two tankards of hot rum," Cassandra gloated, holding up a pair of fingers. "And you said people aren't kind."

"I know. That's what bothers me," Merlyn returned dryly and reached for his drink.

"That's your trouble. You see evil everywhere," Cassandra admonished. "Not everyone must have a gain for every service done. Some people are good and give of that goodness to honest people in need."

Merlyn leaned forward until his lips were within inches of her ear. "My dear young lady, you can hardly call your performance in the yard just now one of unfailing sincerity. 'Father would not hear of my marriage to a cobbler,'" he aped in her high soft voice. "Gad! And you call me a sham. What difference is there between a lie and outright theft?"

Cassandra's cheeks flamed scarlet. She hadn't stopped to consider when her pleas had changed with embellishments to lies, so much was she enjoying herself. She looked up at Merlyn through a forest of dark lashes. "Do you think I should tell them that we have the diamonds?"

Merlyn moved back so quickly he nearly overset his chair. "Feed your son, madame. 'Tis better you not think at all."

The ham was longer in arriving. It was delivered by Josh Tinker, who was still wheezing from the exertion of emptying his wagon. He was a short, thin man with ruddy cheeks and a great bulbous nose out of which grew amazingly long hairs.

Cassandra's fascination with this peculiarity prevented her from realizing that she offered the innkeeper an equally fascinating display. It was Merlyn who reached across her and drew the corner of her cloak over her naked breast at which Adam sucked greedily.

"The missus says ye look in need o' a spot of supper. 'Twas left over after the main meal. We was as like to throw it out in the mornin'."

Two greedy eyes fell once more on Cassandra's bosom before he set the plates down beside the half-empty rum tankards. "We got an extra room at the back. We rent it to tinkers and tax men." The last was said with a wink at Merlyn. It meant that the room was an airless hole with a bolt on the outside. "Ye're welcome to it."

"Oh yes. That would be lovely," Cassandra answered with a wonderful smile for the man.

"Right," he replied. One small glance below her chin and he was gone.

"My goodness," Cassandra breathed when he was out of earshot. "I thought he would crawl right down my bodice."

Merlyn glanced at her. "You've a sweet pair, my love," he said lazily, "but 'twas else that caught the innkeeper's eye." He reached out and removed the cloak.

Cassandra glanced down at her bosom and then at her left hand which she used to position her swollen breast for Adam's ease. "The ring," she said, looking up at Merlyn.

Merlyn shrugged. "If the night was clear I'd drag you out this minute. As it is . . ."

Cassandra made a moue. "As it is, you've lost your bet. I produced hot rum, and that's ham bits in the beans. My reward will be—"

Merlyn cut her off with a quick smacking kiss. "Don't be too eager to claim your reward. There're some proprieties to which even I prefer to bow."

"Oh! You!" Cassandra sputtered, but it quickly turned to a giggle. She was too pleased with herself to let anything he said or did alarm her.

An hour later they were shown to the small room. There was nothing in it but a straw mattress which looked bug-ridden. "There's not even a window," Cassandra protested under her breath to Merlyn.

Merlyn himself was about to voice a similar complaint when he was suddenly shoved in the back with great force. He saved himself from falling into the room by a grab at the doorjamb. He was not so lucky in saving himself from the expected blow. The full wine bottle caught him just behind the right ear. He heard Cassandra's scream, but it echoed faintly behind the explosion inside his head. The second blow went wide, glancing off his shoulder. He heard more screams, tightened his grasp on the doorframe, and hauled himself to his feet. Turning, he saw a sight that might have made him laugh had it not nearly stopped his heart in fright.

Cassandra had been slightly ahead of Merlyn when the blow came. The innkeeper had been carrying a bottle, but it had not seemed a weapon until it was too late. The first blow had struck with a sickening thud. She turned to find Merlyn crumpling at her feet and Josh Tinker raising his arm a second time. With a cry of horror, she dropped Adam onto the straw mattress and grabbed the innkeeper's arm. The blow went wide, and the force of it sent the pair of them to the floor in the hallway.

The innkeeper began bawling curses at her, but Cassandra locked her hands about his waist and hung on for dear life, hampering his attempts to rise.

A moment later they were both hauled upright and the innkeeper peeled away from her. Merlyn dug one hard fist into the man's belly and a second lifted his chin, forcing him back two steps before he collapsed.

"Are you hurt?" Merlyn demanded of a winded Cassandra, who shook her head. "Grab Adam and come on, then," he said as he pulled his knife from his boot and took a few steps down the hall. Cassandra snatched up her squawling son and followed.

A moment later, Mrs. Tinker appeared in the kitchen doorway bawling, "Silence the brat, Josh, afore he rouses the guests." Her look of consternation fell into openmouthed surprise when she saw it was not her husband who stood in the hall. Merlyn took a step toward her, but she gave a cry of fright and slammed the door in his face.

"Come on, she'll not come after us," Merlyn said as he hurried toward the back door. They found the backstairs without any interference.

Not until the faint lights of the village were eclipsed by the hedges of the meadows did they pause for breath.

"Are you badly hurt?" Cassandra asked, reaching out to touch Merlyn's brow.

"I deserve having my head split open," Merlyn said roughly and pushed her hand away. "Of all the idiotic, harebrained mistakes I've ever made! To think he might have gotten away with it if my skull were a bit thinner!"

Merlyn continued in this manner of self-abuse for some time, and Cassandra kept pace with him in silence, knowing that his anger stemmed from hurt, a sense of failure, and damaged pride all at once.

"I'm sorry," she said when he at last subsided into a sullen silence. "What did he want?"

Merlyn slowed his pace. "Ransom, no doubt. Your

story of an irate parent and a runaway daughter gave them the idea. They thought to rescue you from me and make a tidy sum for their trouble."

Cassandra was silent a long time. So, he blamed her foolish impulse for their woes. "I still think there are those who would aid us out of generosity of heart."

"No doubt you still believe in Saint Nick, too," Merlyn answered acerbically. "So, until we come upon the jolly man himself, we'll return to doing things my way."

Cassandra swung around to face him, guilt prodding her words. "Oh, why don't you just leave? Twice you've nearly been killed protecting us. Why do you stay?"

Because I love you! The words nearly burst from him, but Merlyn locked his jaw against them. She was not yet ready for such an admission from him. The very fact that she had asked the question proved it. "You're tired and badly frightened. I won't leave you, not while you persist in believing that God protects all children and fools."

Cassandra had not the heart to protest. Neither did she protest when he stopped a little later under the protection of a great oak and sat down at its base, drawing her with him and cradling her head on his shoulder.

"Pleasant dreams, gentle spirit," he whispered and gently kissed the top of her head.

Chapter Twelve

"YOU CAN'T BE SERIOUS? BATH IS A GREAT CITY FULL OF important people. We would be recognized in an instant."

Merlyn had been listening to Cassie's protests for the better part of the morning as the rise and fall of the land around them grew steeper.

"Besides, just look at us. A fine pair we make."

Merlyn slanted an uncritical gaze at Cassandra. Her hair had been tightly drawn back from her face and braided before it was tucked into her wilted mobcap. Her gown was caked with mud at the hem and the kerchief tucked into her bodice was soiled in several places where Adam had burped milk upon her. "You look fine," he assured her blandly.

"Well, you don't," Cassandra snapped back. "Your shirt is yellow with wear and your breeches are soiled. You need a shave, too," she assured him.

Merlyn lazily rubbed his cheek. He had not shaved

since they left Chatham. Long curly whiskers twined about his fingers. "Shall I keep it, do you think?" Her expression of horror made him laugh. "You're vinegar for a man's ego, my love. Thought it might begin a new mode. Wouldn't it be a delight if bushy chins were required for entry into the Pump Room at Bath hereafter?"

Cassandra looked at him as if he were mad. "It's the sun," she said, nodding her head sagely. "This return of summer heat so late in the year has turned your brain. Or perhaps"—her eyes grew wide and she caught at Merlyn's sleeve to turn him to face her—"'twas the blow to your head."

Merlyn allowed her to reach up and tenderly quest the back of his skull for the week-old lump that had long since disappeared. It pleased him to feel her small fingers in his hair. He had to bend slightly to bring his head low enough for her, and as she stood on tiptoe with an arm raised, her bodice gaped open and he had a full unrestricted view. He nearly leaned down and kissed the hollow between her breasts, but he knew he dared not. The torture of living beside her daily had taken its toll on his self-control. Yet there were benefits of that self-discipline. She no longer shrank from him when he touched her nor did she seem wary when he pulled her tight against him on cold nights for their mutual sharing of body warmth. She felt able to laugh with him, to tease him, to touch him as now.

He'd never known this easy camaraderie with another single living soul. Now his defenses were down, he was open and vulnerable, and he liked the feeling. Yet his bond with Cassie seemed as fragile as his shaky hold on his lust, and he did not want to test it just yet. The pain of her rejection would hurt him more deeply than before because he could finally admit to himself that he longed for her approval. Rather than be a rutting boar he would remain awhile a spaniel puppy, content to have his ears scratched by a lovely winsome girl.

"You'll live," Cassandra pronounced coolly after a moment and resumed walking.

"You don't sound as if that thought gives you any pleasure," he answered in mock dejectedness.

Cassandra shook her head. "You'll get no sympathy from me. You think a great deal too much of yourself as it is."

A saucy smile curved her mouth. She had enjoyed the feel of his satin-soft curls between her fingers. His skin had a salty tang that was not unpleasant, and the tender curve of his mouth had almost persuaded her to sample it. If only he would rid himself of that patch!

She cast him a sidelong glance. It was disconcerting to look into a single eye when she knew he had a perfectly good second. Sometimes his gaze was emerald, as deep and dark a green as the moss that grew thickly at the base of huge oaks. Sometimes his gaze was as vivid a blue as that in the autumn sky at evening when the colors deepened and richened to vermilion, amber, and sapphire. How miraculous was his gaze when nothing obstructed its full power!

Cassandra looked away. If only she could trust him completely, as her instincts urged. He told her he kept the secret of his parti-colored eyes because of past crimes. But if he truly meant to give up his past, why did he not begin with the truth? What were his plans for the future?

They walked a few miles farther in companionable silence until they came to the bottom of a hill. The afternoon sun slanted golden rays through the limbs of the trees overhead, but the weariness of weeks suddenly descended upon Cassandra and she could find nothing of cheer in the mild day. Sighing, she shifted Adam's small bulk from one sore shoulder to the other.

Merlyn saw this and reached out for the babe. "No!" she snapped in weary temper. "You've carried Adam more than your share today."

Merlyn immediately turned off the path, up the slope of the hill, and Cassandra wondered briefly if she had somehow offended him. She had her answer at once in the laughter that floated back down to her, and quick upon it his dark-bodied baritone moved to song.

> Take, O take those lips away,
>   That so sweetly were forsworn;
> And those eyes, the break of day,
>   Lights that do mislead the morn:
> But my kisses bring again, bring again;
> Seals of love, but seal'd in vain, seal'd in vain.

Merlyn turned and called after her, "Come and see the view."

Muttering an unladylike oath, Cassandra marched after him. She was in no mood to sightsee.

It took them the better part of five minutes to crest the hill, and just before they did Merlyn turned to her again. "You've wondered why we've walked halfway across England when it was my original intent to sail to France. I thought of a better stratagem. We'll be safe by the close of day." He took her hand and drew her up the last few steps to the ridge. "Our new home."

Cassandra did not realize he had deliberately chosen this place to introduce her to Bath or that for hundreds of years visitors had found Breechen Cliff the most dramatic entrance into the stepped valley below. All she knew was that, suddenly, the gold and green countryside harbored a magic valley. In the center of the town below, the majestic gray stones of Bath Abbey with its vertical spires were highlighted by the sun. Fanning out from the Renaissance cathedral in ever-widening, gently rising circles like ripples in a pool were the shops, houses, and terraces of the ancient city of Bath. Winding through it all, a river of silvery green, was the venerable Avon.

"It's beautiful!" Cassandra declared breathlessly.

"Will you be satisfied to live here?" Merlyn questioned lightly.

"Oh yes!" Cassandra spun around to face him. "That is, can we afford it? How will we live?"

Merlyn did not miss her use of *we*, and it warmed him more fully than the sun, but he did not comment upon it. Time for that later. "I believe I have a friend or two who'll be willing to aid us."

"Friends like Meg?" Cassandra asked with a narrow look.

"You'll make me believe you're jealous," Merlyn teased as he tweaked her nose. "Besides, you liked Meg. However, the answer's no. We'll be in noble company if Hugh still abides in Bath. It's not the fashionable season for Bath, but Hugh prefers the city's quiet elegance to London."

Cassandra bit her lip. "Suppose someone recognizes us."

Merlyn gave her a sharp look. "You told me you knew no one of the beau monde. Not that it matters. Lord Hugh Mulberry is not a town dandy. He seldom mingles with his own class. You may find him something of a novelty. He is a writer, a playwright to be exact."

"Like Jonson, Dryden, and Shakespeare?" Cassandra questioned innocently.

Merlyn's face lit up in unexpected pleasure. "You know something of the theater?"

Cassandra shrugged. "The library was one of the few diversions Briarcliffe offered. I'm not as ignorant as you would think me. For instance, I know those lines you spoke a moment ago. They're from *Measure for Measure.*"

"Bravo," Merlyn replied with a nod. "Now, the test. Quote me a passage."

Cassandra's brow puckered in thought a moment; then she looked up at him with an impish grin.

"They say best men are molded out of faults,
And, for the most, become much more the better
For being a little bad."

Merlyn's brows shot up in amusement, and she could see that her hasty quote had revealed too clearly her thoughts. "We'd best move on," she said quickly and moved away.

Merlyn came up beside her and gently lifted Adam out of her arms. "We have a short detour to make. You were right when you said we dare not show our faces in Bath in our filth. I know a woman—a very old woman, my love—who lives on the outskirts of Corston who will help us. Hurry, we've much to do before sundown."

Two large tears slid over Cassandra's lower lashes and trickled down her cheeks as she watched Adam being bounced on the knee of Ebba Lane. "I can't do this," she whispered.

"Of course you can," Merlyn answered impatiently. "We've no choice, and you know it." His tone was sharp, but not in anger at her. He had known Cassie would not approve of his scheme, but he also knew that Nick Briarcliffe would not soon give up looking for the pair of them, particularly if he now knew the marquess was also searching for them.

"You're not to worry, dear. Ebba Lane has raised a score of babes. Master Adam is in fine hands."

Cassandra blinked away her tears the better to see the small woman who had spoken to her. From her snow-white hair to her long, slender neck and frail body encased in a simple dark gray gown to her slim feet shod in simple leather boots, she appeared to be a gently bred woman. Only her hands gave away the fact that she had lived a hard life. The knuckles were enlarged from menial labor and the arthritis of age, and protruding blue veins crisscrossed the backs. The woman noticed her stare and tucked her hands under the baby in her lap.

Cassandra was immediately contrite. "I beg your pardon. I am rude. You've been very kind to allow us in your home. It's not that I don't believe you would be good to my son; it's only that I'd not leave him with anyone, as Merlyn clearly knows." And she shot Merlyn a quick glance.

"I know you're being foolish, and after you promised to do things my way," Merlyn promptly answered.

Cassandra's dark honey eyes flashed in anger. "I've no intention of blindly following you when my heart tells me otherwise. I've let you take care of us because there's no other way. Now that we've arrived in Bath, I'm certain we can find shelter. I can still ply a needle."

"Not while you're in my care!" Merlyn shot back.

Cassandra rose to her feet. "Of all the arrogance! Who do you think you are?"

"Gently, gently, children," Ebba admonished in a quiet authoritarian tone. Her gray eyes, as soft as dove's wings, moved between them. "Shame on you, Master Ross. I never taught you such shabby manners." Her gaze switched to Cassandra in time to catch the girl's startled look at Merlyn. "And you, my dear. I'm persuaded by the very look of you that you've been taught a wife's position is to second her husband in everything."

If possible, Cassandra's eyes grew even wider, but Merlyn silenced her with a look. "As I told Ebba before you came in, Cassie, you've had little chance to be a wife, for all that you are a mother. Ebba knows that I was forced to leave you shortly after our wedding day and only recently were we reunited."

"Really?" Cassandra answered him coolly, the dimple in her chin deepening in stubbornness. "Then she knows the reason why you deserted your wife and child?"

If in doubt of her mood before, Merlyn was now certain. "We've no time for the contrariness—"

"Now, that'll be quite enough from the pair of you," Ebbe scolded, rising from her chair. "I've known Merlyn since he was a boy of ten, Cassie. While I don't approve of everything he does, I know if he left, there was good reason."

"He was in jail," Cassandra blurted out like a willful child just to see the reaction.

Ebba turned to Merlyn and shook a gnarled finger at him. "Didn't I say one day you'd pay for it?"

"You mean you know that—that he's a thief?" Cassandra asked in surprise.

Ebba gave the younger woman a slow smile. "So I should. Dirty as the River Styx he was the day we met, and cussing something fierce. Took a fresh bar of soap to that mouth before I scraped him clean."

This new look at the superbly self-confident man she knew made Cassandra laugh. "But how, where did you meet?" She looked up at Merlyn. "You told me you were a workhouse child and that none knew about your eyes."

Merlyn regarded her with a distant look and Cassandra knew she'd been reckless in her question. "It isn't a pretty story," he said, his black lashes hiding his bright sapphire eye. "I was put in the workhouse at eight years of age. At the age of ten I escaped and, in the process of trying to survive, snatched the purse of a nobleman. He caught me. Instead of turning me over to be hanged, he took me home with him, said he liked the look of me." Merlyn's voice grew colder. "It was at his country estate I met Ebba. She boxed my ears, scrubbed my neck, and taught me to read."

"Why?" Cassandra asked when he hesitated.

Merlyn gave her a sharp look. "Boys of ten are not so quick to question why. It wasn't until two years later that I learned the real purpose. My nobleman—names are unnecessary—had unnatural desires. For boys."

Cassandra's eyes darted to Ebba and he said angrily, "Don't blame Ebba. Our benefactor was careful to choose his boys as well as his employees from those who had no recourse but to accept his offers. The boys were brought in early, taught the social graces, how to read and speak languages. Then, later, they were given or sold to those with tastes that matched his own. Several reside quite comfortably in France, I'm told, a few in Italy. I did not wait my turn."

"And no one ever tried to stop the disgusting creature?" Cassandra was incredulous.

Ebba shook her head knowingly at Merlyn. "She's just a child, Merlyn. You've lived a thousand years beyond her understanding."

"It's why I must have her," Merlyn answered in a quiet voice.

She smiled at Cassandra and rocked the child in her arms. "It's like seeing Merlyn as I never knew him." Her clear brow wrinkled suddenly with dozens of creases. "I hope you were not to blame for the crime that sent him to prison. He'd steal the crown jewels for someone he loved."

"I? Oh no," Cassandra answered, embarrassed that the woman had made so much of Merlyn's small lie. "I don't like his thieving."

Ebba's brow smoothed out. "Good. Give him a half dozen little mouths to feed and make him take up a trade. He's a fine metalworker. Made me the loveliest brooch once." She lifted the corner of the kerchief at her neckline to reveal a small beautiful carbuncle set in a delicate lacing of gold filigree.

"You made this?" Cassandra asked, looking up at Merlyn in wonder and admiration. "Why do you stoop to thievery when you've so great a talent?"

Merlyn shrugged off her question. The answer would have upset her. *Because nothing I've ever done before seemed important to me. Until now.*

"You'll leave Master Adam with me until you've found a place to settle down?" Ebba prompted when the silence grew.

"It's not so simple as that," Merlyn answered, his gaze never leaving Cassandra's upturned face. "There're men after us, for reasons I'd rather not explain. We need you to keep Adam safe. Can you do that?"

"I'd like to see somebody try to take him from me!" Ebba declared in a ringing voice. "Your son's as safe with me as in his mother's arms."

"Safer, I hope," Merlyn said under his breath. To Cassandra he said, "You see the wisdom of it. We won't be far. We'll come and get him, once we've established ourselves in town."

"You mean that?" she asked.

"Of course he does," Ebba answered. "Can't you see how proud he is of his son? He's just popping to show off the boy as his."

Cassandra's doubtful glance was answered by a smug look from Merlyn. "How will you feed him without me?"

The solution was as quick and easy as Ebba's handiwork. In exactly five minutes Adam was pulling at an improvised bottle made from a goatskin pouch. "He likes Nanna's milk," Ebba said, referring to her cow.

"Perhaps," Cassandra breathed reluctantly.

"Without a doubt," Merlyn seconded and dropped a kiss on Ebba's white hair at the crown. "You're still a witch, Ebba. I knew you'd have the solution. Now, wife, we must see to ourselves."

"What do you have in mind?" Cassandra asked, almost certain she would not like his answer.

The hour was late, the day nearly spent, as Cassandra knelt on the bank of the River Avon and washed her soiled dress. Beside her in two piles were her scrubbed petticoats and Merlyn's shirt. Clad only in her sacque, she felt the breeze stir in chilly eddies across her shoulders and back. Merlyn lay on his side, one arm propping up his head, and watching. "Will they be dry by morning?"

"With a touch of a hot iron they'll be fine," she answered.

When the last flash of the red-gold sun slipped behind the hill Merlyn rose to his feet. He made no noise as he shucked his breeches. Cassandra didn't move till he dropped the garment in her lap. "That's the last," he cried as he sped past her.

Cassandra looked up in time to glimpse a broad naked back and pale buttocks before he took a flying leap into the autumn-chilled river. A moment later, his shiny head, streaming water in inky trickles, broke the surface. "The soap," he called after her.

Cassandra tossed the cake in his direction and managed a hoarse "You'll catch your death."

Mercy! she thought in stunned reflection. He was more magnificent than she remembered. Not an ounce of fat on him, yet he was full-fleshed, hard and firm, with nicely rounded buttocks, the kind a woman would long to cup in her hands. The thought made her blush furiously and she was glad of the dark. She began scrubbing his breeches, only to remember that they were in daily contact with the part of him which she so greatly admired, and her hands trembled so she was forced to stop. This was madness. They had lived side by side for weeks and she had managed to forget him as the lover who troubled her dreams and complicated her life. Except for that aborted night in Chatham, they had not so much as kissed. And, oh, how she longed to kiss that firm, warm mouth!

But no, she would not shame herself again by wanton display. Though her hands shook and her thighs were melting with desire, she would not allow herself to give in to the passion he stirred. There was only her pride left, as she'd told him before. If she gave that up he would think her a liar and weak-willed. He would tire of her, and then she . . .

"What are you thinking, Cassie?"

Cassandra looked up to find Merlyn squatting before her in the shallows. She doubted those few inches of water would have shielded any of him from her view had night not descended. But still she looked, as though she had the vision of a cat and could make out through the smoky haze of evening the shape of his long thighs, the slim hips, and the tantalizing dark triangle at the base of his belly.

Merlyn reached to touch her folded hands with one of his. "Join me."

"It's too cold," Cassandra answered weakly, vividly aware of his hand on hers.

"Can you swim?" he asked suddenly.

Cassandra giggled like a little girl caught at mischief. "I should say no, but I can. The woman who kept our house when I was younger was from Torquay and she could swim like a fish. I begged her until she taught me."

Merlyn's grasp on her hands increased. "Come on. There's none to see but me, and I'll never tell a soul."

It was a sore temptation. For days she had walked, eaten, and slept in her clothes, stopping only to rinse her hands and face when water presented itself along their journey.

"Turn your back," she said at last and rose to her feet. To her profound discomfort he also rose. When she spun away his deep laughter rolled over her. "Little prude," he called softly and dove once more into deeper water.

A moment later Cassandra shed her sacque and, turning, ran quickly to the edge of the river. She was knee-deep before the icy cold of the water registered in her nerves and she squealed. But it was too late. Merlyn had watched her progress and leaped forward to grab her by the waist and drag her fully into the water.

Cassandra gasped at the stinging cold that shocked every nerve ending and made tight goose bumps of her skin.

"Stand up and be bathed like a good girl," Merlyn instructed. Cassandra found her footing on the slippery bottom only a second before he released her and began applying the cake of soap to her shoulders.

"What do you think you're doing?" she asked in dismay.

"Bathing my wife, of course," he replied amicably as his sudsy hands slid from her shoulder blades around to the front. He lathered her, fingers playing along her collarbones and then reaching lower to cup each full breast. "Why, you are freezing!" he exclaimed, feeling the hard pebbles her nipples made in his palms.

"Don't—oh! I can bathe myself!" Cassandra cried in mortification and reached for the soap, but he held it over her head.

"No. This is a pleasure I reserve for myself. Oh no you don't!" He caught her by the wrist. "You're here now, and you'll stay until I've finished. It's not as if I haven't done this before."

Feeling part fool, part wanton, Cassandra stood quietly under his hands as he lathered every inch of her skin. Once when his hand slid intimately between her thighs she gasped, but he calmly washed each leg. Then he moved to her belly. The feather touch of his fingers here made her giggle, and before either of them realized it, they were laughing and struggling in the water like a pair of children.

At last Merlyn captured her hands by her sides and lifted her off her feet. His embrace clasped their bodies together from knee to shoulder. "Ah, Cassie, you feel so right," Merlyn murmured just before his lips touched hers.

His lips were cold from the water but after only a moment they warmed as she drew breath from him and the hot honeyed taste of his mouth filled hers. She did not shrink from the womanly instinct that guided the gentle writhing of her body, and the springy hairs on his chest teased her naked breasts until she caught her breath in tiny quick gasps of pleasure.

Merlyn waded to the bank and sank down in the thick, slick grasses with Cassandra in his arms, and then they lay on the bank, his sweet heavy weight a blanket for her nakedness. In that moment there were only the two of them and the kisses they shared in mutual delight.

She wanted this, wanted it so badly the wanting became a physical ache. Would it not be perfect, she thought, if she could whisper in his ear, *I love you?* What would he say? Would he laugh at her or merely make love to her? What then? Once she yielded to that love burning in her heart and loins, would he want her after that?

Suddenly Merlyn released her and sat up. "I'm sorry. I promised myself I wouldn't force you again." He stood up abruptly and picked up his soaking-wet breeches. "Come. Ebba will be waiting for us."

Confused and frustrated and hurt, Cassandra scrambled to her feet, too bewildered to give any thought to her nudity on the bank of the Avon. It was Merlyn who finally reached down and handed her her sacque. "You'll catch cold," he said stiffly.

Cassandra yanked it over her head so quickly she heard it tear, but she didn't care. Couldn't he tell that she was not being kissed against her will? Didn't he know that she had been as eager as he? Had he been teasing her to see how she'd react? She tried in vain to see his expression but could tell nothing in the dark.

When she had collected her belongings she fell into step beside him, but she neither spoke nor would accept his arm about her shoulders.

Merlyn moved a pace aside, all too aware of his nagging conscience. He had caught her off guard, without the protection of her good sense. The kisses were a game to her. That must be the reason she returned them so readily, he decided. She hadn't realized that they would inflame him almost past reasoning. He didn't want to frighten her. Damnation! He wanted her to learn to love him. Was that possible? He glanced at her. In profile he saw her chin was sunk nearly to her chest and he knew his misery was shared. It was his problem that he'd fallen in love with her. It was her problem that he had no intention of ever allowing her to leave him.

Ebba handed Cassandra a wicker hamper of cold ham, biscuits, and beer. "You may find Bath a more difficult place to earn a living than you think, and I'll not have it said Merlyn Ross stole to feed his own when Ebba Lane was within hailing distance."

Cassandra smiled at the woman who had in less than twenty-four hours' time proved to be a friend. "You're very fond of Merlyn, aren't you?"

Ebba patted the younger girl's shoulder. "Almost as much as you are, my dear. I don't know what's between you two young people, but you'll work it right. Merlyn's a different man. It's been my constant prayer he'd find a woman to love. He's found you at last."

Cassandra looked away from the keen gray eyes observing her. "He's never said he loves me," she whispered in a guilty breath.

"Ah," Ebba said with a smile. "So that's it. You're young. You've not known him long. He feels things more deeply than most men. Have you told him how *you* feel? Hm. I can see you haven't, and yet you've a lovely son to show for the physical pleasure you share. You must find the courage to expose your feelings. If you're waiting for him, you'll never hear it. Pride can be a form of cowardice, Cassie. Think about it."

Cassandra was thinking about it as Merlyn appeared in the doorway. "Where did those clothes come from?"

Merlyn brushed an imaginary speck of dust from his suit of dark green velvet. The coat fitted his shoulders so snugly it appeared to have been made for him. He flashed her a broad smile which showed strong white slightly uneven teeth.

"I've been to town. Left a wardrobe in care of Hugh a year ago. Do you care for the figured waistcoat?" He opened his coat to reveal a white silk waistcoat embroidered with trellis vines.

Cassandra looked dubiously at the transformation. His hair had been carefully combed and tied back with a flat satin ribbon, but the smooth raven color had not been touched by powder or curling tongs. One bright blue eye regarded her quizzically. He was so virilely handsome her heart ached with yearning, but "Who are you today?" was all she could think to say.

Merlyn's smile cracked slightly but he did not react in any other way. "Merlyn Ross the actor. I've just returned from a tour abroad. I've brought with me a gently bred young lady who found herself in dire circumstances in Venice when her duenna suddenly died. Do you sing?"

"A little," Cassandra answered.

"Delightful," Merlyn returned in a sardonic tone. "I told Hugh you are an aspiring singer."

"A whore, you mean," she said angrily. "I'm tired beyond endurance of your games. Sometimes I am your lady wife, sometimes I'm your mistress, now I'm to be a theatrical trollop. Well, I won't! I wish to be myself."

Merlyn took this in good part, aware of Ebba's eyes on them. "My love, you are my wife. Ebba knows, however, that news of my marriage would carry back to London within a week. I do not wish to draw attention to myself just yet." The look he gave her said, *Steady, Cassie, remember why we're running.*

Cassandra shook her head in resignation. "Am I to sing for my supper for Lord Mulberry?"

"A smile or two will do, I think," Merlyn answered with a wink. "Ebba's done a fine job on your gown. I only wish there'd been time to arrange for your wardrobe. I will simply say you were separated from your luggage when we docked."

"Your ability to lie astounds me," Cassandra said disapprovingly.

"I know. It's a talent," Merlyn replied blandly. "To Bath."

Chapter Thirteen

IT WAS SHORTLY PAST SEVEN A.M. WHEN CASSANDRA descended the steps of Lord Mulberry's town house in St. James's Square and hastily found seclusion in the closed sedan chair which waited for her at the curb. When the two chairmen, one in back and one in front, hoisted her up to bear her down the steep incline of Gay Street toward the Queen's Bath, she looked back. The honey-colored Bathstone walls shining in the early light consisted of twenty-five houses which boasted a Corinthian colonnade and elegant sash windows.

"I shall never tire of looking at it," she whispered to herself. The architecture, she had been told by her host, was the work of John Wood and his equally talented son, as were the Hospital of St. John the Baptist, the Chandos Buildings, and the magnificent Prior Park. All of it was new, as bright and clean as her budding hopes for the future. What better place to begin a new life than in this fairy-tale city built on the grand design of ancient Rome? It made one believe dreaming was possible again.

Just then the bells of Bath Abbey pealed out a welcoming which always alerted the city to the arrival of important newcomers. Cassandra sat back to enjoy the ride, remembering the bells had rung little more than a week ago when she and Merlyn arrived in town. Lord Mulberry had paid the ringer's fee on that occasion just as he had made a present to the city waits, who sang for them as they arrived in St. James's Square. Until that day, she had given little thought to Merlyn's prominence as an actor. Yet only yesterday, in the Pump Room, she had overheard two ladies discussing his last appearance on the London stage two years earlier.

"Quite as powerful an Othello as any," the young woman had confided to her companion. "If not for that disfiguring patch, he might give Garrick a run for his money."

Cassandra smiled to herself as she rearranged the stiff folds of her bathing garment made of yellow canvas. The last ten days had been like paradise. If not for the fact that she missed Adam with an aching that matched the pain of her milk-swollen breasts, all would be perfect.

"I will ask Merlyn to take me to Ebba tonight," she said to herself.

The thought of Merlyn made her smile momentarily waver. She had not missed Lord Mulberry's lingering gaze upon her when Merlyn introduced them. He thought them lovers, no doubt. The fact that they did not insist upon bedrooms on the same floor had not quite erased that look, but in the days following it was tempered by speculation of a new sort that made her equally uncomfortable. She did not care so much what Lord Mulberry thought as much as she cared that Merlyn not be embarrassed. For that reason, she saw little of Merlyn beyond their formal meetings in the Pump Room after the daily ritual of the baths.

The separation had given her time to think, time to reflect on Ebba's words and to understand the truth of the many conflicting feelings that had made a maze of her mind and a mystery of her actions even to herself. Just the night before, as she lay in bed remembering the vivid beauty of Merlyn's eyes, she had come to a momentous decision. She was glad that it was reached in the quiet solitude of this span of days, far from the mercurial hypnotic presence of the man it concerned.

"Here you are, then, miss," one of the chairmen called as her chair was set down before the Queen's Bath.

The metallic odor of the natural hot springs water wafted into the street to meet her, making her wrinkle her nose.

A few minutes later she was wading waist-deep in hot water that wilted her linen cap and tinged her cheeks with blood. The long sleeves of her gown dragged in the water, but the voluminous skirt billowed about her like an umbrella so that no part of it clung to her body to reveal her shape. All about her women laughed and chatted in the communal bath, but she held herself apart. The attack in Chatham was fresh in her mind. The marquess was not a man to give up easily. Her narrow escape would only intensify his determination to find them. It was for that reason, also, that she refrained from accepting Lord Mulberry's offer to secure a maid for her. Until the swelling of her breasts disappeared, she feared the conclusions that would be drawn from them.

She did not linger long in the bath. The water, though lower in temperature than that of the King's Bath, which both Merlyn and Lord Mulberry preferred, made her sleepy and dull-witted, and she needed every wit sharp to face Merlyn. As she ascended a private stairway leading from the water pool she was met by two pleasant-faced women who served as guides. One unfastened her canvas gown while the other flung a flannel nightgown over her head, keeping her covered at all times. The women never saw their customers unclothed.

When Cassandra reached a dry step, slippers were placed on her feet and then she was led into a slip where a great fire blazed. As she sat in silence to steam dry, she plotted what her first move should be. She must find a private moment with Merlyn. A slow womanly smile spread across her damp face. No, it must be longer than a moment. If her desire was granted, they would need the uninterrupted hours of a night.

Thirty minutes later, wrapped in a woolen blanket, she reentered her sedan chair, which had been brought around for this purpose, and then her chairmen appeared, slipped their staves in place, and bore her back to St. James's Square.

Cassandra did not linger in her warm woolen cocoon

but quickly donned the loose muslin gown laid out on her bed. She was to meet Merlyn and Lord Mulberry in the Pump Room precisely at nine A.M. When the last of her heavy dark hair was piled up on her head and a bonnet secured beneath her chin with its ribbon, she drank a cup of hot chocolate and nibbled a biscuit before turning and hurrying back downstairs.

"Really, Hugh. You press me unfairly about the girl. She's nothing more than one of my good works."

Hugh Mulberry, Earl of Glastonbury, eyed his walking companion dispassionately. "You've done no good works that I'm aware of, Ross."

Merlyn chuckled. "Then say I'm turning over a new leaf in my middle years. Miss Lane," he continued, using Cassie's new surname, "is a refreshing young lady, don't you agree?"

Hugh lightly fingered his pronounced widow's peak, a habit that betrayed his thoughtful mood as well as drew attention to his extraordinary eccentricity. For, as all Bath and London knew, the young lord had adopted the remarkable habit of wearing his own hair dressed as a wig. His hair of natural rich brown had been waved and powdered to resemble a scratch-bob. The severe but excellent cut of his clothes was offset by his fondness for rings, which covered all but the thumbs of each hand. These caught Merlyn's eye, but he resisted the impulse. He did not steal from those he liked, and the number was so few that he was seldom bothered by the fact.

"Tell me why you've brought her to Bath in the off season," Hugh continued after a moment. "If she's as talented as you say, she should be put to the test in London."

"Ah, that's the rub," Merlyn answered. "She's not professionally trained." At the young lord's knowing look he added, "That is, she's afraid of crowds. Haven't you noticed how she hides herself?"

Hugh nodded a greeting at a passing couple but did not check his stride. "I've noticed. I thought perhaps you had warned her away from me."

"Should I?" Merlyn's black brows drew together. "She's no lightskirt, my lord. I'll have that understood."

Hugh exclaimed in mild surprise, "Sits the wind in that quarter?"

Merlyn's expression betrayed vexation. "I will say I'm taken by a certain charm in the lady, but I have not paid court to her and would ask that you remember that."

The two men regarded one another in silence. Nearly of the same height, the difference lay in their expressions. Lord Mulberry had a well-featured face that most often displayed a faint boredom for the world around him, but it was etched in concentration at the moment. Merlyn's face, not so well favored but more immediately compelling, was a little angry.

"Very well, Ross. I'll defer to you for the time being," Hugh said finally. "However, I shall proceed as the future dictates. I mean to know the lady better. If she should betray an interest also . . ."

Merlyn smiled charmingly. "Of course. The field is open. I meant nothing more."

It was thus that Cassandra found them, two elegantly but casually dressed young men, facing one another in the middle of the Pump Room. Entering from the abbey churchyard through one of the five arched doorways, she walked over to where they stood beside the Pump's marble font.

"I hope I did not detain you," she said breathlessly, stopping by Merlyn's side.

Both men turned with delighted expressions to greet her.

"You appear to have taken well to the atmosphere of Bath," Merlyn said as he took her hand and brushed it with his lips.

For an instant his sapphire eye met her burnished gold gaze and Cassandra knew the breathless sensation she often felt when there were only the two of them. Her cheeks were tinted pink by the lingering heat of her visit to Queen's Bath and the curls at her temples beneath the brim of her black straw hat enhanced her femininity.

Cassandra smiled at him, pleased by the admiration in his gaze. One quick look about the room would have confirmed her suspicions that she was less expensively gowned than most of the ladies present, yet she knew she looked her best.

"Miss Lane," Hugh intoned warmly, and also saluted her hand.

"Lord Mulberry," she acknowledged with a shy smile. His eyes, the serene gray of a cloudy day, were fixed with more than casual regard upon her, and the color in her cheeks deepened.

"We were just commenting upon which should be

your first opportunity to display your talent," Hugh said, watching her closely.

"Talent?" she asked blankly, seeing Merlyn's warning look too late.

"I am told you sing?" Hugh inquired politely.

"Oh, that." Cassandra gave Merlyn a blighting glance. "I regret to say it was the folly born of desperate circumstance. When Mr. Ross found me I was anxious to secure funds to return to England."

"But you found the funds?" Hugh suggested. Only his pleasant smile struck the sinister undertone from the question.

"Yes, Mr. Ross has proved a vast friend, though I don't know when I'll be able to repay him properly," she answered hesitantly, wondering all the while why Merlyn left her to roast slowly over this questioning.

"Perhaps it is more than enough repayment to know he has helped a damsel in distress. We of the theater are incurable romantics, I fear," Hugh said, adroitly turning back from the probing of his earlier comments. He was satisfied when Merlyn did not come to her aid. Certainly Ross would not have let the girl stammer painfully if he feared she might betray their liaison.

"Hugh, dear boy! And—can it be? Merlyn Ross!"

The three turned simultaneously to see a strikingly beautiful young woman coming toward them through an archway of the Pump Room. It was a measure of her belief in her own beauty that the woman wore her titian hair unpowdered. In contrast, she dressed in the height of the beau monde, in a satin gown of pale blue lined at the bodice and sleeves with gold and with an underskirt of white taffeta ruffled at the hem.

All of this was noted in an instant. Even before she reached them Cassandra saw that the woman's blue eyes, as bright as diamonds, were fixed on Merlyn. When she reached him, she threw her arms brazenly about his neck in a manner that sent a wave of astonishment through the Pump's visitors.

Cassandra believed herself to remain the only one unmoved by the demonstration. This error was corrected by Lord Mulberry.

"My lady, you've crushed your nosegay," he observed in a mildly humorous tone just before he, too, received the lilac-scented embrace of the redheaded woman.

"Enough, Caroline. Beau Nash will have us thrown out," Hugh protested halfheartedly as he disengaged her arms from about his neck.

"Lud! That dull man," she exclaimed in a voice that carried even into the gallery where six musicians attempted to provide a pleasant background for the conversation below. "Don't scold me, Hugh. Oh! I should call you Lord Mulberry in public, shouldn't I?" She gave him a arch look that made the young nobleman uncomfortable.

"Really, Caroline. You'll say anything to shock your admirers. Now behave while I introduce you to my houseguest. May I present Caroline Lambert, Miss Lane? Perhaps you are familiar with her work? She has quite taken the London stage by storm these two years."

Cassandra did not miss the importance given her name in the introduction, and neither did Miss Lambert. "Miss Lane, did you say?" the actress asked in a voice dripping with false friendliness. "Haven't we met before? You are from London, perhaps a niece of Lord Mulberry's?"

Cassandra smiled. *Cat,* she thought. Yet something puzzled her, too, something terribly familiar about the woman, yet just beyond her recall. She chanced then to glance at Merlyn, and he, too, appeared deep in thought, for a scowl rode his brow. "No, I am not Lord Mulberry's kin, and I'm afraid I am a country mouse. Yet I am happy to make your acquaintance, Miss Lambert. Lord Mulberry's flattery is noted for its sincerity."

This seemed to momentarily mollify the tall, voluptuous woman who had completely won the attention of the entire assembly at her arrival.

"What brings you to the country, Caroline?" Merlyn inquired. "The season has begun."

"I've been sent here to rusticate," Caroline said in a throaty timbre, her long lids sweeping shut over her eyes. "I caught a chill two weeks ago. Lost my voice entirely, just two nights before I was to open. Nothing would seem to cure it. Finally, I knew I must retire to Bath to take the cure."

"You mean your theater manager would not succumb to your blandishments to alter your contract," Hugh supplied amicably, laughing outright as her eyes flashed in anger.

"You're a cad, Hugh," she snapped.

"Nothing so mean-spirited, my dear," Hugh answered. "You forget I've a finger on the theatrical pulse. Wind of your squabble with the play's backers precedes you. They would not come to heel, so you're playing the sickbed miss. Bravo, I say. Let them stew a few weeks with no proper lead to start their season. They'll soon see reason."

"Do you really think so?" she asked, then answered herself. "Of course they'll see reason. They'll come running out here by the end of the week. And I'll refuse to see them at first, pleading illness. After a few days they'll be begging me to return. And I may condescend . . . for twice my original demand."

Cassandra did not like the brilliant mercenary gleam in the actress's eye, but she smiled politely as the two gentlemen guffawed.

"You never change, Caroline," Merlyn observed. "You only grow more bewitching with time."

"And you, my lothario," she purred, tucking her arm through one of his. "How do you grow with time? I seem to remember you grew well and fine and quickly."

Hugh had the grace to look embarrassed, but Merlyn favored her with a lecherous smile. "Softly, jade. There are tender ears about."

For the second time Caroline looked fully at Cassandra. "You are a friend of Merlyn's?" she bluntly questioned.

"We are acquainted," Cassandra replied more coolly than she felt.

"Merlyn is responsible for Miss Lane's presence in my home," Hugh added helpfully, an innocent look on his face.

"Really?" The word held a note of challenge.

"You're not to sharpen your claws on children," Merlyn admonished her with a grin, then turned to his friend. "When is your concert breakfast to begin,

Hugh? The waters have left the taste of rotten eggs on my tongue and a vast emptiness in my middle."

Hugh looked from Caroline to Cassandra. "You have not yet drunk your three glasses."

Cassandra shuddered delicately. "I own I'd prefer a cup of hot chocolate."

"Then it's time. Caroline, you must certainly join us," Hugh added gallantly.

"By all means. Merlyn and I have much to catch up on." And she tugged on the man's arm to draw him ahead of the other two. "You really must allow me to tell you of the most extraordinary gossip circulating about London. It all began at an occasion I attended up in Derbyshire last summer," Cassandra heard the woman murmur as they moved away.

"Is something wrong, Miss Lane?" Hugh inquired at Cassandra's sudden gasp.

She turned a pale face to the man beside her, not really seeing him for the tumult of her thoughts. "No—that is, I think the waters were too warm for me this morning. Perhaps I should have warmed myself more thoroughly."

She took the arm he offered and leaned on it a little. Clammy perspiration broke out on her upper lip, and her heart galloped with fear. She now remembered where she'd seen the red-haired beauty. Caroline Lambert had been one of the marquess's guests at the christening ball!

Surely Merlyn remembered, Cassandra told herself. He had been at Briarcliffe that evening, too. Did the actress know nothing of Merlyn's disguise as the Comte de Valure? Perhaps, and perhaps the woman did not recognize her either. Was that why Merlyn had deliberately drawn the woman's interest to himself?

Cassandra's worried glance moved to pick out the couple moving rapidly away from her, and she frowned in annoyance. Caroline Lambert's flame-bright head was inclined intimately toward Merlyn's shoulder. She preferred to return to St. James's Square, but she knew the only way her questions could be answered was by following them to the concert breakfast.

Dish after dish of lovely exotic fare passed before Cassandra's view, but she could barely maintain the presence of mind to place a few items on her plate. The thought of consuming lobster patties and crimped salmon, broiled kidneys and dried haddock, before so potent a threat as Caroline Lambert made her feel ill. Instead, she sipped hot chocolate and nibbled an apricot tart which tasted like dry leaves in her mouth.

Suddenly, Cassandra heard her name called pointedly and she looked down the length of the table to see the actress's diamond-chip eyes on her. "I said, you are a singer?" Caroline Lambert questioned in a tone that implied she had asked the question before.

"I am tolerably able," Cassandra replied with a half smile.

"Then, by all means, you must sing for us," the actress said. The younger woman's start made her smile deepen. "My dear, you would not be so boorish as to decline a request made by your host." She gave Hugh an encouraging smile. "Do ask her, Lord Mulberry. I'm eaten with curiosity to hear your new songbird."

The hackles rose in Cassandra's neck, and she would

have declined in no uncertain terms had she not spied Merlyn's pained expression.

He thinks I can't do it, she realized in pique. *He picks a profession for me out of thin air and is embarrassed now because he believes me incapable.*

Cassandra rose to her feet and turned to Hugh, who sat by her side. "Is it the custom, Lord Mulberry?"

Hugh stood when she rose. "It is. The informality of Bath allows that any person, even a guest, may publicly perform for the entertainment of all."

"Then, if it would please you, my lord," she said sweetly, "I will sing." She did not trust herself to glance a second time at Merlyn. *Let him stew,* she thought.

The little orchestra which had been hired for the day by their host was composed of two violins, a bassoon, a horn, a viola, and a harpsichord. Cassandra allowed Lord Mulberry to lead her to them for an introduction.

It was quickly arranged that she would sing one of her favorite pieces by Christian Bach, the youngest of the famous musical family. It was a gay, light tune, fitting for a morning's entertainment. Only once, when she turned to face the twenty-odd breakfasters, did her confidence suffer a crack. Caroline Lambert had once more threaded her arm through Merlyn's and she was studiously turned away from the stage, her lips raised to whisper in Merlyn's ear. It was Lord Mulberry who encouraged her with a smile and a nod.

From the opening bars Cassandra knew she had chosen wisely. Accompanied only by the harpsichord, her voice rose clear and high over the assembly and the murmur of voices died almost at once. The constriction of fear at the base of her throat eased as the familiar words sang forth. She did not try for exciting embellishments, trills, or warbling scales to enhance her audience's appreciation. Good sense warned her not to risk a mistake with an unrehearsed accompaniment.

Even before the last notes died away, she saw Lord Mulberry rise to his feet, a broad smile on his face and his hands raised in applause. But it was not his reaction she feared. Nibbling her lower lip in anxiety, she swung her dark honey gaze to Merlyn.

He, too, had risen to his feet, but he was not smiling. Only Cassandra could see fully the expression on his face, and it made her knees weaken. There was no denying the look. The passion that made other men smile foolishly or turned their expressions to leering masks did not so mar his. The concentrated power of that single sapphire eye held—her heart quickened in hope that she was right—longing as well as desire.

Cassandra released her tremulous lip, wondering if the desires of her heart were so plainly written on her features for all the assembly to see.

"You've an excellent voice, my dear," Lord Mulberry said when he'd come to stand before her.

He blocked Cassandra's view of Merlyn in that instant, and it was as if he had eclipsed the sun. Her senses drained of the heady magic of Merlyn Ross's gaze. "Thank you, my lord. I fear I'm a trifle rusty. It's been some while," she murmured to cover the conflagration of emotions passing over her.

"Yes. Isn't she clever?" Caroline Lambert said, coming up behind her host. She favored the younger woman with a stingy smile. "You may do quite well in something light, comic opera, perhaps. But, my dear, I must warn you to do something about your dress. Your stature is indifferent, and the color of your hair common. Pretty singers are a shilling a dozen. You must cultivate originality. Don't you agree, Merlyn?"

Cassandra's treacherous pulse raced out of control as she again met Merlyn's look. But this time, his was cool, indifferent to a point that made Cassandra wish, suddenly, impulsively, to slap his face. How could he be so calm a scarce moment after she would have sworn he had been as moved as she?

"You will favor us with something else?" was all he said. A flickering of the actress's lids made Cassandra smile. So, the woman thought more of her talent than she admitted.

"Yes, do," Lord Mulberry urged. "Something gay, something lovely."

Cassandra looked from him to Merlyn. "Something romantic?" she suggested, and he answered softly in a quote, "'A love song, a love song. . . . Ay, ay; I care not for good life.'"

The cue gave Cassandra the courage to be daring, and she turned back to the musicians. "Do you know 'O Mistress Mine'?"

The song was easy to sing and Cassandra unabashedly concentrated her full heart on the words, hoping one particular listener would hear the invitation in her voice.

> *O mistress mine, where are you roaming?*
> *O, stay and hear—your true love's coming,*
>   *That can sing both high and low.*
> *Trip no further, pretty sweeting;*

Journeys end in lovers' meeting,
  Every wise man's son doth know.

What is love? 'Tis not hereafter;
Present mirth hath present laughter;
  What's to come is still unsure.
In delay there lies no plenty—
Then come kiss me, sweet-and-twenty.
  Youth's a stuff will not endure.

Not until the song was begun did she realize just how apt the words were. They were surely at journey's end and she now as never before desired this lovers' meeting. Yet what lay before them was unsure. Perhaps their coil would come right as easily as it did for the lovers in Mr. Shakespeare's *Twelfth Night*.

For a moment, at the song's end, she closed her eyes. When she opened them and looked toward Lord Mulberry's table her spirits plummeted. Merlyn's chair was vacant. Only just did she catch sight of his broad back as he strode through the exit. In the next moment she was surrounded by a throng of vocal admirers. Confused by Merlyn's actions, she mechanically acknowledged the many words of praise. At last they melted away and Caroline Lambert's face swam before her. One angry suspicious look from the woman made Cassandra's heart soar. Merlyn had left without the actress, and whatever explanation he had given had failed to soothe the woman's pride.

"Well, my dear, you've quite outdone yourself." Caroline smirked. "You've won the house and managed to scare off my leading man in the same breath.

Really, Miss Lane, you should practice your theatrics on lesser game. Merlyn Ross need hardly wait for favors thrown out by amateurs."

"Caroline," Hugh Mulberry said dampeningly, "you've said quite enough. Merlyn had a noon engagement for a private game of faro." He turned to Cassandra, a smile of tender regret on his mouth. "Forgive me for being so frank, Miss Lane, but Merlyn confided in me that he did not fare as well on the Continent as he had hoped. He earns his living by gaming these days. While it's not as noble a profession as his first, it serves to pay bills."

"Lud! I told him he'd never make a go of it in Paris," Caroline exclaimed in glee. "He doesn't know a thing about the language and his accent is abominable."

Cassandra said nothing to this. If Caroline did not know that Merlyn in the guise of the Comte de Valure spoke French like a native, this was certainly not the moment to enlighten her.

She gently pressed her fingers around Hugh's slim hand. "I'm pleased you enjoyed my small effort, my lord. If you will excuse me, I am to meet Mrs. Holmes and Mrs. Pickwick at the lending library. I hope to see you again, Miss Lambert," she added as an afterthought.

"But you will, my dear," the actress cooed. "Hugh has invited me to stay at St. James's Square, and Merlyn was anxious to second the invite."

Touché! Cassandra smiled, nodded, and turned on her heel. Merlyn had seconded that cat's invitation, had he? Well, that was all the more reason for her to speak with him at once.

But that was not to be. When the interminable afternoon dragged slowly toward dusk, Cassandra returned to St. James's Square to find that Lord Mulberry had planned an impromptu party to honor Caroline's surprise appearance in Bath.

The final surprise was in entering the salon at dinnertime to find that ten of the eleven guests were male. Cassandra had to begrudgingly admire Caroline's gown. It was of the sheerest turquoise silk with an underskirt of pink. Turquoise ribbons decorated the elbows and formed a row down the front of the low-cut bodice. Once, when she leaned over the dinner table to catch at Hugh's sleeve, her breasts nearly popped free of their confinement.

At that moment Cassandra looked up at Merlyn, who sat across the table, and discovered his sapphire eye hard upon her. *Tonight,* he mouthed and then looked away so quickly she wasn't sure he'd formed the word.

For the rest of the meal Cassandra tried in vain to catch his eye, but it was as if he knew it and deliberately never looked across at her again. After the meal, he took Caroline by the elbow and steered her into the music salon. For the next hour, Merlyn stood and turned pages, smiling down every now and then into the actress's face, while she subjected the company to a recital of her own.

When at last Cassandra felt able to make her regrets and escape upstairs without offending either her host or the center of everyone's attention, she was so angry she slammed the door and threw down her fan in disgust.

"What does he want?" she fumed. "Did he say

'tonight,' or did I imagine it? And what does it mean? Am I to waylay him in the hall or . . .''

Cassandra paused. Had he invited her to seek him out?

"Well, I won't," she muttered, reaching for the lacing at the back of her figured muslin gown. "I would be a fool to be found roaming the halls when all are supposed asleep. What if I should encounter Lord Mulberry?" She drew the gown over her head and laid it on a chair. "If he thinks to play games with me after he's cuddled that overblown trollop before my eyes—"

Cassandra stopped in midsentence, appalled at herself. She sounded every inch the jealous wife. She swallowed, choked, and burst into giggles. Well, that was how she felt. She had watched for the past two hours while the man she loved fawned over that actress, smiling down tender smiles that should have been hers, giving intimate little pats to Miss Lambert's arm or waist that once he had given her. She was jealous. She wanted to rage at the other woman, to tell her to keep her coquettish ways for other men, that Merlyn Ross belonged to her. He was hers by right of a bond they shared, the dangers, and their child.

Cassandra's mouth drooped. Adam! Oh, how she missed him, his glossy black curls and pink mouth and wiggly damp fingers that caught in her hair and grabbed at her breast.

"I must see him. Tomorrow!" she vowed in a whisper.

It took her no longer than the time it took to change into her night sacque of fine gauzy linen and slippers to determine what she would do. Grabbing up her cloak, she pulled the hood over her hair and slipped out into the dark hallway.

Heart in her mouth, she made her way to the servants' stairway and climbed to Merlyn's floor. Which door was his? In panic she put her hand on the first door handle. It gave without a sound. A moment later she gazed upon stacks and stacks of luggage. Trunks and bags lay open everywhere, spilling petticoats and gowns and slippers onto the carpets. Caroline Lambert's room. She shut it at once, grateful that the actress was still belowstairs. Perverseness of nature made her choose the door just beyond on the same side. This latch, too, gave instantly under the pressure of her hand and the faint scent of vetiver greeted her. Cassandra pursed her lips in annoyance. Merlyn's room was adjacent to Caroline's. Who had arranged that?

A noise farther down the hall made her scoot inside a scant second before she heard voices. Caroline's throaty laughter was unmistakable. The room was not dark, for a fire blazed below the marble mantel. On tiptoe, Cassandra made her way to the huge four-poster bed and stepped into the shadow of its hangings just as the door opened partway.

"What do you mean, I'd better not come in?" Caroline's petulant voice inquired. "I don't care a fig what Hugh thinks. He knows I'd sooner warm your bed than his. Besides, he's had his eye on your little squab the evening long. I doubt he'll know we're here."

Cassandra caught her breath in outrage, but then Merlyn's deep smooth voice said, "You try me hard, Caroline. I think you like to see me suffer. If Hugh were to find us *flagrante delicto,* I'd find myself without a home. For all his urbane manners, he's as jealous as the next man, and you are here as his guest. Besides, I need Hugh's good graces just now. I'm out of work. Two years away from London has taken its toll. I need a part, a good one, the kind Hugh could write for me if he's of the frame of mind. I'll not spoil it, not even for an hour between your luscious thighs. In London, *chérie*. 'Tis a promise."

Cassandra silently ground her teeth as she heard the pleasurable moans of a long kiss. Her hands balled into fists as she flayed Merlyn in her thoughts. How dare he promise to bed that strumpet in London sometime hence. Reprobate! Scoundrel! Libertine!

Several short smacking kisses followed the first torrid exchange before Cassandra heard Caroline say, "You will at least escort me to my room. You may be tempted to change your mind."

"I'm certain to be tempted," Merlyn replied with a chuckle just before the door shut behind them.

Cassandra let out her breath in a ragged sob. "How could I have been so foolish!" she whispered angrily. "To think that this time it would be different. Are there no true men in all this great world?" The pain of this fresh betrayal made her head pound and she slumped down on the bed, holding on to a post for support.

The tears were quickly spent and a calmer temper replaced them. Cassandra shrugged out of her cloak and wiped her face with her hands. The reasons for her coming were not abated by her discovery. She still needed Merlyn's help to return to Ebba and Adam. And her warning against Caroline was more necessary than ever.

That she had been tricked by love once again was a private matter, a matter that no one but herself knew. It did not make the pain any less, but the shame was less. She would not run and hide her face in her own pillow. She would stay and make Merlyn hear her out—whenever he chose to return.

Chapter Fourteen

MERLYN SLAMMED THE DOOR TO HIS ROOM WITH NO thought for the other sleepers in the house and gave his neckcloth a savage wrench. "Damnation! Where could she have gone?"

He swore under his breath as he jerked the crisp linen from his neck with one hand and began working open his waistcoat with the other. For the better part of an hour he'd cooled his heels in Cassie's room, but she wasn't to be found.

He shrugged out of coat and waistcoat together and flung them carelessly onto a chair before stomping over to the mantel, which he grasped tightly in both hands until his knuckles whitened. There was only one explanation: Cassie had gone to Lord Mulberry's rooms. And yet his heart would not quite let him credit it.

"She wouldn't! My shy little dove fears to singe her wings. She couldn't expect Hugh to treat her more kindly than I. By God! If she's giving comfort to her host when she offered invitation to me . . ." The tirade veered off into profanity spoken low and methodically.

The slammed door had awakened Cassandra, who now sat up in bed with a great yawn. It took her only a second to realize where she was, and the realization made her stomach flip-flop as she heard the string of curses being dealt out by the room's owner. Immediately, she leaped from the bed into the shadow of the bed hangings, her satin slippers making only a whisper of sound on the carpet. It was enough.

Merlyn's head swiveled around at the sound and another curse whispered past his clenched teeth. "Well," he demanded harshly after a moment. "Don't coquette, Caroline. Present yourself."

O God, she begged silently, *don't let him turn me out.* She moved, a shadow separating itself from the others, hesitated, and then stepped fully into the fire's light.

"Cassie!"

"Good evening, Merlyn," she voiced in false calm, but she could not smile at the angry man. She cast a glance about the room, measuring the distance to the door. "It's uncommonly cold," she said inconsequentially.

Merlyn's gaze lowered from her face to the thin night rail she wore. "You wore nothing more?"

Cassandra heard the astonishment in his voice and realized that she was not the only one uncertain of herself. She moved forward two steps. "I wanted to talk," she began, "but if you're—"

Merlyn's look stopped her. She did not know how transparent her gown appeared in the firelight. The full ripe thrust of her chilled breasts stood out in sharp relief beneath, every curve of her revealed for his warm regard.

"Perhaps another time," she added as the silence played havoc with her nerves. Why, oh, why had she not waited? He was obviously in search of Caroline. Why, he had just addressed her by the woman's name. The thought sent anger gushing through her veins, loosening her tongue. "I didn't know that you expected other company this night."

When he did not reply she reached for her cloak and started toward the door. Nothing, she told herself, would make her stay after the insult she had just suffered. But Merlyn moved from the mantel when he saw what she was about. Two long strides brought him before her and he halted her with a heavy hand on each shoulder.

"Don't be an idiot," he said in the cold, flat tone Cassandra had learned to fear.

Dread crept over her and she trembled beneath the hard grasp of his lean fingers. "You're hurting me," she said.

"Am I?" Merlyn seemed to consider this a moment, his fingers still on her flesh. Finally they loosened and his hands slid down from her shoulders to her wrists, which he clasped gently. "Forgive me, I'm out of sorts. But that's passing." She thought he nearly smiled, but the twitch straightened into a hard line. "Where have you been this last hour?"

She swallowed. There was no sense in lying. "Here."

"All the time?" he insisted with a gentle shake of her wrists.

"Entirely," Cassandra answered.

Something in her inflection alerted Merlyn. "An hour. Then you heard—"

"Heard Miss Lambert's warm invitation to share her bed," she finished for him, allowing her anger to show. "Did you find it—enjoyable?" she asked defiantly.

For the first time he smiled, and it was Cassandra's heart that did a nervous flip-flop this time. "Well, well," he said with a hint of mockery and good humor. "This would seem to be my cardinal day. The Fates present me with two tempting offers, and I nearly missed out on both."

Cassandra tried to shrug off his touch, but he would not release her hands. "I'm no fool, Merlyn. I heard you leave with that—that wretched woman. Don't pretend you've stood in the hallway this hour trying to gather your courage."

"Softly, my lover," he cautioned in amusement. "or that wretched woman may hear you." His laughter was gentle, taking away the sting of his taunt. "Would you believe, Cassie, that I've spent the last hour sitting before your fire, waiting and gnashing my teeth? I, too, had hopes for this evening. You wanted to talk?"

Cassandra's gaze fell before his and fastened on his shirtfront. Slowly she became aware that his shirt was open nearly to the waist. His skin appeared very tan against the starched white linen. The impulsive desire to reach through the opening and touch the crisp black curls was so strong that she raised a hand.

"Don't."

The softly uttered word made her start and her eyes rose to his face once more. He was not smiling now.

The hard ridges of his high cheekbones showed prominently in his harsh-featured face. "There'll be no turning back if your small hand touches my flesh."

All at once Cassandra understood with certainty that he had not been with Caroline but had gone to seek her own bed. The knowledge sang through her like the flush of strong spirits, and she smiled the smile of triumph. "I came to tell you something," she said softly.

Merlyn's belly quivered at the sound of her voice. "What was it you wanted to say, Cassie?"

Cassandra took a breath. He was so close his wide shoulders blocked her view of the room beyond him. It was as if the world had ceased to exist beyond the length and breadth of him. And she wanted it so. It made possible the words she spoke to him now.

"I love you."

She saw the pulse quicken beneath the brown skin at the base of his throat, but he said nothing. The moment stretched out until she began to wonder if she had spoken at all. "Perhaps I'd better go," she began, but his hands moved; one caught her chin and the other threaded its fingers through the heavy weight of her hair at the back of her head.

He tilted her face up to meet his. "You've been a long time learning what I've known in my heart always," he said. "No, I'll not spoil the perfection of your wondrous vow with glib words. 'My love's more richer than my tongue,'" he quoted softly as his mouth came down on hers.

His lips were hard with desire, their touch ungentle, but Cassandra did not care. There was only the wonder of their magic, the fire of their branding, their fiery mystery that made this man the one, above all else, she loved. ˉ

She heard the whispered rustle of her gown as it slipped from her shoulders to the floor, and then the cool night air stirred on her bare skin. Oh, but she was warm, and warmer still, wherever his hands touched her. She melted into his touch, opening her mouth for his skillful tongue and offering the weight of her body against his.

He might have possessed all the skill of witchcraft and magic of his wizard's name, for now she knew this moment had been inevitable. From the moment she had rushed headlong into his arms in Newgate and touched this dark, inscrutable man, she should have known that her safety and her doom were bound up in the violent tenderness that was Merlyn Ross.

They spoke no words, the time too long since last touching, the moment too full of anticipated fruition. Hands and mouths, bodies urgently eager to possess and be possessed, pressed and touched and kissed. Then there was only the powerful demand of his strong, hard body on hers and her astonishment at the sweet, fierce invasion of her body that made one union of their beings.

When the moment was not so full and Merlyn's dark head lay quietly against the lush softness of her breast, Cassandra knew, without the needed reassurance of his voice, that she loved and was loved equally in return.

The peace did not last long. After only minutes his silky black head moved against her, raised a little so that he could tease a nipple with his lips, and she felt him harden against her thigh. "No, wait, love," she whispered raggedly when he raised up on his elbows. "There's something I must tell you before I forget it."

Merlyn took her hand from his shoulder and teasingly bit into the fleshy part of her palm before he said, "I thought all had been said."

Cassandra moaned in pleasure as his tongue licked the sensitive tips of her fingers. "Oh, Merlyn—stop!"

He raised his head and looked into her flushed face. "What is it, Cassie?"

Cassandra smiled and touched his cheek, wanting to touch all of him, to roam freely and confidently over his warm, hard body as he did hers, but she held the passion in check, her trembling fingers still on his cheek. "I don't want to say these things. I would forget all—but for Adam."

"What is wrong?" Merlyn sat up higher, his black brows drawn low. "Has Ebba sent a message? Is he ill?"

Cassandra shook her head, indescribably pleased that he should care as passionately for their child as she. "No, but my troubles concern him. I know Caroline Lambert. That is, I have seen her before."

Merlyn nodded once. "In Derbyshire, at Briarcliffe."

"You remembered, and yet you said nothing?"

Merlyn let his fingers roam idly over the satin skin of her breasts. "What could I say? Should I have asked her if she remembered me dressed as the Come de Valure? Come, Cassie, it was enough that she did not."

"What of me? She said I was familiar. Tomorrow, perhaps, she will begin to remember why."

Merlyn chuckled. "If Caroline remembers anything, it will be that I was ungentlemanly enough to decline to share her bed. That, my love, is what will concern her most."

Cassandra's anxious look changed to thin-lipped annoyance. "Don't you dare speak to me of that trollop and her lures. I heard her, remember? And—I heard you kiss her. It didn't sound as if you were eager to be quit of her. Luscious thighs, indeed!"

Merlyn smothered his laughter in the valley between her breasts. "Oh, love! You've changed. My frightened little mouse can roar." His hand moved from her waist to her hip and down to the inner velvet of her thighs. "Here's all the lushness I desire."

"Mer—lyn," she breathed unsteadily as his fingers began to work their magic again. "Listen, I am serious. She may remember. I heard her begin to tell you at the Pump Room about that very trip. She said there were rumors circulating in London."

Merlyn frowned. "That's true. Nick has taken a beating in the gazettes. Those cartooners can be the very devil when they seek to lampoon a fellow. No names were named, but conclusions were quickly drawn when the announcements of Adam's birth made the society columns. Perhaps I shouldn't tell you, but Caroline says your sainted Nick has fought several duels over the matter."

"Oh no!" Cassandra shook her head, the exquisite pleasure of the last moments fading. "I didn't want any of this to happen. I told the marquess his scheme was a mad one. Adam is my child, mine alone."

Merlyn bent and kissed her mouth. "Not quite, my love. I seem to remember a night in Newgate—no, don't turn from me. Once I wondered if I should be ashamed of that act. But I've seen how dearly you love the child I gave you, and I've never been sorry since. You belong to me, Cassie, just as Adam does. Never again can Nicholas—who was no husband—come between us." He cupped her face with his hands. "You will stay with me, live with me as my wife."

"I want that," Cassandra answered. "But it can't be here, as I'd hoped. We must go where the marquess can't find us."

"Precisely." And Merlyn kissed her again. "I've been thinking of France. In few days, a week or two at most, I should have won enough at the faro tables—Did you hear something?"

Cassandra had heard a soft click like the opening of a door, but when she and Merlyn sat up and looked around the edge of the bed hangings, his door was shut. Merlyn hopped nimbly from bed and went to the door and listened. After a moment he turned the key in the lock and came back to bed. As he looked down at Cassie his expression turned curiously hard. "I'll have no disruptions this night. I want you here to make love to as much and as often I can manage it."

Cassandra lifted her arms to him. "Come, then, my love. Whatever you want."

Merlyn's face lit anew with pleasure and he knelt quickly over her. "What, do you not demand protestations of love? Will you not need assurances that it is your bed alone I shall seek after this?"

Cassandra shook her head. "I've asked too much of love before. I'll accept what's given me this time."

Merlyn lowered himself against her, glorying in her soft warmth. "You underestimate yourself, Cassie. If I do not swear to love you above all the others, it is because there have never been any other loves. There was even a time when I didn't like myself so well. But you're reforming me, as a good woman should. I can almost say I will never steal again, unless your safety and Adam's demands it, and I will strive to be a good father and husband."

"Then there is one more thing I would ask of you," Cassandra said as her fingers slid through the thick black hair at his temples. "Take off your patch. Let me see you as you are, with no illusions between us."

Merlyn allowed her to remove the leather patch, conscious that none other had ever done that before. It was a curiously erotic moment, one in which he revealed himself to her in a way no one else ever suspected.

"You have my secret," he whispered, his emerald and sapphire gaze darkening with desire. "When we are safe, I swear to you, I will throw that patch away."

Cassandra sighed and moved across the space in the bed, but her seeking hand met nothing. Instantly, her eyes flashed open and brilliant sunlight made her close them again. How quickly came the dawn these days, she thought as her face relaxed into a smile. Every night for the last eight, Merlyn had come to share a part of it with her. He said that, of the two, it was better if he risked being found roaming the halls. Hugh would not approve of him seeking to press his attentions on a female guest, but it was excusable in a man.

Cassandra hugged herself with joy. Merlyn loved her; it was there in every look they shared, in every unspoken word that gave their silences worlds of meaning. Once or twice he had even been able to slip off and meet her at Ebba's cottage for the afternoon.

Cassandra rolled over on her stomach and hugged her pillow tight against her. She missed Adam, the funny ache in her heart was never quite gone. It would not be long now, Merlyn promised her. His luck at the betting tables was paying off. Soon they'd have enough funds to purchase tickets to France.

She sat up at the sound of a knock on her door and quickly looked about to make certain Merlyn had taken all of his clothing with him. Just the day before he had forgotten his cravat and she had nearly left it lying by the bed when she went out. The maid would have made quick gossip of that!

"Come in," she called just as the door opened.

"Oh, you're still sleeping." Caroline popped her head through the door as if expecting to catch Cassandra unprepared. Her painted smile drooped a trifle. "Did I hear voices?"

Cassandra smiled. "Why ever would you think that?"

Caroline straightened and sailed into the room, wearing a lovely creation of russet taffeta which, surprisingly, clashed with her hair. "Oh, I know," she said, spying the girl's look, "but it's the newest color from Paris and I thought perhaps a lace collar would dampen the effect."

She curtsied to display the deep plunging decolletage which revealed most of each rounded breast. "Merlyn, of course, dismissed the idea. What do you think?"

She's testing me, Cassandra realized in alarm. She and Merlyn would need to be more careful in the future. "I think Mr. Ross should know what best becomes a beautiful woman," she answered truthfully. Let the woman wear the hideous color. If it did not dim her beauty, nothing would.

Caroline made a moue. "You sweet child. Do you think me beautiful? I've seen the way your eyes—What is that?" The last words were said sharply as her brilliant eyes fastened on Cassandra's gown.

Cassandra looked down with a sinking feeling, knowing even before she saw it what had caught the woman's gaze. Reluctantly she touched the emerald and sapphire ring that she kept pinned inside her bodice at all times. The collar of her night rail was unbuttoned and it had fallen to the outside. "It's a keepsake," she said calmly, not knowing what the woman knew.

The actress's eyes narrowed to slits. "I had wondered what happened to Merlyn's ring. I supposed he'd been forced to sell it in Paris in order to eat. But I see, instead, it was used to purchase relief from another kind of hunger."

Cassandra held her head proudly. "Who paid for your new gown, Miss Lambert?"

The woman's porcelain complexion reddened to an unbecoming shade. "Why, you little minx!" Then suddenly she threw back her head and laughed. "You almost had me convinced. You little whore! So that's why Merlyn neglects me. I should have guessed. Well, I should be angry, but I'm not. I'll have him again, soon."

This speech was calculated to hurt, but Cassandra remained calm, for the woman's temper rang a false note in her. The anger was contrived, as if she'd acted on cue. The consummate actress Miss Lambert's performance would have been flawless to the casual audience, but Cassandra's nerves were tuned to the tiniest hum of nuance and she knew at once that the actress had known of her liaison with Merlyn for days. It was then that she remembered the click of the door latch the night she'd spent in Merlyn's bed. They had thought someone had tried to enter. Perhaps, instead, someone had closed that door!

"What do you plan to do with your information, Miss Lambert?"

The actress's eyes widened. "Do? Why, nothing. I like you, Cassie." She came and sat on the edge of the bed. "If you please Merlyn, then it pleases me, for he is talking to Lord Mulberry about a new play. If Merlyn takes a lead, then so will I. You keep him here and happy, and we'll both have what we want." There was a malicious glint in her eye as she added, "But I would be careful. Merlyn is a jealous man. Your long afternoon walks in the country might be misconstrued."

This got the reaction the actress had expected the first time. Cassandra's face paled of color and her eyes grew enormous. "You're not going to cry?" the actress exclaimed in annoyance, afraid she might have gone too far too quickly. If Merlyn learned what she knew, then her little trap might spring too late.

She rose and made a great production of shaking out

the folds in her skirts. "I don't pretend to know where you go. I don't care. Just keep Merlyn here and happy. Adieu." A moment later she was out the door.

Here and happy. The line echoed in Cassandra's mind as she sprang for the door and locked it behind the vicious woman. "Why should she want Merlyn to remain?" Cassandra strained to recall what she and Merlyn had said that night. Had Miss Lambert heard everything? Or was she just jealous of their love and wished to see them squirm?

Cassandra hurried her dressing, but Merlyn and Lord Mulberry were gone when she went in to breakfast. Later, in the Pump Room, she could not find them. It was there she learned that they had gone up into the hills on a hiking expedition. Exasperated, angry, and frightened, Cassandra spent the interminable afternoon in the lending library thumbing through a quite shocking book entitled *The History of Tom Jones, A Foundling* by Mr. Fielding. Her heart was not in the misadventures of the lovable rogue. She had one too nearly like him on her conscience at the moment.

It was not until a full twelve hours after Caroline's veiled barbs had stung her that Cassandra found herself, miraculously, alone with Merlyn. She had come down early for dinner, and he was the first after her to make an appearance in the salon.

"Merlyn!"

The inflection in her tone made him instantly aware that something was wrong, and he came quickly across the room to her after a look over his shoulder at the closed door. "What's wrong?"

Cassandra grasped the hands he held out to her.

"She knows, Merlyn! Caroline knows that we are lovers."

Merlyn did not immediately reply. He was caught and held by the rich dark eyes on him. "You are so lovely, Cassie. I feel myself drowning in the warm sweet honey of your gaze."

Cassandra pulled her hands free and turned away, miffed that he had no concern for her fear. "Well, I can see you do not care who knows about us."

Merlyn shrugged, but his eyes never left her. "Do you care so much? Are you beginning to think you've made a mistake? We're no more married than we ever were. I thought you'd worked through that for yourself. If you will start each time someone guesses we're not wed . . ."

"Oh no!" Cassandra turned back to him, reaching out to touch his sunburned cheek. "You must never think that. I'm not ashamed of loving you and sharing that love; it's that I believe she overheard us the night I came to your room." Then she repeated the morning conversation.

When she was done, Merlyn shrugged. "I don't see the cause for alarm. As long as she doesn't know about Adam we've nothing much to fear." His eyes crinkled in the corners as he smiled. "I don't want a part in Hugh's new play."

Cassandra drew in a breath to protest, but the door opened and Caroline swept in on Hugh's arm, her new gown billowing about her. "Do we interrupt?" she questioned in glee. "Look, Hugh. Miss Lane is blushing. Merlyn, you rogue, were you making violent love to the girl?"

"Of course," Merlyn returned at once and raised Cassandra's hand to his lips. "Detestable gown," he murmured with a wink as he lightly saluted her hand.

It was just the bracing Cassandra needed, and she laughed.

Annoyed by their private moment, Caroline moved forward with Hugh in tow. "Nothing naughty, Merlyn. Hugh has just been telling me that he finds Miss Lane excessively pretty."

Hugh looked skyward and Cassandra smiled. "Two suitors. My, my, it must be the fresh air."

It was not until much later, in the privacy of her bed, with Merlyn's black head on her breast and her fingers laced gently through the heavy silk of his hair, that Cassandra spoke again of what was uppermost in her mind. "We must leave, Merlyn. I want to go tomorrow."

Merlyn stirred, the weight of his naked body curling down more tightly against hers. "We cannot, my love. I cannot afford much more than the trip to Plymouth. We'll have nowhere to go."

A film of tears blurred her vision. "I'm so afraid. Caroline is too pleased with herself. She wants us to remain. We must leave."

Merlyn raised his head and kissed the dimple in her chin. "Don't worry, Cassie. Just a few more days, I swear it. You won't allow me to steal Hugh's ring collection, so it must be done slowly, a hand of cards at a time. There's to be a rout at Prior Park in two days' time. After that we'll leave."

Cassandra said nothing more. She could not deny the

need for money. Adam was growing; he needed to be kept warm and dry and well fed. They would wait because they must.

After a few minutes, she ceased to think at all. It was quite extraordinary, she thought, how easily a man could be aroused. She had merely brushed her hand along the inside of his thigh, touching him as lightly and familiarly as he touched her, and she heard his breathing change and felt the stirring of his manhood.

Merlyn lifted his head once more and kissed her damp cheeks. "Love, my love, I love you so."

Cassandra decided not to take the baths the next morning. A dread had come to overlay her joy, and when Merlyn vacated her bed just before dawn she could not find the peace of sleep. It was well past sunrise before she fell into a disturbed slumber that changed into an aching head by midmorning. Before lunch, in an effort to shake off the feeling, she had a hearty snack packed for herself and set out for Ebba Lane's cottage.

"Hasn't he grown?" Cassandra said proudly as she held up her four-month-old son.

"That he has. He's going to be every bit as tall as his father," Ebba said. "Only, I'm a wee disturbed about his left eye. Bring him out into the sunlight and you'll see. It's changing to a greenish hue."

Cassandra wrapped Adam in his blanket before carrying him out into the sunlight, but she noticed from his vigorous kicks that he longed to be free of the confining wraps. "He'll be crawling soon," Cassandra said and received a nod of confirmation from Ebba. "Merlyn must get us away. I've missed too much in the weeks we've been apart."

By the end of the afternoon, the shadow that had marred her day was gone, flown as completely as the shrouding fog of early morn.

It was Caroline who burst in upon her peace as she shared a before-dinner glass of wine with Hugh and Merlyn.

"You'll never guess the news!" she greeted them, sweeping in in a gown of midnight blue. "Hugh, you will remember the scandal of the bastard heir?" She spoke to her host, but her eyes were on Cassandra. "Well, you'll never credit it. The cuckolded husband has been killed in a duel!"

If she had not been sitting, Cassandra knew, she would have fallen. Instead her world tilted wildly and from a great distance she heard Hugh exclaim, "Miss Lane, you've spilled your wine!"

"Blast you for a stupid cow!" Merlyn's deeper, angrier voice roared, and then Cassandra felt herself being pushed swiftly forward till her head hung between her knees.

"What did I say?" Caroline's voice was full of affront. "Certainly you cannot blame me for a fit of the vapors. Lud! Men! One simple swoon and—" Her voice ended in a choked gasp, but Cassandra could not see by whom or how she was cut off.

"Ring for brandy," Hugh said in the quiet authority of a nobleman. "Well, Caroline, make yourself useful."

"No . . . please," Cassandra managed thickly and

tried to raise her head, but the pressure of a large hand kept her bent forward.

"A moment longer," Merlyn said near her ear. "It'll pass."

"I feel . . . so silly," Cassandra murmured.

"Too much sun," Hugh suggested. "I noticed her flushed cheeks when she came in this afternoon. She must be put to bed. Ah, there you are, James. Brandy for Miss Lane. Then ring for Harriet. Miss Lane is feeling unwell."

"Never mind." Merlyn reached down and scooped Cassandra up into his arms. "Steady, Miss Lane," he said in warning in case she forgot herself before the others. "I'll carry her upstairs. Which room, Hugh?"

Caroline's unladylike snort of derision was ignored by both men, and Cassandra gave up to the pleasure of the strong arms about her and dropped her head against his shoulder.

Only when they reached the safety of the hall did she raise her lips to Merlyn's ear. "She knows."

"Yes, blast her!"

"Oh, Merlyn, if it's true!" Cassandra found she couldn't go on, didn't even want to acknowledge the faint flutter of hope struggling in her heart. A man was dead. That was terrible.

"Quiet, my love. We'll know in time. Say nothing more," he whispered, then raised his voice. "Miss Lane has fainted, Harriet. Follow me to her room. She'll need help undressing."

"Rest," Merlyn commanded when he laid her on the bed.

Cassandra opened her eyes to see his dark face above her, the slash of his patch cutting diagonally across his brow. "I hate that patch," she whispered inconsequentially and closed her eyes again.

Hours later, when the room was dark, Cassandra again opened her eyes. This time she did not feel the welcome weight of Merlyn's long body beside her. It was as if he understood her need to be alone.

A quick cut of memories flashed through her mind, memories of a beautiful golden-haired man who had once seemed the limit of all her best dreams. Little remained in her memories of him at their last meeting. That had not been real for her. Just as she now knew the love she had felt for that bright knight had never been real.

The reality of love had been found in the arms of a dark, passionate man who was no saint, not even an honest man, but one who loved her unequivocally as she was.

The tears that dampened her pillow were for the old life, falling away from her now like the shredded images of a fading nightmare. She had loved the good in Nicholas, but there was none. It was for that good that never was that she mourned.

Chapter Fifteen

CASSANDRA DID NOT LEAVE HER ROOM THE NEXT MORN-
ing. She didn't care what conclusions Caroline Lambert
might draw from her actions. Without a personal maid
she was free to begin packing. No one would know until
the last minute that she planned to leave Bath. She
didn't expect Merlyn to leave with her—that would
draw too much attention to her departure. But he
would follow in a few days, she was sure. In the
meantime she would go and stay with Ebba and Adam.

Her life held a breathless hope. If not for a nameless
nagging at the back of her mind she would have danced
a jig on her carpet. As it was, a simple song sprang to
her lips, a shamelessly bawdy ditty that Merlyn had
taught her.

It was the unusual sound of carriage wheels on Gay
Street that finally brought her out of her self-exile and
made her turn to the window. There were few personal
carriages in Bath, since the steep incline of the streets

made travel by wheeled vehicles uncertain and dangerous in unskilled hands. Those who did not prefer sedan chairs most often took to horseback.

The sight that met her inquisitive gaze surprised her. It was a military vehicle, a coach with barred windows and an escort. As she watched, a squat, plain-faced man in a red military coat emerged and came straight up the steps of Lord Mulberry's town house.

Cassandra drew in her head with a frown as she heard the scurrying of feet below. She had not bothered to dress, but now she reached for the plain dove-gray walking dress she had laid out and slipped it over her head. It was demure of neckline with unfashionable long sleeves, a compromise with the black mourning she would have worn under other circumstances.

A few moments later her slipper-shod feet skimmed over the carpeted stairs. Even before she reached the main floor a strange tightness began to squeeze her chest. Standing in the hall, their backs to the front door, were two uniformed soldiers, their muskets at the ready.

It has nothing to do with me, she told herself, but she did not believe it. Intuition told her that it did concern her, and Merlyn. Her eyes went to the closed salon doors and she knew that behind them played the drama of which she was shortly to become a part.

She had just put a foot in the hall when those doors swung open and the man she'd seen in the street emerged. A second later Lord Mulberry followed, and then Merlyn and two soldiers. Her gaze fastened in horror on Merlyn's face. His eyepatch was gone.

"Sorry about this, I am, Your Lordship," the officer was saying. "Only doing my duty as it was given me."

"I quite understand, Sergeant. A most unpleasant business—Why, Miss Lane!" Hugh stepped uncertainly toward her, as if to shield the spectacle from her view. Cassandra moved past him, not about to be waylaid.

"What's the matter?" she demanded, her eyes going once more to Merlyn's face. It was expressionless and he did not look toward her.

Hugh cleared his throat uncomfortably and reached out to take her hand. "I'm sorry that you were disturbed, my dear, particularly since you were ill last evening. It's my sad duty to tell you that Mr. Ross has just been arrested."

Cassandra felt the returning upsurge of vertigo, but she fought it, knowing that she must not fail Merlyn. "I—I don't understand. Arrested? Why? Has some poor loser at cards accused him of cheating?"

Hugh shook his head regretfully. "I'm afraid it's more serious than that. It seems we were mistaken in our company, Miss Lane. Word has it that Merlyn Ross is a common thief, and more, that he is an escaped prisoner, a man condemned by the courts for the crime of murder."

Time suspended its orderly measure. Cassandra did not know how long it was before anyone spoke again. It might have been a second or an hour. She was only aware of the aching cry that burst through her mind. *Oh, Merlyn! Oh, my dear! We were so close! So close to perfect happiness!*

"It's been my pleasure to arrest a notorious thief," the sergeant said proudly. "He's a wily one. He's had the Bow Street Runners searching for him five years, but it took Sergeant Baker to show them how 'twas done." The soldier pulled Merlyn's eyepatch from his pocket. "That was the trick. It came off in the struggle. Imagine, the bloke's got two-color eyes!"

Yes, I know, Cassandra nearly answered. Instead, she moved toward Merlyn, only to have one of the soldiers put out a warning hand. "I wouldn't do that, miss. He's a tough customer." And he indicated the length of chain he held which was attached to Merlyn's wrists.

Now Cassandra noticed the tiny trickle of blood at one corner of Merlyn's white-lipped mouth. Still he would not look at her. As if confronted by a naughty boy rather than a condemned man in chains, she took a handkerchief from her sleeve and gently dabbed away the blood from his lip.

Only then did Merlyn move, the granite expression melting into unfathomable sadness as his emerald and sapphire gaze lowered to her face. "Thank you." It was all he said, but it was enough.

Cassandra moved back and reached for the steadying influence of Lord Mulberry's arm. "I know this man," she said to him. "He's not guilty of the crime of murder. For the other I cannot say, but I believe him innocent of the greatest of his charges."

"My dear," Hugh Mulberry began soothingly and patted her hand. "You have such a tender heart . . ." Cassandra turned such a look of furious disdain upon him that he faltered. "Well, perhaps you are right, Miss Lane. I will make inquiries, but you must understand, theft also carries the death penalty. Do not mistake it."

Cassandra heard herself say, as if from afar, "Would you not rather die for that which you have done rather than for that of which you're innocent?"

Hugh Mulberry gave her a curious look, but she did not know or care. Her whole heart had gone out to the man being escorted out of the door and perhaps out of her life forever.

"Good Lord! What is happening?" Caroline Lambert appeared at the top of the stairs as the doors closed behind the soldiers. "Was that Merlyn I saw arrested?"

She received no answer from the two people below. When Cassandra climbed the stairs and moved to pass her without a word, she grabbed the smaller woman by the arm. "What's going on? Answer me, I tell you!"

Cassandra looked up into the avid face with its bright blue malicious eyes and knew what to do. She slapped the beautiful woman full across the face before moving on.

Cassandra thought herself to have suffered the worst of shocks, but the day was not yet done. An hour later, a knock came at her door. "Who is it?"

"Let me in, you little bitch," Caroline Lambert growled, her beautiful pear tones dropped at last.

Cassandra hesitated. Now that she'd had time to think about it, striking the taller, no doubt stronger woman had probably been an act of folly. Yet she unlatched the door.

Caroline entered slowly, her eyes on the girl. "Back off, you street-mannered wench. I'll not be mauled by you a second time!"

The declaration reassured Cassandra and she relaxed. The woman feared her. Good. "What do you want? If you've come to say a word against Merlyn I'll—"

The actress backed up a step, but she did not flee. "Oh no. I care nothing for your precious Merlyn. He's a thief. All of London will know it soon. I'm only glad I had the good sense not to link my name with his. The scandal might have set back my career. As it is"—her eyes went up and down Cassandra's straight-backed form—"I can say I knew the strumpet he bedded. That makes my gossip so much juicier."

"Is that all?"

Caroline blinked. "You're a cool piece, I'll say that. Your lover's about to swing, and you have shed not a tear."

"Theatrics do not come easily to me," Cassandra countered and smiled as the imprint of her hand deepened in color on the other woman's cheek. "But you have not come to exchange insults, I think. What do you want?"

"Oh, I come to bring you more news." She saw the girl tense and she smiled for the first time. "Do you know who brought the warrant for Merlyn's arrest? You don't, I see. Allow me to enlighten you. 'Twas the Marquess of Briarcliffe who served the papers on the sergeant. Ha! That sticks you, doesn't it?"

She took a step forward. "You're the bitch who sprang the marriage trap on Nicholas. God knows how you managed it, little brown wren that you are. I overheard you and Merlyn one night in his room. Brazen baggage, you had the gall to climb into his bed under my very nose. I knew I should have remembered your face that day in the Pump Room. But it wasn't until I heard you two scheming that I placed you. I was at the christening ball for your bastard.

"Oh, yes, I have many friends in high places," she said, preening. "The morning after you disappeared, the marquess had a fit. He accused all his guests of conspiring against him, but none of us could guess the reason for his distemper. Who'd have thought the old boy would go so far in his feud with his son that he'd put a bastard forth as his heir?"

"You sent a message to the marquess." It was a statement, for Cassandra had no doubt.

"Of course. It was my duty as a friend. How was I to know Merlyn was an escaped prisoner? Just wait until London learns 'twas I who caught the notorious Sorcerer?"

"What?"

Caroline shrugged, enjoying herself now that she was the center of attention again. "Didn't Merlyn tell you? That's the name the beau monde gave the thief who robbed them of their jewels and left no trace. It suits him, does it not?"

"Yes," Cassandra answered quietly, thinking of how thoroughly he had bewitched her. Merlyn was, indeed, a most capable sorcerer.

"So I've come to say that I'm sorry that Merlyn will hang. It was not my intention." She looked momentarily stricken. "I liked him. He was a fascinating bed partner." She looked up through her lashes. "You'll miss him, too."

Cassandra did not answer. This woman's self-serving lust could not compare with the deep abiding passion with which she loved Merlyn Ross.

"Oh yes. Hugh says to tell you that the marquess will be present for dinner. You're to present yourself to him, prepared to return to Briarcliffe immediately after. There's just one thing I wish to know. Where's the brat? Did you give it away, or did you kill it?"

Caroline escaped without another mauling only because Cassandra wished her gone more than she wished to do violence.

When the door was once again safely bolted, Cassandra sagged against it. Now the tears came, great heaving sobs that would have pleased her enemy had she stayed to witness the victory.

The afternoon dragged by, but Cassandra had a great deal of thinking to do and welcomed the sluggish passage of time. When the sky clouded over just before dusk, she sent up a small prayer of thanksgiving. She knew that she could not leave the house before dark. Not only Caroline but Lord Mulberry also was now aware of who she really was. She didn't know what her status was as Nicholas Briarcliffe's widow, but she knew the marquess well enough to know he wouldn't let her slip out of his hands until he had her son. It would be a matter of pride with him to know that he could not be beaten. The game of father against son was ended, but the game between the marquess and herself had one desperate round yet to be played.

An hour before dinner, she rang for a servant and asked for her best gown to be pressed. The news would go straight to Lord Mulberry, of course, and he would assume that she was cooperating. Then she packed a small bag which included the Briarcliffe diamonds. In her desperation she hoped there might be someone to bribe for Merlyn's freedom. If not, she had still to get away, for Adam's sake.

The escape from the house was ridiculously easy. The steady drizzle of cold rain leadened and dulled the last of the evening's light, blurring distant figures and blending them to sameness. In her long cape with the hood pulled close she attracted no notice.

"Dear girl, you're soaked," Ebba cried when Cassandra's knock brought her to the door.

Cassandra rushed inside and turned to the woman. "Shut and latch the door! I've much to tell you, and I need your help."

"Poor child," Ebba said when Cassandra had stumbled through her long and complex tale. "Merlyn's gone to Bristol. That's where they'd take him. We must go there."

Cassandra heard this simple declaration in amazement. "You'll still help me, knowing what I am and what I've done?"

Ebba's face was full of gentle candor. "My dear child. Did you think I swallowed Merlyn's Banbury tale whole when he brought you to me? I'm old but no fool, and I've known Merlyn far longer than you have. He's always lied his way through this life. But there's one thing he couldn't hide from me. He loves you and little Adam. I saw it in his eyes while his clever tongue told me a world of lies. That was all that was important to me. And you love the boy I raised but could not save from himself. For that alone, I've given far more than you've asked of me. What would you have me do now?"

"I must go to Bristol. I must see Merlyn before—" Cassandra's voice faded before the horror of her thoughts. "Well, I must see him. We had no chance to speak."

"We'll need a coach. I can't have you and Adam exposed to that bone-chilling rain." She rose and went to her room and came back with a small purse. "It isn't much, but it's my life savings."

Tears sparkled in Cassandra's lashes. "I can't take it. It wouldn't be fair when I don't know if I could ever repay you."

Ebba scoffed, "As if I'd accept it. Let me tell you 'tis little enough for what Merlyn's done for me. If not for him I'd be in debtors' prison. He saved my life. After that wicked scoundrel I worked for died, there was none would hire me. Word gets about, even when the main story's not told. Merlyn found me in the work-house and brought me here over twelve years ago. Since then, it's been his generosity that's kept a roof over my head. If he's guilty of crimes, then I've contributed my part. I took every cent he sent me. If I seemed hard on you when we met, 'twas only my own guilt riding me. I didn't want to see the lovely man saddled with another grasping woman." Ebba sniffed lightly and nodded her head decisively. "So we'll hear no more of debts. I've just to go up the lane a bit to the coach house. You bundle up Adam, and we'll go when I return. Now hurry!"

Cassandra was glad to have someone take charge, if only for the moment. It made fear of the future less terrible to bear. Surely, with two women who loved him, Merlyn was not yet lost.

Half an hour passed before Cassandra heard the knock at the door, and, laying Adam in his crib, she rushed into the outer room to open it. "Oh, Ebba, I thought you'd—"

"Move back from the door, Lady Briarcliffe." Kendal Dermont put a foot in the way a scant second before Cassandra tried to slam the door. Putting his shoulder to it, he forced it open again. With the pistol in his hand he waved her back. "That was foolish. You might have forced me to shoot you. Now back up. That's right." He sent the door flying shut with a kick.

Cassandra looked at him, dumbfounded. The rain had darkened his fair hair and it clung to his head like a skullcap, but beneath the fringe of hair his pale eyes gleamed with the malevolence common to all Briarcliffes. "Why are you here? How did you—? Miss Lambert told you, didn't she?" Cassandra cried, wishing now she had beaten the woman to an insensible pulp when she had had the chance.

"No, that interfering slut didn't tell me." He wiped the rain from his face with the back of his hand. "I set a watch at St. James's Square the moment we arrived. We followed everyone who left Lord Mulberry's house. 'Tis a particular skill o' mine the marquess finds useful."

Cassandra backed up into a chair and sat down heavily. "So you've come to take me back to the marquess."

"No, lady, not that." Suddenly he roared at her, "Why didn't you leave England when you had the chance? Stupid girl! I tried to scare you off that night in Chatham.

"Oh yes," he continued at her gasp. "Didn't you guess? The men were hired to kill Merlyn Ross. I couldn't afford to have him set blackmail upon the marquess. The old fool's gone mad. Thinks that bastard you whelped is his blood kin. No one can talk sense to him. It didn't take long to guess you'd used the Comte de Valure to help you run away. Good riddance, says I when I heard it. But the marquess wouldn't let be. He sent me to London to track you down. 'Twas easy enough to locate the comte's rooms. 'Twas harder to catch him there. When we did, he brought me straight to you."

Kendal's gun hand began to tremble. "I let you go, do you know that? I *let* you! 'Twas easy enough to squeeze your destination out of the woman in Lewknor Lane."

"You killed Meg?" Cassandra whispered in horror.

Kendal's chuckle was as thin as the rattle of dry leaves. "Nothing so final. She has a fondness for Blue Ruin. Two bottles and she wept on me shirtfront for her lost love. You stole her benefactor and she didn't mind telling me she'd never see him again, not with him taking the coach to Dover."

"Why are you telling me this? What matter can it be now?" Cassandra took a deep breath, tried to steady her pulse. "I must come with you. I've no choice."

"You don't, but I do," Kendal answered. "You don't see it yet, do you? You don't know why I can't let you go. If not for the bad luck of tipping your hand to that

Lambert wench we'd both have what we want." He shrugged. "I freely admit I lost your trail after Chatham, but I supposed I'd frightened the pair of you into permanent exile. The marquess wanted you found, but he wasn't doing the looking, I was. He had to take my word for it that I'd tried my best."

His smile stretched into a hideous grin. "He never suspected I'd use my skill against him. He's never given me credit for a man's feelings. I'd have let you rot in Newgate if it hadn't served my purpose to have you home again safe."

His smile turned ugly. "When I heard what plans the marquess made after he learned your sluttish ways had gotten you with child, I could have killed you with my bare hands. But I'm a patient man. There are enough hot tempers in the Briarcliffes, and they've served me well."

He paused, running his tongue over dry lips. "But that's another tale. In a few days or weeks the world will learn just what Kendal Dermont's made of. The marquess can't last long." His eyes glittered. "I've you to thank for it. You've taken your toll on his temper and his nerves, ground him down slowly. No one's ever bested him before, not even his son. You were first, but I'll be the last. When he's gone, Briarcliffe will belong to me."

Cassandra had taken her eyes off him for a moment, straining to hear the faint sounds of Adam's awakening. It was the last thing she wanted, to draw Kendal's attention to the boy. "What did you say? Briarcliffe will belong to you?"

"Aye. That's so, once your son's been put where he can do me no harm."

Cassandra stood up, pushing her chair back so that it loudly scraped the floor to distract the man from the increasingly fretful stirrings in the other room. "I don't understand. Surely you know my son cannot inherit. I wouldn't want him to, in any case."

"But you've no say, lady. 'Tis the marquess's doing. He signed the will naming the boy his heir. After that comes Cousin Nicholas. I'm third, as ever. But that'll change." His fair lashes flickered repeatedly over his pale eyes. "Some of the marquess's gold went into the pocket of a professional murderer. Nicholas has fought three duels this year alone. The Briarcliffe temper. He won't walk away from the next."

Cassandra looked down quickly before he could see the look in her eyes. Nicholas had not walked away— but this man didn't yet know it. "If all you want is Briarcliffe and I want no part of it, let me go." She raised her head. "I swear I will leave England and never return."

Kendal's lids fluttered again. "Leave England? For how long? You know little of the lengths to which poverty can drive a man—or a woman. You may leave, but years have a way of turning the mind to other thoughts. Were you to find yourself cold and hungry and could remember the wealth and splendor of Briarcliffe you might be persuaded to return, for your wee one's sake."

Cassandra did not bother to deny that. For her child's sake she had dared much. Without Merlyn—but no!

She would not think of that, not now. "You were willing to trust me before. Why not now?"

"You had a man before," Kendal answered simply, and Cassandra understood. "Your son stands between me and Briarcliffe. I'm a patient man; I can wait for the marquess to die."

"You can't murder us."

"Aye, that I can," he answered pleasantly. "Once I could have let you go. Now it's different. As long as there's a chance you're alive the marquess will keep up the search, spending money that should be mine. No, I must know where you're to be found. In a year, maybe two, your bodies can be dug up and presented if necessary. Victims of highwaymen. Who'll know different?"

Just then Adam wailed out in hunger, the tenseness of the moment climaxing in that small human cry.

"So the babe's awake." Kendal's gaze swung from the woman to the open doorway of the second room and he smiled. "Too bad. I'd rather have smothered him in his sleep."

The horror of that statement, so matter-of-factly pronounced, sent a wild, surging revulsion through Cassandra. She did not think of the futility of her action but flung herself at him with a scream of desperate fury.

He had turned away, did not expect the physical assault of the small woman, but it was not surprise alone that made him stagger against the weight that careened into him and buckled his knees. Terror and fear for her child had given Cassandra an extraordinary share of strength. Even as they fell together to the floor she grabbed the wrist that held the gun and sank her teeth into its flesh.

Kendal cried out his pain and brought his other fist up to smash her face, but he fell on his stomach with her on top and he couldn't find the room to swing his arm. He heaved under her to throw her off, but Cassandra quickly straddled him and jerked his gun arm back as hard as she could. A muffled oath burst from him, maddening him beyond endurance, but before he could rise under her weight she bit his thumb and he involuntarily dropped the pistol.

The heavy metal weapon bounced and clattered across the floor, but Cassandra had no time to reach for it. Kendal was a man, a sinewy farmhand, and it was not to be expected that she could long overpower him. He gained his knees quickly and threw her from his back. She landed with an impact that winded her, but she struggled to all fours. A moment later his fist landed with a sickening stun on the side of her head and she sagged back to the floor, dazed.

"That should hold you," she heard him hiss as the world behind her closed lids swirled and dimmed, bucked and dipped, with nauseating rapidity. She tried but she couldn't move, not even her lids would open. Chains seemed to weight her to the floor, and then she heard his retreating footsteps.

"Adam!" She didn't know if she cried out loud or if the scream sounded only in her thoughts, but she found the chains melting away and she struggled to her knees. He was smothering Adam! She must stop him.

She saw it lying on the floor beside her. She'd never

touched a pistol before in her life and she had no way of knowing if it would fire. She picked it up, the weight of it like an anvil in her trembling hands, and staggered to her feet.

He was silhouetted in the rectangle of light beyond the doorway, a tall figure bent over her son's crib. She did not cry out or warn him. She did not ask him to stop. She lifted the pistol with both hands and pulled the trigger.

The bump and rattle of the Bath coach was surprisingly easy on Cassandra's nerves. Adam lay against her breast and she absorbed with her body the worst of the jolts.

"It won't be long now," Hugh Mulberry said to break the long silence since his last comment.

Cassandra looked across at him. She owed him so much, as much as she owed Ebba, who sat beside her. "I don't know how I'll ever repay you," she said.

Hugh held up a hand. "Dear lady, please. You would make me out to be better than I am. I have done so little and fear that I may fail you in your greatest need." His eyes were kind, but sadness lurked there. "I will do all that is within my power to gain Merlyn a new hearing, but that may take months. It's better if you don't tempt fate by remaining in England until then."

Cassandra nodded, telling herself yet again that she must be grateful that she had not killed Kendal Dermont. Had she not simply wounded him, no one would have believed her story. She shivered in remembrance of the marquess's face when he learned of his son's death. The pale ice-water eyes had closed briefly but, she knew, not in sadness. His hatred for his son was complete. It was the spoiling of his victory he mourned, that and the fact that he'd been beaten by the one foe he'd never understood he had: Kendal Dermont.

"I can't believe he let me go," she said aloud.

Hugh leaned forward to take one of her small hands in his and found the fingers icy cold. "You're shivering. You don't quite believe it's over, do you?"

Cassandra shook her head. "How can it be over when I am about to embark on an ocean voyage to a place I've never been, alone and with a son to care for? Do not think me ungrateful, Lord Mulberry. I long to put an ocean between myself and the marquess. I know that he no longer has any jurisdiction over me, but in my heart I cannot shake the dread his very name invokes. He is responsible for Merlyn's arrest. I can neither forget nor forgive him that."

"Miss Lane will be with you," he reminded her. "And I'm sending letters with you for every member of my family in the Massachusettes. They will take an instant liking to you. You must leave behind old memories and begin anew."

Anew. Cassandra closed her eyes. She did not want to begin anew if it meant a life without Merlyn.

"The ship leaves at dusk tomorrow." Hugh saw her blink in astonishment. "That's right. There'll scarce be time to put you aboard. That's why I sent a messenger on horseback. Whatever else, you must be aboard."

"I wish to see Merlyn first," Cassandra replied.

Hugh shook his head. "Absolutely not!" At her

shocked expression he frowned. "Do you think Merlyn would have you see him behind bars?" Her crooked smile made him blush as he remembered the long incredible story she had told him in the wee hours of the night following Kendal's attempted murder. "Still, he wouldn't, not this time. You must be Patience herself. You will wait for him in America."

Cassandra said nothing more. How could she fight against the man who was trying to save Merlyn's life? But it was the hardest sacrifice yet.

The city of Bristol went by her window unnoticed. The boarding of the ship took but little more of her attention. When they set sail the next day with the evening tide, she did not have the heart to watch the shore disappear behind her. Instead, she huddled in her bunk with Adam, staring into his dear little face, so very like the one she ached to have beside her.

"We must be Patience herself, my son," she whispered just before tears obscured her vision.

"It isn't right, and what's more, you know it," Ebba scolded her charge. "Five days at sea, and you've yet to take a breath of fresh air."

Cassandra sighed and picked up her fork, but the thought of food made her green. "I can't be happy, Ebba. I've tried and I've tried, but I'm not that brave."

Ebba clucked her tongue. "Don't speak to me of brave. I'll never know how you managed it, wrestling that pistol away from the man. And giving him his own shot for the trouble, besides." She chuckled. "Merlyn knew what he was getting when he picked you. No, don't cry, little lamb," she added quickly and reached out to put an arm about the younger woman's shoulders.

After a moment she said, "This simply must stop. You've got me all teary-eyed, too. Tonight's our first night beyond the sight of any land. We're in international waters. It's a grand spectacle to view the sea all about you, the captain tells me. Now I want you to wash your face and go up to have a look. Scat!"

Cassandra huddled in her woolen cloak as she leaned against the midship railing. The wind off the North Atlantic was bracingly cold, numbing fingers and toes within minutes. It would be a long, hard crossing, two months perhaps, Hugh had told her. No other ships would sail from England to New England until after the spring thaw.

Cassandra closed her mind to everything else but the rolling gray sea before her. Little caplets of white rode the tips of the larger waves and icy spume occasionally raked her cheeks, but she stayed there staring, willing herself to forgetfulness until the blue-gray of evening passed into the wintery black of night.

"Miss! Miss!"

Cassandra turned at the sailor's cry.

The burly seaman came up to her and smartly touched his cap. "The cap'n's orders, miss. You're to go below. 'Tain't safe after dark. You need a guide?"

Cassandra merely shook her head and he backed away, saying, "Soon, miss. Don't tarry."

Cassandra flung one last look back at the inky waters and turned toward her cabin.

She felt him in her being before she saw him, the tall, dark figure wrapped in a long coat against the frigid night air. And it was as before.

Shadows dulled his features, but she had the impression of a harshly handsome face. And power, a power so strong that her fear momentarily subsided. There was only the feeling of power, of security, of safety, that she had felt once long ago in the arms of another.

Then a spasm of horrifying clarity shook her and, with a wail of fright, Cassandra swirled about and would have fled the ghostly presence of all her fondest dreams.

"Cassie!"

That voice! Cassandra swirled about so quickly her skirts tangled at her knees. He was coming toward her and she knew—knew beyond reasonability or plausibility—that it was "Merlyn!"

He stopped within inches of her, staring down into her face with the emerald and sapphire eyes she saw even in her dreams. "Well? Is this all the welcome I'm to receive from my loving wife?"

"Merlyn." Cassandra could barely whisper the words past the tears in her throat. Suddenly she could not speak the words to make him know her joy or her terror or her love for him, so great that it threatened to burst her small frame with the sheer magnitude of it.

There was no need. He simply opened his arms and, miraculously, she was in them, enfolded against the warm masculine heat of his body. She felt him tremble and it was as if the world trembled, so closely were they bound by each other's arms.

"I thought I'd lost you!" she whispered when she could find breath.

"Have you so little faith?" She heard the rumble of laughter deep in his chest and gloried in the sound so dear and not lost to her.

"Hugh said it would be months and months!" she wailed against his shirtfront, her fingers clutching the material of his coat.

"Easy, love," he whispered hoarsely next to her ear. "Hugh wasn't sure he could bribe enough turnkeys to set me free."

Cassandra raised her head. "How did he manage it?"

"Oh, a few pounds here, a few there. He's quite an interesting fellow, actually. We must invite him to visit us when we're settled in the New World."

Cassandra cried then, uncaring that the sound of it carried to the sailors nearby. "That will hardly repay him for all he's done for us."

Merlyn smiled, but his embrace did not relax even a fraction. "You've already repaid him, Cassie. He told me he's finally at work on his new play. It's to be a kind of beggar's opera about a jewel thief who falls in love with a nobleman's wife."

"He wouldn't!" Cassandra gasped.

"Oh yes, I rather think he will, and make a fortune with it. Five nights in the hold of this ship have quite convinced me that the jewel thief will reform by the play's end. We're in international waters. I'm free, Cassie."

Merlyn stared at her a moment, mesmerized by her gaze. "Has anyone ever told you how absurdly beautiful you are?"

Cassandra shook her head. "No one's ever been that foolish."

"Then they've never seen you as I have, Cassie, my love."

He kissed her then, in the wind, in the cold, in the dark of the night in the midst of the North Atlantic.

Tapestry
HISTORICAL ROMANCES

Breathtaking New Tales

of love and adventure set against history's most exciting time and places. Featuring two novels by the finest authors in the field of romantic fiction—<u>every month</u>.

Next Month From
Tapestry Romances

DAWNFIRE
by Lynn Erikson

MONTANA BRIDES
by DeAnn Patrick

POCKET BOOKS

If you've enjoyed the love, passion and adventure of this Tapestry™ historical romance...be sure to enjoy them all, FREE for 15 days with convenient home delivery!

Now that you've read a Tapestry™ historical romance, we're sure you'll want to enjoy more of them. Because in each book you'll find love, intrigue and historical touches that really make the stories come alive!

You'll meet brave Guyon d'Arcy, a Norman knight ... handsome Comte Andre de Crillon, a Huguenot royalist ... rugged Branch Taggart, a feuding American rancher ... and more. And on each journey back in time, you'll experience tender romance and searing passion... and learn about the way people lived and loved in earlier times.

Now that you're acquainted with Tapestry romances, you won't want to miss a single one! We'd like to send you 2 books each month, as soon as they are published, through our Tapestry Home Subscription Service.℠ Look them over for 15 days, free. If not delighted, simply return them and owe nothing. But if you enjoy them as much as we think you will, pay the invoice enclosed.

There's never any additional charge for this convenient service— we pay all postage and handling costs.

To begin your subscription to Tapestry historical romances, fill out the coupon below and mail it to us today. You're on your way to all the love, passion and adventure of times gone by!

HISTORICAL *Tapestry* ROMANCES

Tapestry Home Subscription Service, Dept. TPTP05
120 Brighton Road, Box 5020, Clifton, NJ 07012

Yes, I'd like to receive 2 exciting Tapestry historical romances each month as soon as they are published. The books are mine to examine for 15 days, free. If not delighted, I can return them and owe nothing. There is never a charge for this convenient home delivery—no postage, handling, or any other hidden charges. If I decide to keep the books, I will pay the invoice enclosed.

I understand there is no minimum number of books I must buy, and that I can cancel this arrangement at any time.

Name

Address

City   State   Zip

Signature   (If under 18, parent or guardian must sign.)

This offer expires January 31, 1984.   TAPBC5

Tapestry™ is a trademark of Simon & Schuster.